Ada Lovelace
the Countess who Dreamed in Numbers

Shanee Edwards

Ada Lovelace: the Countess who Dreamed in Numbers

Published by The Conrad Press in the United Kingdom 2019

Tel: +44(0)1227 472 874
www.theconradpress.com
info@theconradpress.com

ISBN 978-1-911546-44-3

Typesetting and Cover Design by: Charlotte Mouncey, www.bookstyle.co.uk
Cover design based on Watercolour portrait of Ada Byron by Chalon, Alfred Edward 1780-1860 held at the New York Public Library in the Carl H. Pforzheimer Collection of Shelley and His Circle.

The Conrad Press logo was designed by Maria Priestley.

Printed and bound in Great Britain
by Clays Ltd, Elcograf S.p.A

What is imagination? It renders Earth tolerable; it teaches us to live. It is that which penetrates into the unseen worlds around us, the worlds of science.

–Ada Lovelace

Author's note

Ada Lovelace was born Ada Byron in England on December 10, 1815. Her father was the poet Lord Byron. Ada's mother, Lady Annabella Milbanke, was a devout Christian who was educated in mathematics, earning her the nickname 'Princess of Parallelograms' from her husband. The severely ill-matched husband and wife divorced shortly after Ada was born. To prevent Ada from developing a wild imagination like her father, Annabella narrowly focused Ada's education on mathematics and science. Ada was kept away from her father, who died in Greece when she was just eight years old.

On June 5 1833, when Ada was just seventeen, she met the inventor Charles Babbage, who was charmed by her beauty, wit and mechanical aptitude. Together, they worked to find funding for his machine, the Analytical Engine, which was the world's first true digital computer. Ada, who called her own approach to the study of science and mathematics 'poetical science', was the first person to understand the enormous and wide-ranging significance a computer would have in human society and culture.

She walks in beauty, like the night
Of cloudless climes and starry skies;
And all that's best of dark and bright
Meet in her aspect and her eyes:
Thus mellow'd to that tender light
Which heaven to gaudy day denies.

One shade the more, one ray the less,
Had half impaired the nameless grace
Which waves in every raven tress,
Or softly lightens o'er her face;
Where thoughts serenely sweet express
How pure, how dear their dwelling-place.

And on that cheek, and o'er that brow,
So soft, so calm, yet eloquent,
The smiles that win, the tints that glow,
But tell of days in goodness spent,
A mind at peace with all below,
A heart whose love is innocent!

Lord Byron

1

All my life, I've been terrified my talents would be wasted. Not only do I have an aptitude for numbers, machines and scientific discovery, but they are my life's passion. Curious to a fault, independent – no, downright stubborn, I have a mind that constantly questions the world around me. Though it may seem as if these skills would have created a wealth of opportunities for me to build, create and invent exciting new mechanical wonders, there was one simple thing standing in my way: I was a girl.

Standing on the roof of the home where I had lived for nearly all my seventeen years, looking over the edge, feeling the breeze whip through my tangled, auburn hair, I couldn't help but think what an exciting time it was to be alive. It was 1832 and everyone in England was looking for new ways to harness the power of steam. Steamboats stormed the seas and steam trains rolled over earth, but I knew steam power offered so many more possibilities. The world was changing fast and I wanted to be a leader of that change. Numbers were exciting on their own, but I wanted to apply them to something meaningful, something extraordinary. More than anything, I wanted to harness their power into the science of flying machines in a new field I called Flyology.

For weeks, I had toiled from the early morning until the wee hours of the night on a project I called 'The Carrier Pigeon Endeavour.'

The Carrier Pigeon was a hand-built air glider intended to allow humans to fly. To make the wings, I stitched together horsehides around a frame I constructed using wood from my old childhood desk that I broke apart. Then, I made a harness to fit my torso out of an old horse saddle. I carefully attached the harness to the wings with leather straps and the glider was finally ready to test. The Carrier Pigeon was an odd-looking contraption, pieced together with scraps of leather, metal hinges and screws, but I was proud of it.

Today I would soar over the tree-lined grounds of my home, Fordhook Manor. Carefully, methodically, I strapped my contraption onto my torso and cinched the straps at both my wrists and shoulders, before pulling the harness straps tightly around my chest.

'Wish me luck,' I said to Puff, my ginger kitten, aged three months, who had followed me onto the roof.

With a meow, Puff trotted in the opposite direction, scattering the birds. Their flight sent a breeze toward the fox-shaped weathervane that suddenly pointed eastward. 'All I need is a little wind,' I said, and took in a deep breath.

A tingle of excitement ran through my body. I knew that once I leaped off the roof, I would need to keep my legs and torso as straight as possible to prevent drag. I had practised this numerous times by leaping onto my bed, keeping all my joints stiff and rigid.

I took a deep breath and surveyed the horizon in front of me. The sun was high and golden, practically smiling its light down on me through clear blue skies. I could see the grove of oak trees at the edge of our property and visualized myself soaring high over the treetops and beyond. If I were successful today, flying over the English Channel would be my next feat.

A strong gust of wind blew my hair forward. It was time.

Determined, I backed up, squeezed the harness with my fingers, sucked in some air and said a little prayer just to be on the safe side. I then gathered all the courage I could muster and took a giant, running leap off the rooftop.

My feet left the shingles.

I was in the sky.

It was glorious.

As the air rushed beneath my winged body forty feet above the ground, I stiffened my spine and legs, just as I had practised. I spread my arms out wide and straight. The wind whipped through my hair. My heart was pounding, but by God, I was in the air.

I'm flying! I really did it!

Everything looked so small on the ground below. The green rolling hills off in the distance looked like tiny anthills. I felt proud. What an achievement I had made for England! A million possibilities flashed through my mind. The King would want to meet me, of course, and there would be the obligatory visits by countless dignitaries. Mother would be jealous of all the attention I would get, but she would just have to resolve herself to it.

I pushed the thoughts of fame from my mind, though, and refocused myself on flight. I'd been in the air a few seconds already, the most triumphant 3.4 seconds of my life. At 3.5 seconds, however, I knew something was horribly wrong. Instead of thrusting forward, I was suddenly losing altitude – fast.

I panicked. This can't be happening, I thought. I began flapping my arms, hoping the horsehide wings would catch the wind. I flapped harder and harder, but it was no use. Like a giant, winged acorn, I was falling to the ground. While I knew crashing my flying machine was going to be bad, I never could have imagined exactly how *very* bad it would be.

2

There was no time to brace myself for the impact. There wasn't even time to ask for the Lord to take me should my head be smashed to bits. There was just time to realise I was plummeting like a brick, which created a cold lump of fear in my belly that I'm sure only made me fall faster.

I landed in the hedge not far from where my mother, Lady Annabella Byron, and Dr. Poole, her long-time companion, were seated. As I collided with the bushes, I could just make out that I had travelled a mere six feet. When I hit the spiny, Berberis hedge, my carefully designed wings busted with a loud crunch. All the air was forced out of my chest. I felt my ankle twist.

'Ow!' I finally screamed in pain, once I was able to draw oxygen back into my lungs.

'What in heaven's name?' said Mother. 'Ada?' she called as she raced over to the hedge. Her honey-coloured ringlets bounced as she ran while lifting the hem of her black silk brocatelle dress. Her face still held a fragile beauty even though it bore a worried expression. Dr. Poole, in a tailored brown jacket and wide cravat, followed right behind.

As I spat the purple Berberis leaves out of my mouth, I had no way to know how many thorns had penetrated my flesh. I did know that the pain in my ankle was increasing and now ran up my entire leg. I squealed in agony as Dr. Poole picked me up, broken wings and all, and rushed me towards the house.

In his mid-fifties, Dr. Poole was a tall man with handsome features, copper eyes and a full amber beard that was peppered with grey hairs. He always smelled clean, with a hint of lemon-mint. Typically, he was a very decisive man, able to solve problems quickly, giving him an air of confidence. If he were ever at a loss for what to do in a particular situation, he would look to scripture to guide him, as was the case in something I call the 'father/grandfather incident.' Let me explain.

When I was little, I asked my mother if a father and a grand-father were the same thing. For some reason, the question really got her kettle boiling. She gathered up all my dolls and said she was sending them to shoeless orphans in Ireland who had neither fathers nor grandfathers. I couldn't stop crying. On the third day of listening to my wretched sobbing, Dr. Poole read Mother a Bible verse from the Book of Mark that said a family splintered by feuding would fall apart. She took it to heart and finally returned my dolls – the orphans went without. Bless their poor little souls and feet.

I must have blacked out for a moment after hitting the Berberis hedge, because the next thing I knew, Dr. Poole had already carried me past the parlor and was well on his way up the staircase. Although I couldn't see her, Mother mustn't have been far behind because as we reached the second floor, I heard her bark to our housemaid, 'Miss Stamp, Ada fell off the roof!'

'But why was the girl on the roof at all?' asked Miss Stamp as she jumped into action and followed us into my bedchamber.

'Testing my flying machine,' I called out to her.

'Needs work, I take it?' replied Miss Stamp, for which Mother shot her an irate look.

Dr. Poole poured me onto my Celestial blue duvet and I told myself the pain in my ankle was only temporary, simply part of the scientific process. All great scientists had made personal sacrifices. Had Galileo never poked an eye while staring at the heavens through his homemade telescopes? Had Sir Isaac Newton never bruised his skull while waiting for apples to fall from the tree? Certainly my damaged ankle would be a small sacrifice to make in the name of scientific discovery.

My bedroom wasn't a typical girl's bedchamber. The floor of my room was littered with broken wood panels, hinges and paper wings in a multitude of shapes and sizes. Tools of all kinds, from an iron farrier's rasp to blacksmith tongs, were also strewn about. My walls were filled with my sketches of birds in flight, insects buzzing and a highly detailed sketch of a steam train with wings – the result of countless hours of work. My prized pigeon skeletons sat on a shelf between a motley beetle collection and jar of mostly live moths. Once in the middle of the night, I accidentally stepped on a saw-tooth fireplace trammel but had to stifle my need to cry out in pain for fear Mother would force me to move my collection of tools to the stable, preventing me from working until late into the night. My heel still bears the jagged scar.

To outsiders, my room probably appeared to be nothing more than a rat's nest, but to me, every langoustine shell and dissected bit of sheep's bone had its place. It was on those treasured shelves I now focused my eyes as Mother argued with Miss Stamp about whether or not the poor woman knew of my plans to throw myself from the roof.

With the pain from my ankle now radiating up my leg, I hardly noticed as Miss Stamp fumbled to untie the leather straps of my flying machine, or as she pulled the broken horse-hide-and-wood wings off my arms.

'What on earth were you thinking?' Mother asked, while I went over the event in my mind. My wings were directly proportional to the pigeon's wings that I had dissected months ago. I had wind and speed. What was I missing?

Dr. Poole removed my right boot, which I have to admit, hurt quite a bit. I reluctantly howled in pain. He examined my bare ankle as Mother sunk her head into her hands as she sat on the edge of the bed. 'She's going to be hard enough to marry off without being a cripple,' she said.

'I almost made it!' I said with indignation. At least I had tried. What efforts had she ever made to invent a new method of transportation? To invent anything? The woman gave me no credit for my efforts at all.

Dr. Poole interjected, 'Everyone calm your nerves. Though it's growing quite swollen, it appears to be just a sprain.' Mother sighed with relief. 'She'll need to stay in bed for a least a week,' Dr Poole added.

An entire week? I moaned again, this time in misery at the thought of spending a whole week indoors. No, that wouldn't do at all. 'But tomorrow I'm fixing a pair of wings on a steam engine,' I said in a panic, 'This was just my first Flyology experiment – I need to conduct six more.'

That was when Mother picked up a hand mirror from my dresser and held it in front of my face. The mirror's handle was made of cast iron and the back of the looking glass had a hand-painted scene of a French lady and gentleman sitting in a garden overlooking a small pond. I had always liked the picture, though it was the reflective side and not the portrait she held in front of my eyes.

'Look there. What do you see?' Mother asked.

'See?' I asked, not grasping her meaning.

'In the mirror, child.'

I saw my own reddened face, wet with the fat, shameful tears gushing from my eyes. Even though I was embarrassed at my own crying, I couldn't help but notice that my crystalline eyes appeared even bluer in contrast with my blotchy pink flesh. My russet-coloured hair was a tangled mess.

'Me,' I said.

'Anything else? Feathers? A beak?'

'No.'

'Of course not,' quipped Mother, 'Because you are a girl. Girls do not fly.' And with that, she thumped me hard on the head with the mirror.

Clearly, she didn't understand the greater purpose of all this and needed me to explain, and why does it matter that I'm a girl? 'Flyology will change the world!' I told her.

But Mother, as usual, wouldn't listen. Once she had an opinion in her head, there was no changing it, and she obviously had many very, very strong opinions rushing through her head right now. As she huffed with aggravation, she stepped over papers, rocks and bones on the floor to collect various books of mine from the shelf. She made quite a show of collecting them, all of which, she then handed to Miss Stamp.

'Use these as kindling,' she said.

I cried out in protest but Mother ignored me. Then, using a white silk handkerchief she drew from her bosom, Mother reached for a dead crow on my shelf.

That's when I knew my circumstances had gone from bad

to worse. Mother would never in a million years lower herself to touching a corpse of any kind, no matter how many silk handkerchiefs she had at her disposal. Seeing her reach for the decaying crow meant Mother was about to discover something truly terrible, and it nearly sent me into an epileptic fit.

'Don't touch that!' I shouted as I jumped up to stop her, but my injured ankle gave out and I fell short. The pain was like a hundred sewing needles piercing the flesh, muscle, tendon, and bone that made up my ankle all at once. But even as I lay there, blinded by the pain, I knew I was in mortal trouble because underneath the crow was a book – a book more forbidden than the roof I had just launched myself from moments before. I was in illegal possession of something I was never supposed to see or read and Mother was about to see it below my dead crow. Why hadn't I hidden the book better?

For a moment time froze, as my Mother stood there—crow in hand and completely dumbfounded at how any daughter of hers could be so passionate about a dead bird—and I thought perhaps heaven was about to take pity on me and keep my Mother from turning her face back to the shelf, but then I remembered that time is the only constant and that it can never be frozen. My mother looked at my face, recognizing instantly that it wasn't the crow I was worried about. She whipped her head back towards the shelf like a bee-stung pony and sucked all the air out of the room in shock.

Mother glared at the book, realizing my crime. A slow fury built on her face, turning the pink in her cheeks to a dangerous crimson. Her lips pursed together and she let out the tiniest of huffs. A stranger might interpret such a huff as a good sign, but I knew it was a sign that a storm was building within. Saliva gathered at the corner of her lips. The hand holding my crow dropped it to the ground as if it had never held the bird to begin with.

The book at the center of my Mother's rage was *The Collected Poems of Lord Byron*. For a moment, I wished I had broken my neck in the glider fall, because I knew Mother's reaction to discovering that book in the innocence of my bedroom was going to be a fate much worse than death. I looked to Miss Stamp, desperate for help, but she quickly scuttled herself out of the room, unable to bear my impending punishment.

Dr. Poole also felt the need to escape, offering, 'I'll get a cold compress,' as he left the room. No soul with a sound mind wanted to witness the tongue-lashing that was sure to follow.

Mother closed her eyes and nodded her head. 'Now I understand everything.'

I climbed back up onto my bed, wincing at the sting from the thorns still in my flesh. It took a moment for me to gather my courage. So today was the day we'd finally have the mother-daughter battle I knew was so long overdue—and I'd have to fight it bleeding and on one leg. Part of me was terrified. The other part was ready to argue. I had lived so long under her rule, following her every command that I scarcely knew how to be my own person. I knew what I wanted – to succeed with Flyology— but my failure to get my flying machine functioning properly was proof that I needed freedom to follow my own instincts as an inventor. How else would I ever accomplish my goals? Sadly, freedom was in short supply at Fordhook Manor. I steadied myself and looked her in the eyes.

'Is it so wrong for me to read my own father's poetry?' I

asked, trying to stay calm, and trying not to cry from the pain in my ankle.

The question hung in the air for what seemed like minutes, unlike my flying machine, and I again had to remind myself that time does not slow. I forced myself not to look away, hoping she would see that I was so much more than a child now. I wasn't prepared to see the anguish in her face.

For seventeen years, Mother must have anticipated this question, secretly hoping I would have the sense never to ask. But of course I couldn't appease her wishes—I was too curious, too wild, too much like *him*. If my heritage was so grotesque that she wanted to pretend it never happened, perhaps the day of my ill-fated flight was the perfect time for her to finally illuminate the dark family history she had been alluding to all these years.

'Lord Byron was so dangerous a poison, I do not wish his name to even cross your lips,' she said with a solemn certainty I hadn't witnessed from her before.

'But Miss Stamp says he was the most brilliant and handsome man in all of England,' I said.

Mother's delicate facial features grew severe, 'Then perhaps Miss Stamp needs to be reminded that she is under my employ and I am not paying her to fill your head with nonsense.' I had a sudden sinking feeling in my stomach for the dressing down poor Miss Stamp would surely receive later.

My mother wasn't finished though. 'Your father was a monster. There's a reason God marked him with a clubfoot. His mangled toes were evidence of his vile soul. He...' Her voice trailed off, she could not finish her sentence. Emotion filled her eyes as she seemed caught up in a memory that was too painful to speak out loud. After a moment, the memory seemed to pass from her mind, as though it were terrified of her strong-as-oak will. Quickly, Mother stood and, after looking my dusty, leaf-ridden self over once more, simply left the room, taking the book of Lord Byron's poems with her.

'Please, I need that book!' I called out, but Mother was gone. I considered going after her but then remembered I couldn't put weight on my ankle. I almost laughed at the poetry; here I am without a foot to stand on and apparently it's a trait I shared with my father. Mother said he had a clubfoot. But what exactly was a clubfoot, I wondered? Could it be walked on without the assistance of a cane? Could it be repaired by a surgeon? Or should it be amputated altogether? A clubfoot must look like a club, but how much so? Does it have all five toes? Are the toes monstrous? Or, is a clubfoot a regular foot that appears to have been beaten with a club? My thoughts were rushing along so fast I could scarcely keep track of them, so I put my hand to my head to check for fever. I was relieved to find my forehead cool to the touch, even though my curiosity was on fire. If only I knew more. Cursed or not, Lord Byron was my flesh and blood – my father.

Standing in my ransacked bedroom without the books I loved, I couldn't help but feel as if I had inherited a curse by being forced to live with Mother.

My parents' marriage legally ended when I was less than a year old, so I had no memory of my famous father. Growing up, I created numerous fantasies in which he stole me away to go adventuring with him. We would travel the world, invent marvellous machines, and hatch entire universes together! Sadly though, he died while fighting with rebel forces in Greece when

I was only eight-years-old. His absence created an enormous hole in my heart. Maybe that had something to do with my determination to be part of the scientific community. He was as celebrated and esteemed in the literary world as I hoped I'd one day be in the scientific one. I just wanted to inspire others, as he did. Why couldn't mother see that desire was a good thing?

I don't know the exact circumstances of their divorce, only that my mother managed to gain custody of me, which is a rare occurrence in a legal system known for favoring men in such situations. Father must have done something pretty awful to give Mother the upper hand. Or maybe the judge took pity on her for being so young and vulnerable. I've been told she was considered quite beautiful in her youth.

I looked at the dust-lined shelves, now empty, and felt hot tears returning to my eyes. Not knowing my own father as a little girl had been the greatest travesty of my life and it was all Mother's fault for keeping him from me during those years. She married the 'dangerous' Lord Byron, after all, chose him to be the father of her child, probably even loved him once. Surely, he couldn't have been *all* bad.

Just then, Miss Stamp entered my room, bringing me a supper of cold sausage with a buttered roll. I watched her set down the tray, but I wasn't interested in food.

'Your mother is mad as hops. Didn't I tell you to keep to yourself and not to aggravate her today?'

'Tell me again about my father,' I begged her. She looked at me, eyes wide in disbelief.

'Darls, after all that's happened today, shouldn't you have your nose buried in scripture?' she said.

'Please, tell me something, anything,' I said, 'It's cruel for you to keep such information from me.' Miss Stamp hated when I called her cruel.

Miss Stamp closed the bedroom door and sat a whisper's distance from me on the edge of my bed.

'I've already told you everything I know,' she chided.

'Tell me again, please,' I said.

She sighed, seemingly resolved not to say anything. Then a devilish grin crossed her lips. In her heart of hearts, Miss Stamp was a gossip and I took advantage of that any chance I could.

'Lord Byron was said to be breathtakingly handsome,' she said. 'A dandy, he was. I never saw him myself, but the way ladies go on about him, surely it must have been true. They said his lips were the colour of pomegranates and that his eyes literally twinkled like the belt of Orion. He dressed in the most expensive fineries, like embroidered silk shirts and tall leather boots imported all the way from Italy. Some people claimed he had a bear for a pet and drank wine out of a human skull.'

'Where did he get a human skull?'

'I don't know, love.'

'What about his poetry?'

'You've read it yourself.'

'Just that one book. What about the rest?'

'Gentlefolk and scholars alike say he was gifted beyond any other poet of our time.'

Then I asked her another question. One to which I was afraid to hear the answer.

'Do you think he loved me?'

A tender look of pity came over her face. She began to brush a lock of my hair behind my ear. 'Of course your father loved you, Ada. Why wouldn't he? It's your mama who kept you two apart. She was very hurt by him and didn't want the same to happen to you.'

'Do you think he ever wanted to see me?'

'I'm certain of it.'

'It's not fair!' I said, more tears beginning to well in my eyes. 'Sometimes I think she kept him from me all those years just to make me suffer. I feel so stifled in this house. I'm unable to do my work as a scientist, unable to develop my mind the way I see fit. She's squeezing the life right out of me.'

'Ada, slow down. By God, you're only seventeen. Once you're grown and married, you will have more options at your disposal. Until then, do try to please her. Everyone will be happier that way,' she said, shooting me a warning look. 'Now, I must prepare the leeches for your mother's treatment. She's developed a severe headache and Dr. Poole is eager to bleed her,' she said.

I nodded, knowing that Mother would have a fit if Miss Stamp were late with her leeches. Mother used leeches to treat all of her ailments, and there were many, some real, some probably imagined.

'Go, then,' I said, wiping the tears from my cheeks. Miss Stamp exited the room and I felt my resolve begin to stiffen.

So what if they won't tell me what I want to know? There was nothing keeping me from finding out more on my own. I began to hatch a plan.

I would escape from Fordhook Manor and see the world, and no one—not Mother, nor Miss Stamp, nor the kindly Dr. Poole—would stop me. As the plan took shape in my mind, I felt a grin spread across my face. My first destination would be my father's ancestral home, Newstead Abbey.

3

Several days after my disastrous air drop, I still couldn't walk on my ankle. This made escaping from Fordhook pretty difficult, but I was still doing research and didn't mind waiting to recover. Science, it turns out, is all about research. It's very important to do thorough research or your whole hypothesis could be thrown out. I learned this the hard way when I was studying anatomy.

I had recently been fishing when I was ten, and thought that the delightfully slippery, eight-inch long jack pike at the end of my fishing rod would be a perfect subject for dissection. I wanted to see how its skeleton compared to that of a shark, having found an illustration of the toothy beast in one of my anatomy books. Not having the time for research that afternoon, I put the fish aside, and merrily went about the rest of my day without first planning the anatomy experiment out. It took me three days to finally do so, and by then my room stank to high heaven. Miss Stamp had to replace all my window dressings.

So it was with great care and attention to detail that I set about researching my escape plan. I knew the Byron family – my family – had a home called Newstead Abbey in Nottinghamshire, and according to a map in our library, the journey there would take several days on horseback. I began to pack a modest leather travel case with clothing and other items, but then unpacked it for fear of Mother discovering it. I decided I'd be better off quickly packing on the morning of my departure instead. I kept a mental list of all the things I would need to bring: food for the journey, extra stockings, books, and a warm coat for although it was summer, England always seemed to be cloaked in cool air… the list was growing longer by the day. I would escape in the middle of the night, but I began to wonder how I would ever sneak so heavy a trunk down the stairs without waking anyone.

And although the risk of capture was high, I couldn't stop thinking about seeing the home where my father lived for so much of his life. Surely there would be clues about my father at Newstead, artifacts even… perhaps some of his fancy garments still remained at the Abbey and I would be able to bury my nose in them in the hopes of uncorking the memories they surely held.

So many ideas about my father ran through my mind that I almost didn't notice the long days spent still as stone in bed. I wanted to be walking within the week, so I followed all of Dr. Poole's instructions to a T. I'd been in bed for four days and hadn't once upset Mother (a new record) when I heard the sound of a carriage approaching our house. Someone must be here, I thought. I hopped on my left foot over to the window and looked out at the surprisingly sunny day just in time to see the carriage arrive. But the identity of its passenger remained a mystery as the ornate carriage passed under the oak tree branches.

I hopped to the edge of the window, bending low in the hopes of seeing through the branches. That's when the man, perhaps in his late teens or early twenties, stepped out of the car. He carried at least a dozen books with him as he made his way up the walkway to our house. A brown, leather satchel hung on his shoulder. I felt a sudden flutter in my stomach. Mother didn't receive many visitors. Surely, his arrival had something to do with my latest disobedience.

His arrival was unsettling enough to push all fantasies about visiting Newstead Abbey to the back of my mind, and I slowly hobbled out of my bedroom to the top of the stairs (hopping as quietly as I could) in order to spy on the young man's entrance.

From my perch, I watched as Miss Stamp answered the door to greet the stranger who introduced himself as Mr. Stephen J. Spencer from Oxford University. I felt a sigh of relief wash over me and I finally let out the breath I'd been holding. He must be my new tutor and a tutor was much better than a doctor from the Bedlam lunatic asylum called by Mother to take me away. I inched closer to the stairs to see if I could get a better view of him, trying not to give my position away with an ill-placed hop on one of the creaking floor boards. I crouched down on my knees to see through the gaps in the railing.

Mr. Stephen J. Spencer had sandy blond curls peaking out from under his cap and a pencil behind his ear. His square chin fit his face rather well, giving him a sturdy, handsome appearance. He wore a wool, Oxford-embroidered scarf and hat, despite it being a warm day.

As Miss Stamp went to find Mother, Mr. Spencer nervously took off his cap, ran his fingers through his hair before taking the pencil from behind his ear and gnawing on it slightly. Mr. Spencer, in his green jacket and heavy brown boots, stood straight, had the skinny legs of a boy but the broad shoulders of a man. In my opinion, he looked less like a tutor and more like one of the cricket players I once saw play a match in Sussex. I couldn't help but wonder if he ever played the sport.

When Mother and Dr. Poole entered to greet him, Mr. Spencer took the pencil from his mouth and put it back behind his ear as he followed them into the spacious, hunter green-coloured parlor where they exchanged greetings.

'Good afternoon, Mr. Spencer. We hope your ride here was a pleasant one,' said Dr. Poole as he shook Mr. Spencer's hand.

'I couldn't have asked for better weather to make such a journey, though it took much longer than I anticipated,' replied Mr. Spencer.

'I'm sorry to hear that,' said Mother, 'Please, may I pour you some tea?'

He nodded and she tilted a pale blue Wedgewood teapot that depicted some lively Greek gods over an empty cup, filling it with Darjeeling.

'How old a man are you?' asked Dr. Poole.

'Twenty years, sir. But I have passed all my exams with excellent marks. And many people agree that Oxford is the best University in the modern world, producing the most sought–after academics. It is quite a stimulating place,' said Mr. Spencer.

'We hope you won't find country life too dull, Mr. Spencer,' said Dr. Poole.

'Nonsense. I have a journal of statistical mathematics as related to the principals of uncertainty I'm planning to write – in my spare time, of course – and the bucolic pace of the country shall provide an outstanding environment to do so,' he said. 'Now, in regards to the education you would like me to provide for your son—'

'Daughter,' said Mother, 'I have a daughter. She is seventeen and has been carefully sheltered from the outside world.'

Mr. Spencer paused a moment, evidently trying to understand. He tilted his head to one side.

'I am to teach mathematics to a *girl?*' he asked as if she had asked him to teach a hog.

'Yes,' she said, 'You don't take issue with tutoring a young lady, I hope.'

He was stumped for what to say. Clearly, he'd never considered it before.

'No,' he finally said, 'If there's anything for which Oxford has prepared me, it is a challenge.'

A challenge? I felt my cheeks getting warm. He hadn't even met me. Was he speaking in earnest? If so, he must think awfully highly of himself. Needless to say, I was angry at his position and also at Mother for not attempting to change his opinion of me. It took every ounce of restraint in me not to toddle down the stairs and make my intellect known to him. How dare he assume I would be a challenge simply because I was a girl. I'll show him a challenge, I thought to myself as I crawled back to my room. My ankle was getting better, but nowhere near ready for adventuring yet. I hopped into bed and pulled the covers over my head, mulling over Mr. Spencer's words and hoping my ankle would heal very quickly so I could get on with of my escape plan as soon as possible. I vowed to myself that there was no way on God's green earth I would let that pencil-chewing dolt think he was smarter than me.

4

I woke up from a nap later that afternoon to find my mother standing over me with a judicatory air. I rubbed my eyes warily. Was I still sleeping or was there a hint of a malicious twinkle in her eye?

'I should like you to know that, as of today, I have employed a Mr. Spencer from Oxford University to be your new tutor. He comes highly recommended. He will be residing in the east guestroom and will begin daily calculus sessions with you this afternoon,' she announced.

So Mr. Spencer's presence *was* meant to be a punishment after all. I felt my stomach recoil at the thought of spending time in his condescending presence. Though I knew any attempt to change her mind would be futile, I wanted to make sure she knew I wasn't in favor of it.

'I'm not in need of any tutor. I am quite capable of educating myself.'

'The state of your swollen ankle implies otherwise.'

'We both know I'm likely more clever than any tutor, even one from Oxford.'

'It is not the reaches of his mathematical acumen with which I'm concerned. It is the keen eye he is to keep on you at all times that shall bring me solace. Lord knows I've tried my best to watch over you. Mr. Spencer will assist me in ensuring that your mind is constantly occupied with the proper subjects.

There is no effort, large or small, that I will not make to keep you from indulging your devilish imagination.'

'Devilish?'

'Indeed. You will receive five hours of tutoring in mathematics daily, followed by one hour of French. Any and all books used in your education will be approved by me. Now put on a proper dress and fix yourself like a lady. I won't have you looking like a guttersnipe in his presence.' She turned on her heels and left the room.

I felt the knot in my stomach double. If I were to stay at Fordhook, which I would not, Mother had just made it clear that I wouldn't be able to read the poetry, plays or narrative fiction that I love, for fear it would further ignite my 'devilish imagination' as she put it.

Fortunately, I had already read nearly all of the Shakespearean plays and sonnets. *Hamlet* was my favourite, as I empathized with Ophelia and her fate in the Danish Prince's tragic game. I, however, was sure I would never drown myself in a frigid river. I had too much work to do, and many scientific discoveries to make as well as discredit the notion that women cannot be great thinkers. Dear Ophelia, if only you had an escape plan such as the one I'm developing. Perhaps one day, I'll write a book for women on how to escape tragic circumstances and not simply give up on themselves.

To satisfy Mother's demands that I dress like a proper lady, I chose one of my fancier dresses, a green, low-necked moiré silk gown. The bottom of the skirt was puffed with quillings of bright yellow satin. With my ankle still painful, I decided against stockings, but I did brush my hair before meticulously braiding it. I then pinned the long braid in a circle, and affixed a gold and pearl diadem on top to match my pearl earrings – a bit overblown, but at least Mother couldn't say I didn't make myself presentable.

Typically, all studying would be conducted in the library, but I needed to stay off my feet. So, for my lessons today, I sat on my bed, propped up by big pillows as Mother and the tutor entered my room at half-past two. Mother's face registered a bit of surprise when she saw that I was so dressed up, but she said nothing about it. She introduced the tutor as Mr. Spencer. He nodded, avoiding eye contact with me.

Without asking me any questions about my education or interests, Mr. Spencer simply went to work drawing an *X/Y* table on a chalkboard and began to fill in a linear equation. As he did this, Mr. Spencer lectured me on the history of calculus and the role Archimedes played in its further development. I knew all this of course, but I let him drone on.

Mother watched him intently at first, but after three quarters of an hour of him prattling on, I caught her swallowing a yawn. Finally, she stood up.

'Mr. Spencer, shall I leave you to your instruction? Or should I remain as deputy?' asked Mother.

'Whatever pleases your fancy, Lady Byron. I am amenable to either,' he said, giving her a polite smile.

'I feel a nerve-storm coming on. I shall have a brief rest and then return. Ada will no doubt be on her best behaviour,' she said, shooting me an icy scowl before she exited the room.

Once she was down the hall, Mr. Spencer took what I considered to be a haughty tone with me. It was a very different tone than the polite one he adopted with Mother, in any event.

'I have a very specific plan for your education, Miss Byron.

I shall be attempting to shape your mind into that of a man, which is going to be quite a challenge for both of us,' he said, shaking his head. 'But I will explain any new fundamental theorems of calculus as slowly and simply as possible. I understand women's brains need to hear information repeated numerous times before it sets into their logic.'

After he finished speaking slowly and clearly to me, he studied his mathematical table on the chalkboard. That's when I noticed his almond-coloured satchel sitting on the bed and I became quite curious as to what was inside. With his back to me, I quietly unlatched the leather strap and slid out what appeared to be a sketchbook.

Mr. Spencer cleared his throat. 'Please tell me the quadratic equation, Miss Byron,' he said, in a slow, scholarly voice. But I paid him no mind as I flipped through the pages of what must have been his own hand-drawn sketches of people, faces, hands, and bowls of fruit.

When he discovered me examining his drawings, he grew agitated.

'That is not yours, return it,' he said as he reached for the book. But I was one step ahead and played a game of piggy in the middle with the book. He was fun to taunt. I loved watching his irritation grow.

'It is of the utmost importance our teacher-pupil relationship begin with you showing me the proper respect.'

But what did I care about showing him respect? He already showed me a discourtesy by patronizing me and, besides, I would be departing in a few days, anyhow.

After a moment of awkwardly attempting to seize his sketchbook from me, he finally snatched it out of my hands. He was so incredibly frustrated, I couldn't help but giggle at him.

Red-faced, Mr. Spencer asked again, only more sternly and slowly this time, 'Tell me the formula for the slope and the Y intercept.'

I glanced up at the X/Y table. My eyes quickly scanned each row of numbers.

'I can't.'

'Please try to follow along. At Oxford it is extremely important to listen to the lecturer at all times,' he said as if he were speaking to a small child. Little did he know that in his hasty judgement of my mental ability, he had provided me with the perfect moment to shine.

'I cannot calculate the slope nor the Y intercept,' I replied slowly, 'because you have made an error.' I took the chalk from his hand, leaned over and changed a negative fifteen in the lower right corner of the table to a negative ten. In disbelief, Mr. Spencer examined the X/Y table more closely. He went over the numbers, mouthing the calculations to himself before conceding.

'You're correct,' he said, perturbed and chewing his pencil, 'but how did you see that?'

'If Y is quadratic, then the change in Y values should form a line, and the change in the line is constant,' I said as I wrote the correct quadratic equation on the chalkboard: $Y = -5X + 15$.'

His jaw hung open.

'But I...But you...No one at Oxford will ever believe a girl can do this.'

Mr. Spencer now seemed to look at me with a mild curiosity rather than disdain. Suddenly, I went from being a known quantity to a variable. Though I still resented his condescending attitude, I felt vindicated. Yes, Mr. Spencer, I can play your game and I may even win.

For the rest of the afternoon, his tone changed slightly. He spoke a bit more quickly and (thankfully) resisted the urge to explain every single mundane detail. Though I never softened my aloof attitude, I could tell he saw me a bit differently than when he first began my lesson.

After our long afternoon of studies, Mr. Spencer retired to his bedchamber at the other end of the manor. I was happy to be rid of him and took a few tender steps around my room to stretch my languishing muscles — as I'd already learned that week, sitting in bed all day can lead to leg cramps and I'd no interest in waking up in the middle of the night with another muscle spasm.

As I hobbled around, favoring my good foot, I kept thinking about my plan to escape. I had spent so much time plotting my journey to Newstead that I hadn't spent much thought on what I would be leaving behind. Would I miss my room, I wondered? Or Fordhook? And what about Miss Stamp? She'd be heartbroken.

I limped over to my window to look out over the grassy grounds and was surprised to see Mother in her tulip garden. She hadn't returned to check on my progress like she said she would, though it appeared that her 'nerve storm' had passed. The more likely scenario was that the ailment had been invented as a way to occupy herself with her own preferred activities.

Mother grew prized black tulips that were such an inky charcoal in hue, they seemed to actually absorb the light. Any room in which they were placed would get darker not brighter. I watched as she bent down and tore weeds from the earth, occasionally squashing an aphid or two with her thick wool gardening gloves. Oh, Mother, I thought. How melancholy you'll be when I'm away. She'd have to send Mr. Spencer back to his beloved Oxford and she would be without anyone to torture. Whatever will she do with all her time? Grow more macabre flowers, I supposed.

Then a strange thought occurred to me – what if she were happy when I was gone? What if my absence were a relief from all the trouble I caused her? The thought was more than a little unsettling, and I considered it for quite some time before remembering my role as the pawn on her chessboard. The truth is, she needed me to sell her woeful tale of divorce.

Without a daughter, no one would pity her. My mother fed on pity the way Dr. Poole's leeches fed on her blood. My presence protected her. It was as if she didn't need to consider her own failings as long as she could obsess over mine. No wonder she never wanted me to know my father and said so many cruel things about him. For if he weren't a monster, her failed marriage would be her fault. It was in that moment that I knew deep down in my bones that my father was a good man and must have had a strong sense of purpose and dignity. The problem in their marriage must have been that he refused to let her control him the way she controlled me.

I prayed to God to heal my ankle quickly so I could begin my journey. After Newstead Abbey, I would go to the continent. I'd go to Paris – no, the French territory in Morocco and test new flying machines in the boundless and forgiving sand dunes. That sounded so divine, I even considered crafting some crutches out of the leftover wood from the Carrier Pigeon, but then told myself it would only be a few more days. A few more days before I'd be free from my captor.

I was surprised when Mr. Spencer joined us for supper that evening. It was proper, I suppose – he needed food after all, but it had been quite some time since anyone other than Dr. Poole joined Mother and me at the table. His presence once again put my stomach in knots. Miss Stamp helped me to the table but my face turned sour as Mr. Spencer complimented Mother on the centerpiece: a crystal vase of black tulips.

Tonight, the menu at Fordhook consisted of rabbit pie baked with whelks, carrots, onions and celery, and a dish of roasted potatoes. Mother typically made chitchat with any guests about neutral topics, always avoiding matters like the King or religion. When guests weren't around, we'd hear an earful, but tonight's keynote seemed to be disease.

'Apparently, a cholera epidemic has broken out on the east side of London. A merchant ship returned infected from Germany and is now being quarantined. The King's men have warned that all should stay away,' she said, as if she were an authority on the subject.

'At Oxford,' said Mr. Spencer, rubbing his ear where he usually keeps a pencil, 'I once saw a play performed called *Love and Fright*. It was about how the paranoia of a cholera outbreak turned otherwise God-fearing, productive citizens into frightful denizens suggesting that mad panic and fear of the disease is perhaps worse than the actual disease itself,' he said.

'Cholera is a dreadful pestilence and should positively fill society with fear and panic. Don't forget the bubonic plague deniers,' said Dr. Poole, always eager to balance an argument.

'Must we really discuss such dreadful things, Mother? Our guest, Mr. Spencer, might begin to think you're a pessimist,' I said before filling my mouth with rabbit.

'Very well. I'm only trying to inform you of the health and well being of our great nation. It would do you some good to take an interest in such matters,' she said. The table was quiet for some time.

Dr. Poole was the only soul brave enough to bring conversation back to the table.

'So, Mr. Spencer, how did your first lesson go today? Was our Ada an apt pupil?' he asked.

'Miss Byron was a surprising pupil,' he said, then paused as if trying to find the perfect way to phrase his thoughts. He turned from Dr. Poole and looked directly at Mother. 'Lady Byron, your daughter doesn't have a typical woman's mind,' he said as cut his potatoes into squares.

'I make no secret that she is a flawed stone,' Mother replied, before sipping her claret.

Flawed? I nearly choked on my mouthful of pie. I was furious she would say such a thing. But then a tiny smile crept onto Mr. Spencer's face, like he had a secret.

'To the contrary,' said Mr. Spencer. Both Mother and Dr. Poole stopped chewing. 'Ada's intuitive grasp of calculus is sharp and clear as a crown jewel.'

Goodness. No one had ever said such a kind thing about me, and certainly not in the presence of Mother. My eyes were fixed on her to see how she would respond.

'Well then, at least your pedagogical talents won't be wasted, as I had feared,' she said as she glanced at Dr. Poole. He responded with an, 'I told you as much' expression.

'Cheers to Ada's unusual mind,' said Dr. Poole as he raised his glass.

'Cheers,' said Mr. Spencer though Mother seemed to lack the same enthusiasm.

It was then Miss Stamp cleared our dinner plates to make way for the delicious dessert course of Spotted Dick with chocolate custard, but I was surprised to feel a contented glow had already washed over me without even taking a bite.

After dinner, Miss Stamp helped me hop on my left foot to my bedchamber. When we got to the stairs, I leaned on her shoulder to steady me.

'Careful, now my lovely,' she gently cooed into my ear. I felt quite lucky to have such a kind-hearted companion. She was always helpful and never afraid to show me affection. I realised I would miss her terribly when I escaped. As she helped me up the final three stairs, I wondered if I could write to her using a secret code so we could correspond without Mother discovering my whereabouts.

I dressed for bed to the sound of Miss Stamp's gossip, laying back in contentment while she applied a minty balm to my wounded ankle. Only when she began giggling about the newest addition to Fordhook did my ears perk back up.

'The lad seemed to be quite impressed by your thoughts, missy,' said Miss Stamp as she returned the lid to the jar of balm before setting it on my dresser. She wiped her hands on her apron and knelt to the ground, where she began sorting through my dirty laundry.

'That was after I showed him I was as smart as any boy. Did you see his pencils? They're all chewed up.'

'I think I could overlook such a trivial matter for a man so handsome.'

'Handsome? Mr. Spencer?' Maybe I had been so fuelled with

anger at him for calling me a challenge, I failed to notice the details of his face.

'Yes, that chin. Those lips,' she said as she made kissing noises.

'Then perhaps he should be tutoring you, because I think he's quite plain, and a bore,' I said, realizing now would be the perfect time to employ her to fetch my father's book for me. Enough time had passed for Mother not to notice if the book went missing. Miss Stamp didn't like going against Mother's wishes, but would if I begged her to do so.

'Such a lovely blouse,' said Miss Stamp as she held up a fine silk blouse with puffy sleeves and seashells for buttons from the pile of laundry. In luminescent pink, the shirt was quite charming. I scooted to the edge of my bed, very close to Miss Stamp's face. 'Keep it,' I said, casually, trying to register her interest in acquiring the garment.

'I couldn't,' said Miss Stamp, though I could tell she wanted it.

'It has a stain,' I said, though we both knew it didn't. That's when I looked deep into her eyes and said, 'I just need one small thing.'

Miss Stamp raised her eyebrows.

'Find my father's book of poems and return it to me.'

'Darls, if you get caught with it-,' she said with a warning tone.

'Just bring me that book,' I said, handing her the blouse. She gave a small sigh but we spoke no further on the matter.

Around midnight, as I was deep in fantasy about my escape route to Newstead Abbey, an envelope slid under my door. I tossed the blankets off of me, got out of bed and hopped over to the note, occasionally touching the wall for balance. I opened the door slightly, expecting to see Miss Stamp, whom I assumed had failed at retrieving the book of my father's poems. But instead, I saw no one.

Baffled, I quietly closed the door and plopped onto the floor. I opened the envelope, expecting to read Miss Stamp's apology, but was intrigued to discover the note was not from Miss Stamp, but from Mr. Spencer. In perfect penmanship, it read:

Miss Byron, I cannot sleep. My mind is galloping with thoughts of your precocious equations, particularly the ones you've written on the blackboard with your dainty fingers. Oh, how I wish my person were the blackboard on which you scribbled all those immaculate integers, so I might feel your warm touch on my skin. You draw your eights with circles so perfectly round and plump, it has become my favourite composite number. The image of the curve of your slope, rising over my straight tangent fills me with a rare excitement. Discovering these free variables would resolve my lonely logarithm.

Stephen

His mind is 'galloping with thoughts' about me solving equations? I felt somewhat confused for a moment, then reread the note. It said I filled him with a *rare excitement*. Did that mean he fancied me? As I read the note a third time, I was convinced he was expressing romantic feelings for me – the girl that was to be a 'challenge' to educate – ha! Before I could determine if his fondness was a good or bad thing, my bedchamber door opened. It was Miss Stamp clutching the little brown book of Byron's poems. As I looked up at her, I couldn't hide my embarrassment about the note. She instinctually knew I was hiding something.

41

'What is that you're reading?' Miss Stamp whispered as she plucked the note from my hands and scuttled over to the candle to read it. When she realised it was a love letter from my tutor, she clucked with laughter.

'Hush! You want to get both of us exiled to the Scottish Highlands?' I said, and quickly took the letter back.

Miss Stamp quoted the letter, mocking Mr. Spencer's teaching voice, 'You draw your eights with circles so perfectly round and plump,' Don't you see? He fancies your bosom!' said Miss Stamp.

'He does not,' I said. 'Besides, I want nothing to do with silly romantic escapades. He's a lowly tutor,' I said, not understanding how the number eight could be a euphemism for my... then I suddenly understood. Oh, my! The letter really was truly amorous.

'He was educated at Oxford, don't forget,' taunted Miss Stamp.

'How could I? He reminds me every hour,' I said, then burned Mr. Spencer's note over the candle. As the paper turned to ash, I grew increasingly curious. Never in my seventeen years had a man expressed his desire for me. It felt strangely exciting. Not that I had any desire for him, his personality was quite stifled in his Oxfordian mind-set. If I were ever to be interested in a man, he would need a powerful imagination, first and foremost, along with a spirit of adventure. But it did feel quite remarkable to be desired.

I took the scandalous book of Lord Byron's poems and told Miss Stamp to go to bed. She playfully pushed up her own bosom with her hands, saying, 'Pardon while I adjust my eights.'

'Go!' I said and shut my door before anyone heard me laugh.

I looked down at my own bosom – they weren't exactly

eights. Maybe a couple of twos. Suddenly, I couldn't help but wonder what it would feel like to run my fingers through Mr. Spencer's blond curls. Or what it would feel like if he brushed his cheek against mine? Before I escaped this den of darkness, the scientist in me was determined to find out.

5

Within a fortnight, my ankle was feeling ready for a journey, though I continued to pretend it still hurt so no one would suspect I was capable of setting off on my own. But the more I spent time with Mr. Spencer, I began to think Miss Stamp was correct about him being handsome. He did have a very masculine jaw line that, by the end of the day, was covered in stubble. And though the left side of his upper lip wasn't exactly symmetrical with the right side, both lips were pink, full and pillowy, and seemed like they could kiss for days on end. Truth be told, I was thinking much more about Mr. Spencer than escaping. On a Thursday evening, I sent Mr. Spencer a note to arrange a meeting in private.

Dear Mr. Spencer,

Thank you for your letter. I should very much like to take my lessons on the far side of the grounds tomorrow, away from Mother's hawkish eyesight, should the weather be pleasant. There, we can discuss your note in more thorough detail.

AAB

Not exactly a love letter, so much as a call-to-action letter, but I couldn't stop wondering if Mr. Spencer, or Stephen I supposed I could now refer to him, had true affections for me. If he did, it's possible he'd help me escape. Of course, that would mean he'd become unemployed and the man seemed quite serious about his employment, so perhaps he wouldn't help me after all. But perhaps Stephen liked adventure and would want to accompany me on my trip. Terribly scandalous, yes, the two of us travelling together, but he could prove a beneficial adversary, considering the trip had many variables. Of course, he'd try to convince me to stop in his beloved Oxford on the way to Nottinghamshire, meaning I would have to convince him there wouldn't be time…

My mind was awash in thoughts of my tutor, and I hardly noticed the passage of time while I waited for his response. Within an hour of sliding my note under Stephen's door, another note slid under mine. It was from Stephen, of course.

Miss Byron,

I am in favor of your request to take your lessons outdoors. Truthfully, I am counting the minutes until I am alone with you. I believe the fresh country air will do both our constitutions some good. May I be so bold as to ask if you would be willing to allow me to make a sketch of you in my book? I shall bring my charcoals and you may tell me your answer when we meet.

Stephen

A sketch? Of me? I supposed that it would be romantic if he were a skilled artist, but Stephen was quite the novice. I had never been casually sketched before, but I decided I would allow it. If the likeness of me were done in a shoddy manner, I would demand he destroy the paper.

The thought of having my face pressed amongst the same pages as Stephen's hastily drawn pears gave me a little thrill, and I was reminded of my father. Perhaps today would be the perfect opportunity to read aloud my father's poems and see if Stephen liked them as much as I did. He did, after all, fancy himself some kind of artist, and don't artists band together? If Stephen thought my father a great writer, he may be more inclined to help me escape from my captor.

The next day, after a light morning's rain that brought out the snails and earthworms, the sun appeared, golden and toasty. A parade of ants marched up the oak tree branches that made long, finger-like shadows at the far end of the garden. I knew this area well, as it was where I would come as a small girl to get away from Mother. Hardly anyone ever made it over to this part of the Manor, as the grounds were less manicured here and the garden grew a little wilder. It was a secret spot all to my own, where I would collect leaves or beetles and the occasional bird's nest. And it was in these familiar shadows that Stephen had neatly set out his charcoal pencils while waiting for me to arrive.

Wearing my yellow dress made of silk taffeta woven with white flowers and a front closure, I watched him from behind a tall tree for several minutes before I made my approach. He kept shifting his sitting position, as if trying to find the best view of the surroundings. He licked his fingers then smoothed the cowlick above his forehead. I walked quietly behind him with the purpose of surprising him. I tapped his left shoulder then stepped to the right as he turned his head to the left. He quickly realised I was teasing him and tried to hide his embarrassment.

'Miss Byron, good afternoon.'

'Good afternoon, Mr. Spencer.'

46

'Have you had time to consider my request to sketch your likeness?

'I have. But, I should like to see your sketchbook before I give you my answer.'

'Did you not see it the other day?'

'Not well enough. I should like to get a better look at the quality of your drawings. To determine if you have any true skill.'

Nervously, he handed me the book. As I looked through the pages, I could tell his eyes were scanning my face, eager for my approval. His sketches were mediocre at best and he knew it.

'These are the work of an amateur,' I said, 'They lack a certain *je ne sais quais*', don't you think?' I pointed to one lifeless sketch of a woman holding her needlepoint.

'Yes, I agree that one lacks some inspiration...'

He paused for a moment, not sure what to say. Then, a thought came to him.

'However, my Oxfordian colleague by the name of James Essinger spent a summer amongst the artists of Paris. In France, it is customary to sketch a woman in the...' he paused, his face turning red.

'In the what?' I asked, having no idea what he was referring to.

He searched for the most discreet word and finally spat out, 'To sketch them *au natural*.'

What on earth did that mean? I had to tread carefully, as to not sound ignorant.

'Do you mean they sketch models in a natural environment? Like these woods? Or by the sea?'

Stephen grew a bit embarrassed, saying, 'Not exactly. The models present *themselves* in their natural state.'

I tried to fully understand what he meant. Then it became clear.

'You mean without garments?' I asked. Stephen nodded. My mind was racing, I had never considered such a thing. Then it dawned on me.

'Are you suggesting you'd like to sketch me -- in the French style?' I asked in a low tone.

Stephen froze for a moment, then muttered, 'No, no, no. I mean...unless that is a possibility?'

'Of course not,' I snapped. But then, a grand idea came to me: we could make a trade. 'Such a thing would never be possible – *unless* you'd be willing to keep a great secret for me.'

Stephen swallowed hard then said, 'I am the keeper of many secrets. My friends at Oxford all regard me as the trustworthiest of the bunch. You may tell me anything and I'll—' he made the motion of locking his mouth and throwing away the key.

From under my dress, I pulled out Lord Byron's book. He looked at the book and asked, 'That is your secret? A book of your father's poetry?'

I smiled, 'I guess I should have said secrets plural, as in, I have several of them. This book is part of an elaborate plan I have to escape this house.'

'Escape? But why?'

'To get away from Mother, of course,' I said, starting to become exasperated by his lack of awareness about my misery. 'Are you quite certain I can trust you?'

'Certain as rain.'

I eyed him carefully. He seemed earnest enough. I took a breath and began to unbuckle my boots. I removed my stockings and began unhooking the front of my dress. Stephen watched me carefully, barely even blinking.

'I've been to many poetry readings at Oxford. Hearing the

words spoken is a delight to captivate one's ears. Why don't you read aloud while I sketch,' he said quickly, as if he thought I might change my mind.

With my dress unhooked, I paused for a moment. This was probably the most scandalous thing I had ever done in my life, but it would be worth it if he would help with my liberation. I grew determined to do it. I lifted my yellow dress over my head, causing Stephen to gasp. His eyes scanned the area in and around the oak trees; no one was around. Seeing him so nervous was thrilling to me. He would most definitely help me with my plan.

Now wearing only my white camisole and petticoat, I laid down on my stomach, the book of poems in hand. Finally, there was someone with whom I could discuss the meaning of my father's writing. Someone who might love his poetry as much as I did – at least, what little I knew of it. Stephen could likely acquire other works by my father and share them with me. Filled with excitement, wearing nothing but my under-garments, I began to read aloud.

'Ah, happy she!' I read, devouring each word like cake. 'To 'scape from him whose kiss had been pollution unto aught so chaste,' I paused briefly to glance at Stephen. His hands shook ever so slightly. His charcoal crumbled after a moment. He nervously searched his pockets for another, finally remembering he had laid them on the ground. Wisps of my hair floated up and down in the lavender-scented breeze.

'Who soon had left her charms for vulgar bliss and spoil'd her goodly lands to gild his waste,' I read, looking up at him again. 'Spoiled her goodly lands...Sounds dangerous. And fantastic, don't you think?'

Stephen's own mouth was so dry from nervousness, he was barely able to murmur the 's' sound in 'yes'. I continued reading.

'Nor calm domestic peace had ever deigned to taste. And now Childe Harold was sore sick at heart. And from his fellow bacchanals would flee--' But Stephen interrupted me.

'The poetry of your form has transcended the angles and curves of my charcoaled strokes on this sheet of paper. I fear I cannot do it justice!' he said with a frustration that brought him near tears.

I looked up at him and saw the pained look on his face. I didn't understand why he suddenly became so frustrated.

'Just carry on,' I said.

'I cannot,' he said then tossed his sketchbook aside and moved daringly close to me. His chestnut eyes were big and wild. That's when I feared he might try to kiss me. My fear was justified. He took my hand and began showering my palm with kisses. He was clearly love-struck in the worst way and before I could pull my hand away from his lips, he took my head in his hands.

'Run away with me, tonight, dearest Ada. We can be married by morning,' he said in an urgent tone. My stomach suddenly rose to my throat as I realised I had made a terrible mistake trying to employ him as an ally in my escape plan. The last thing I wanted was to be married to Stephen! Who knew posing in the French style would ignite such strong passions in a man?

'Stephen, I --,' but he grabbed my hand and began kissing up my arm until he reached my bosom, where he planted his mouth on my chest! I watched him as if I were watching a stage play, like an audience member. His lips were tender on my flesh and his breathing quickened. I wondered what kisses on the mouth would feel like, not that I would let him kiss me there, but before I could render my verdict aloud, the sunlight on my face turned to a dark shadow: a person's shadow.

'Mother!' I shouted, without really meaning to as I saw her standing over us. Panic struck my body, this was going to be worse than her discovering my father's book – much worse.

Stephen was so focused on me, he did not yet see my mother and responded as though I was merely talking about her.

'We'll tell your Mother after we are wed,' he mumbled into my bosom, right before my mother delivered a swift kick to his ribs.

Stephen turned around to see her standing over us, breathing fire.

'Unhand my daughter. You snake!' Mother hissed.

Stephen jumped to his feet. I quickly reached for my yellow dress and began putting on the garment.

'A...a wasp flew under Miss Byron's dress,' said Stephen, 'I was merely trying to suck the poison out of the sting.' I nodded, knowing full well that Mother would never believe such a pathetic story.

'She's been poisoned indeed,' said Mother, 'Slither out of here, Mr. Spencer, before I tear you apart with my own hands.'

'Yes,' he answered and reached to pick up his sketchbook. Mother stepped on the book before he could retrieve it. Stephen then ran off.

I tried to hide my forbidden book of poetry by sitting on it, but Mother saw it and managed to pry it out from under me. She whacked me with the book several times on my head.

'You've wounded me in a way that is unforgivable,' said Mother.

Again, her upset was all about what I was doing to her. But what about what she was doing to me, locking me away in this lonely house, sequestering me from my past and denying me the only father I had? I was furious. And yet, I was also terrified of what she might do to me. Looking up at her rage-filled face, I realised I could fight or cower. I chose to fight.

'You've kept my father away from me my whole life. I'm not a child anymore and I have a right to know his poetry,' I said in my strongest, loudest voice.

'You have no rights beyond what I give to you in this house,' she said attempting to slap my face. I managed to swat her hand away, but she was surprisingly strong. I knew I couldn't live in this house one more day.

Just then, Miss Stamp arrived at the scene, out of breath and pale as a ghost. 'Don't murder her, please!' But Mother swatted Miss Stamp across her cheek, leaving a red mark that I knew wouldn't fade for days.

'I'm leaving this house, and I'm getting as far away from you as possible and there's nothing you can do to stop me,' I shouted.

'And where exactly will you go?' said Mother.

'French Morocco to test flying machines,' I yelled, but as the words left my mouth, I realised how foolish I sounded; how very much like a child.

'Your mad, wicked schemes are going to be the death of me, Ada.'

Mother's anger was leaving her, and in its place was fatigue and… fear. She was afraid for me plain and simple. Suddenly I saw what she saw – a brash, sunburnt young woman with no money of her own and no prospects, threatening to leave the only home she'd ever known, who only moments ago was nearly ravaged by a half-mad scholar. I had calculated all the risks of travel except one: people.

I didn't understand people. Mother, who always confused and angered me, Miss Stamp who had just taken a slap to defend me, and now Stephen whom I had fantasized would help me escape with nothing in it for him, and whom I had assumed I could easily manage… How on earth could I expect to live in this world if I couldn't even predict that a man such as Stephen could behave so wildly?

My resolve began to crumble as I realised that escaping from my home was really just a childish ruse. I was suddenly embarrassed I had said it. But I was so desperate for freedom! The plan made so much sense in my imagination, but it was not a practical plan in any way. I was still just a girl and travelling alone or with Stephen (mad or not), would incite scandal. Mother had won. I knew I would need to prepare myself for the punishment that was to follow, but nothing could have prepared me for what she said next.

Mother turned to Miss Stamp, 'Fetch Dr. Poole. I want Ada's person thoroughly examined,' she said before she narrowed her eyes on me. 'If your maidenhead is compromised, I shall sell you to gypsies.'

How cruel to threaten such a fate! I knew it was hyperbole, but it still made me feel so unwanted. Fighting back tears, I shouted, 'I have nothing to hide!' I didn't bother to fasten the hooks on my dress. Instead, with my undergarments showing, I ran through the grove of oaks, across the garden and to the house. My mind was a flood of frustration, it felt as if an ocean of frigid water sloshed inside my skull, freezing solid any love I had ever felt bubble up for Mother.

I ran into the house, up the stairs and into my bedchamber where I threw myself down onto my bed and howled with tears.

Miss Stamp knocked on my door, wanting in, but I didn't want to see her. I couldn't.

After a few hours, Mother and Dr. Poole solemnly entered my room. I remained motionless on the bed, in a pool of tears. It seemed the inspection of my person was about to begin and would certainly be the most humiliating event of my life.

'Ada, Dr. Poole is here. He'll need—'

'This is not necessary. There has been no carnal breach,' I said.

'Sometimes, a man can accomplish such things without a lady's knowledge,' she said.

What on earth did she mean? Certainly that couldn't be true, could it? I honestly didn't know. The situation was suddenly far more complicated than I had ever anticipated. Dr. Poole spoke up.

'Lady Byron, forgive me, but if I may request some privacy for your daughter. This is a delicate matter and will no doubt be easier to accomplish with fewer eyes on the patient.'

I looked at Mother. She made eye contact with me and I nodded in agreement with Dr. Poole.

'Very well. I sincerely hope the doctor's findings are consistent with your version of the events,' she turned and exited the room, nearly slamming the door behind her.

I was no doubt sweating by now, unsure what was to come. Dr. Poole sat in a green leather armchair by my bed, his shoulders a bit slouched over. His thumb and forefinger cradled his forehead before he cleared his throat. He then leaned forward and spoke very softly. His brows came together in a way that created a deep crease between them.

'Ada, would you say you love Mr. Spencer?'

Was Dr. Poole mad?

'Love him? I despise him. I'm pleased he'll be sent away.'

Dr. Poole was quiet a moment, considering my answer. He gave a tiny nod and said, 'I see,' as he stood, taking in a deep breath.

Every muscle in my body clenched, fearful of what was to come next. Truth be told, I had no idea what they thought Stephen had done to me. I hoped my exam would be over quickly. But then, to my surprise, Dr. Poole began to exit the room.

'But where are you going?'

'The exam is complete. My medical expertise has concluded that your body is pure.'

That's all? No disrobing? No examination?

As he reached for the door handle, he paused a moment, then turned and looked at me.

'Ada, in addition to your status and wealth, you have become quite a lovely young woman. Sadly, there are people in this world who will endeavour to take advantage of your finer qualities. Promise me you will be most vigilant in protecting yourself from such men.'

'I promise,' I said with a sigh of relief.

He left the room and, filled with sweet relief, I quickly fell asleep.

In the morning, I found a note had been slid under my door.

Miss Byron,
Your mother is forcing me to return to Oxford, but it does not diminish the love I feel for you. I have, however, decided to abandon the visual arts for good and only pursue a life of numbers.
Every time I see the number eight, my dearest, I will think of you.

With fondness,
Stephen

6

Over the next few weeks, Mother and I did not speak. If she had a request, she would give it to Miss Stamp to deliver to me and vice versa. I tolerated this arrangement very well, in fact, I preferred it. I was expecting a specific punishment to be administered by her for my crime, but waited and waited. I assumed it was taking her so long because she was spending her days crafting something terribly painful and humiliating. However, no penance ever came. Maybe she reckoned that I had been embarrassed enough with my 'exam.' For the next couple of months or so, life was quiet, and I was sullen. It appeared Mother had finally broken my spirit. Then one night, just as the chill of fall began to cling to the air, a carriage arrived at Fordhook around half-past eight in the evening.

I was in my room, the place I rarely left those days, studying non-Euclidian geometry, when I heard the carriage approach. My eyes lifted from my annotated quadrilateral and I went over to my window to see an unfamiliar man descend from the carriage. He carried a wooden crate.

As the man got closer to the house, I could see he was a bit shabbily dressed. His pants were too short and his jacket wrinkled. He set the crate on the stone porch, tried to smooth out his hair and then knocked on the door.

I went to the top of the staircase, where I could see into the parlor, however it was unlikely anyone could see me since the lantern on the landing had not been lit. Miss Stamp let the man in and Mother greeted him as if she were expecting him.

'Mr. Hobhouse, it's been many years. I hope life has treated you well,' Mother said politely.

'Well enough, I must say. You seem even lovelier now than you did on your wedding day. Liberty from marriage has suited you,' said Hobhouse.

'In ways you cannot imagine,' she said.

'And your daughter is well? Augusta, is it? After George's sister?'

'We call her after her second name, Ada. Indeed she is well, now ten and seven years. She is nothing like her father, for which I thank the kindness of the great Lord Almighty.'

Well, that was a bold lie. This man must have been a friend of my father's, I thought, if he knew about my aunt Augusta. But what was his purpose here tonight?

'Tell me, do you have news on the matter I shared with you in confidence?' Mother asked.

'Yes, but perhaps not the news you'd like to hear. After much investigation, the authorship of the letter you inquired about, the request for a large sum of money, could not successfully be determined.'

'I see.'

'It does give fuel to the rumours, however,' he said with half a smile that exposed two gold teeth.

'Rumours? What rumours?'

'I shan't trouble you with it.'

That's when I crawled as far down the stairs as I could without being seen, desperate to hear about these rumours.

'But, I insist,' said Mother.

'In that case, I shall proceed. It seems some people, close to your former husband, are saying that Byron feigned his own death. That it was a fraud. That he wanted the world to think him dead. I myself think he's too clever to be killed so young,' said Hobhouse.

I gasped. Could this be true? Could my father really be alive? Did the almighty Lord hear my prayers?

'But why on earth would he do such a thing? He loved his fame and all its glory.' asked Mother.

'Seems he fathered a bastard with the poet Percy Shelley's sister-in-law, bringing scandal to the Shelley family. And there were his outrageous gambling debts. He could not stay away from the dice, and after he had been forbidden from the all the dice games, he tried his sour luck on the horses. I myself lent him thousands, only to receive tearful promises the arrears would soon be made solvent, but never were. There's one report of a Greek banker pounding on his front door in the middle of the night, prompting Byron to escape out the kitchen window naked as the day he was born and flee into the next town.'

'That will suffice,' said Mother, as she lifted her hand, motioning for Hobhouse to stop speaking.

'Oh, forgive me, Lady Byron, I shouldn't have said it to such a woman as yourself,' he said.

She waved, dismissing the comment.

'If he did fake his own death, the debt collectors would at least stop trying to hunt him down. It would be one way to find peace,' he said.

'I suppose. Certainly, it's been accomplished before. What is in there?' asked Mother, pointing to the crate.

'Some papers regarding Newstead Abbey. I understand your

daughter is to inherit the property.'

'Yes, when she turns 28. I suppose it was kind of him to remember her, but I'm sure my daughter has no interest in the estate and will simply sell it,' said Mother.

Inheriting my father's property was exciting news but Mother was a mad woman if she thought I'd ever sell my family's estate. 'The crate also contains Byron's portrait,' said Hobhouse.

'What need do I have for a portrait of Lord Byron, Mr. Hobhouse? I stared at his insufferable face quite enough when we were married.'

'Certainly your daughter would like to have it. I understand she hasn't seen her father since she was a wee babe. A girl ought to know what her father looked like,' he said.

'My daughter is much too impressionable. Leave it, though. I'll send it off to Newstead Abbey where it belongs,' said Mother.

Of course I wasn't surprised she didn't want me to have the portrait, especially after all that happened recently. But oh, did I want it. The question became: how would I get to it without her knowing?

'Thank you for your visit, Mr. Hobhouse,' she said.

'My honour, Lady Byron,' said Hobhouse.

Mother took several coins from her purse and deposited them into Hobhouse's breast pocket.

'If there are any more nasty rumours, surely, you'll investigate and keep me informed?' said Mother.

'Yes, m'lady,' said Hobhouse, then flashed a roguish, golden smile and gave her a slight bow.

Then, I was hit by a stroke of pure genius. I would write my father a letter and give it to Hobhouse to deliver to Lord Byron, in the case my father was still alive!

Quickly, I ran back to my bedchamber and took a pencil and a paper.

Dear Father,

It is me, your loving daughter, Augusta Ada. I have just learned you are still alive despite what you have led others to believe. I swear on all that is holy, your secret is safe with me. I must see you!! I only want to know you as the man you are before it is truly too late. Please use discretion in your letter. Perhaps you could write in a mathematical code? I have a talent for sorting numbers. Our correspondence must never be discovered.

Your faithful daughter,
Augusta Ada Byron

Through the window I could see Hobhouse walking toward his carriage. I quickly folded the paper and ran to find Miss Stamp, who was in the sewing room.

'Take this to the gentleman before he leaves. Don't get caught!' I whispered. Miss Stamp shot me a look of consternation. 'Please! My father may still be alive.'

She looked at me as if I had lost all sanity.

'Hurry!' I told her

Finally, she put down her mending, stood up and trotted out.

I went to my window and watched Miss Stamp hand the letter to Mr. Hobhouse. He nodded and looked up at my window before tucking the letter into his breast pocket. We made eye-contact for the briefest of moments.

As Mr. Hobhouse travelled away with the letter to my father, my mind was a storm of thoughts. I felt my only hope for happiness in this life would come from knowing my father.

Spending time with him, learning from him. Surely, he wasn't the monster that Mother made him out to be. Perhaps he could even appreciate me in a way that Mother could not. For the first time since hearing the news of his supposed death, a tiny glimmer of hope lit up my heart.

But just as I turned from the window, I saw that Mother was standing behind me. Did she see Miss Stamp deliver my letter to Hobhouse?

'Mother.'

'What did Miss Stamp just deliver to that man?'

'I don't know,' I said as innocently as possible.

She then looked down at my left hand. I was still holding the pencil with which I wrote the letter.

Mother clicked her tongue and spun on her heels, before heading downstairs, I followed close behind.

'Mother, it's not what you think. Mother, please. I just wrote the man a thank you letter for making the journey out here.' But it was no use.

Mother found Miss Stamp attempting to quietly re-enter the house. She was startled to see Mother in the doorway.

'Miss Stamp,' Mother said quietly.

'Yes, ma'am?' she replied.

'After tonight, your services will no longer be needed at Fordhook Manor,' she said plainly and went back upstairs.

Miss Stamp opened her mouth, but no words came out. She was in shock.

Mother can be spiteful, but this was downright vile and unfair. I had to make that point, even if it would make my own punishment worse. I followed Mother.

'She was only following my orders, as she is required to do.

If you must blame someone, blame me. I told her she must take that letter and not to argue,' I pleaded.

But Mother said nothing. She just walked up the stairs. I followed, as did Miss Stamp.

'She told me I had to, my lady,' said Miss Stamp, desperate to keep her job. So desperate in fact, she began confessing all her indiscretions.

'Miss Byron has forced me to engage in activities that I do not condone, including fetching the book of poems that you did not want her to read. I have tried to show her the error of her ways –' But Mother slammed her bedchamber door in our faces.

The next morning, a carriage arrived to take Miss Stamp back to her hometown of Mousehole in Cornwall. I attempted to say goodbye to her, but she wouldn't look me in the eyes. I began to cry.

'I didn't mean for this to happen,' I said, reaching out to take her hand. A single tear rolled down her face. She said nothing as she climbed into the carriage. I never saw her again.

7

The day after Miss Stamp left, I awoke in my bed to find blood on my nightgown and sheets. My first thought was that Mother had tried to murder me in the night but did not succeed. I searched my body for a stab wound but could find none. So why was I bleeding? I cleaned the blood up as best I could, feigned a headache and just hoped it would stop on its own. After the fourth day of bleeding, I was certain I was dying. I finally told Mother through tears. Her reaction wasn't what I expected.

'You've been having your courses for four days and you're just telling me now?' she said, almost with a laugh.

'Courses? Mother, what is going on with me? Am I dying!'

'You are not dying, Ada. This is simply what every woman goes through each month. You're no better than the rest of us now. As it was with Eve, as it is with me, so be it with you. It is the end of your innocence.'

Then I remembered Miss Stamp often taking a hot water bottle to bed and mumbling about 'bringing on the flowers,' which I thought meant she had spent too much time in the sun while gardening. When I asked her if she might want to wear a broad brimmed hat the next time she weeded, she simply said I'd bring the same flowers when I was older and to stop my squawking.

'But why is this happening?'

Mother looked at me in bewilderment. As if I was asking the most ridiculous question ever asked.

'So you may bear children in pain. It is the Lord's will to punish us for causing Adam's fall.'

'God is doing this?' The idea that He would make women bleed seemed terribly vindictive.

'God should never have put men and women together in the same garden. Now, our sex is left picking up the pieces,' she said as she left my bedchamber. Though I hadn't really thought too much about my own possible motherhood, I was certainly dreading the idea now. In that moment, I decided I would become a spinster.

8

Three lonely, sickly years passed for me. In late January, 1835, I became quite ill with a fever that left red spots all over my body and my eyes sore and runny. I was confined to bed for almost a year. Mother often tried to get Dr. Poole to bleed me, but the very thought of one of those gruesome leeches anywhere on my skin repulsed me. To avoid them, I would barricade myself underneath pillows, blankets, books – anything I could find – to keep him and those foul vampires away from me. My head hurt so much from the fever, though, I often thought my own death imminent. It was in those dark moments I knew I must recover and make a serious attempt to focus my mind on a profession of my own. I decided to give up Flyology once and for all. After my fever subsided and my eyes were no longer red, itchy, and oozing yellow fluid, I began work on a new field of science I called *Poetical Science*. Those two words, 'poetical' and 'science' put together, tying imagination to facts, lifted my heart.

In my bed, I wrote about a theory where numbers and equations explained natural phenomenon. Though I wasn't sure exactly how I contracted the horrible illness that made me an invalid for all those months, I was certain that by examining the natural world as closely as possible, the human mind would one day walk down a path to medical enlightenment. I thought once we figured out how this and other fevers could infect our human bodies, we, as a collective of scientists, could figure out a way of preventing the fevers entirely. Just as there is symmetry and logic in mathematics, surely the same principals must exist in nature, in disease and in cures for disease. They were just waiting to be uncovered, I was certain of it. These ideas gave me a stronger purpose in life and bred a new, more mature view of life.

Remarkably, despite my illness, I grew two inches taller over those years and gained a more womanly appearance. I missed Miss Stamp every day and lamented the fact I was the reason she was forced to leave our home. I thought of Stephen every time I saw the number eight.

My bedchamber now looked much less like a mad scientist's laboratory and more like an Anglican shrine. Mother encouraged me to keep religious items, including a painting of Jesus on the cross and a banner that read, 'Honour thy father and thy mother,' with the words 'thy father' scratched out.

When I was finally recovered, Mother took on the responsibility of my tutelage, as clearly no one could be trusted with me since I was so 'impressionable.' It wasn't long before my mathematical talent overtook Mother's ability however, and I began studying alone. Except for Puff, of course, who was now fully-grown and terrorizing up to four mice per week – poor little creatures. I said a tiny prayer for each one.

For every ten books of calculus equations I completed, Mother let me read one book on Celtic fairies and their magic. Fairies became incredibly popular with the women of English society and new books were being published each month. Fairies weren't only in books, however, their images graced dresses and wallpaper, were featured in jewellry and portrayed in travelling stage shows. I didn't necessarily believe these tiny, winged creatures were real – I would need proof of their existence. Yet, so many books were now being written about them, it seemed they must have some basis in fact. Could there not be a race of small humans, perhaps those with dwarfed ancestors, living in the forest?

Despite the droplets of rain that began to fall from dark clouds, I was actually feeling quite high-spirited today as my health was good. As I sketched a fairy with gossamer wings onto a piece of fabric I would use for my needlework, Mother sat in the parlor. Also three years older, Mother began to rely on newfangled medical treatments, such as Mesmerism, a treatment that involved a mysterious magnetic bodily fluid, and water cures where very cold water would be poured over her person. Today however, she drew comfort from her old acquaintance, a fat black leech feeding in the crook of her arm. It wriggled as its small, slimy body filled with her blood. Dr. Poole was visiting an ill family member in the north, so she had to administer the treatment herself.

An elderly manservant had been added to Fordhook Manor by the name of Mr. Kirby. He had grey and black hair with a short beard. He was easy to make laugh, which I liked, but he often had trouble remembering where things were or what he was setting out to do. He was also hard of hearing and sometimes the kettle would whistle for what seemed like ages before he took it off the stovetop. Today, he seemed alert and cheerfully brought a silver tray to Mother, on which rested a very fancy looking letter with a wax seal.

When I saw the letter, I took my sketch and went to sit next to Mother on the sofa. Seeing me, she rolled down her sleeve to hide the red mark left by the leech, then returned the glutton to a nearby jar. From the tray, she picked up the letter. It said *Invitation from His Royal Highness, King William IV*. She opened it eagerly. I watched her face carefully as her eyes scanned the page.

'What is it?' I asked, wondering if it could be news that my father was found alive, but I dared not say that out loud.

'In one month, the King is to host a ball at Windsor Castle.'

A ball! It sounded so exciting. 'Shall you attend?'

'Yes, and so shall you. It's the perfect occasion to introduce you to society and begin the search for a husband.'

A husband? I remembered my earlier declaration of spinsterhood. I hadn't discussed this plan with Mother, but decided there was no need. Suddenly, searching for a husband seemed so much more exciting than remaining unmarried, especially if it meant attending a Royal ball.

'Mother, do you really think a man will want to marry me?'

'Yes, assuming you are capable of bending your will to him without driving him to the edge of madness with your wild schemes,' she said with her eyebrows raised.

'I'm confident I have matured a great deal, in both body and mind these last few years. Have you not noticed the newfound sophistication I've acquired since I began my monthly courses?'

Mother laughed and shook her head. A rarity, for sure, but it hurt my feelings that she still saw me as a silly girl. Why was this such a humourous topic to her?

'My girl, the world is a big place inhabited by small minds. Having your courses doesn't make you sophisticated. Every mare in our stable can do that. What you need is refinement.'

And in the blink of a horse's eye, my world completely

changed. One moment, I was sketching a sprite and the next, preparing to meet the King. Finally, my health was good and my life was sailing toward shore. I had no idea if I would like attending the ball or meeting Royalty, but no matter what, it was better than spending long, cold days alone.

One week later, on another cloudy Wednesday, a dance instructor from Switzerland arrived at Fordhook. Her name was Frau Schmidt.

9

L ight on her feet, Frau Schmidt hurried from the carriage to the front door. Her ice-blue eyes were large and round and her nose had a bump, giving her a hawkish appearance. Her blondish-brown hair was parted in the middle of her head, lining up perfectly with the sharp tip of her nose. Thin, curled ringlets dangled in front of her tiny ears. In her forties, her cheeks were smooth, though she had deep lines around her lips.

I knew of Frau Schmidt's impending visit and was worried that I would not be very good at dancing. I would have to really focus my attention and listen carefully to every word the instructor said.

Frau Schmidt was pleasant enough as she greeted me with a curtsey. There was no small talk to ease my nerves, however.

'You vant to learn to dance?' she asked in her thick accent.

'Yes, very much so.'

'Zen, letz get ztarted. Let me zee you valk,' said Frau Schmidt.

'But I already know how to walk,' I said.

'Do what Frau Schmidt asks, Ada,' said Mother.

So I walked across the room, very self-consciously. Their four eyes were evaluating my every step. I decided to sweep my hands back and forth as I trotted, in an effort to look more graceful.

'Vat is dis?' hissed the Frau as she mimicked my arms flailing about in an exaggerated way that looked ridiculous.

'Oh, sorry,' I said as I drew my arms down and glued them to my sides. I walked again.

'Now, she looks like a valking schtick!' said the Frau.

'Her father had a clubfoot. She herself has a weak ankle. Do you think there is any hope she'll master at least one dance before the ball?' asked Mother.

The Frau shook her head as she stared at my feet. I knew learning to dance would be difficult, but I didn't realise I was in such dire straits.

'I don't know. Vurst I've zeen in long time. Ve can only try.'

And I began my very first dance lesson.

It started with learning how to stand. And something called 'crowning' where you stretch your neck as long as it will go without raising your chin and remembering to breathe, which was something else I thought I already knew how to do. Breathing was apparently the most important part of dance and heaven forbid if you forgot to do it. I tried to explain that I had never once forgotten to breathe in my entire life, but she snapped her fingers in my face, telling me to 'Schpeak vith za feet.'

After three days, once I had the breathing and the posture down, could relax my shoulders and keep my arms from waving about, I was allowed to learn the actual dance. This required an elaborate diagram.

The diagram had arrows pointing in various directions, sometimes encircling little egg shapes that I believed represented where one was to put their feet. Men were to follow the black eggs and women the grey eggs.

But my mind was too full of questions about the ball to concentrate properly on the chart, which looked more like a picnic blanket crawling with ants than instructions for a quadrille. Attending the King's ball was certainly the most exciting thing that had ever happened in my life. What would I wear? Would Mother embarrass me? Would I be introduced to the King and Queen? So many questions buzzed through my mind until the Frau started yelling at me in German.

This caused Mother to look up from her needlepoint, none too pleased, but, honestly, I could make no sense of the dance chart.

'Forgive me, Frau, but I cannot follow the dance as written on your diagram. Perhaps it is best to forego the illustration entirely and allow me to follow along as you perform the steps. To imitate you,' I said, hopeful to find a solution and be finished with dancing for the day.

'All across Europe, men and vomen schtudy za diagram. It is how it is done.'

Then, the answer occurred to me.

'Numbers,' I said out of frustration, 'I need numbers on the dance chart if you want me to follow it.'

The Frau paused and looked over at Mother.

'I believe it is a good suggestion, Ada,' said Mother in support of my idea. That was a first.

The Frau muttered something in German and took a tea break. With a pencil, Mother and I added numbers to the dance instruction chart, giving it an order I could follow. It worked.

Over the next two weeks, my feet became blistered from my dance instruction. The skin around both Achilles' tendons was red and raw. The nail on my baby toe cracked in half and, much to my horror, soon fell off. But once I had the steps down, I no longer needed the blasted chart.

After a very rough start, I learned three dances – a polka, a galop and a waltz, all to the tap, tap, tap of a clever invention called a metronome, a little box with an arm that would tick and tock like a clock to the same beat as the music. Frau Schmidt continued to bark instructions at me in her thick Swiss-German accent, making me repeat the choreography over and over until I could barely stand.

'Leeft your head! Schtraighten your back! Now, turn, turn, turn. Little baby schteps. Now schtop!' commanded the Frau.

Though I believed I had many talents, dancing was not one of them. I stumbled easily and often, particularly when the metronome was sped up. The first week, Mother watched every dance lesson, helping when she could. But by the second week, she occupied herself with reading Goethe's *Faust*.

Even more embarrassing than tripping over my own feet, I hated that Frau Schmidt also filled-in as my male dance partner. There was no other choice, of course. Mother wouldn't risk bringing another young man into the home, and Mr. Kirby was just too old and probably couldn't remember the steps anyway. The Frau's *sourkraut*-breath and dry hands made dancing incredibly unromantic.

When the day of the ball arrived, I was a storm of nerves. I hadn't slept a wink the night before, so I was exhausted in addition to being severely anxious.

In Mother's bedchamber, she struggled to tighten my corset, causing my breasts to bulge, giving the illusion that I had cantaloupes under the whale-boned harness. I sucked in my stomach and pleaded with Mother. 'Please, please let me wear my fairy dress.' On her bed, I had laid out an amber-coloured gown with green and orange fairies flitting about. The bodice had folds of green lace that gathered in a fan shape. I simply adored this dress. It was my favourite dress of all time.

'And present you to Court covered in wood nymphs? Not a chance,' said Mother, tying off my corset. She then proceeded to remove an eggshell coloured dress from her wardrobe. But this wasn't a new dress. This was Mother's old wedding dress -- and its Napoleonic empire cut and Regency styling were severely out of fashion. Even the lace flower sewn to the waist seemed wilted.

'I'm not wearing that. I'll kill myself first,' I said.

'Must you turn everything into the French revolution?' said Mother as she began to pull the dress over my head. I flopped to the ground in an effort to avoid the dress even touching me. But as soon as my derrière hit the floor, Mother managed to get it over my head. I couldn't believe she was forcing her old dress on me!

'Mother, everyone will know this is an old dress. They will think us impoverished!'

'Most young ladies would be thrilled to wear a dress with such historical significance. And the silk was imported all the way from China. It cost my parents a fortune. Touch it.'

'I don't care if the silk is from the moon, it will embarrass both of us.'

'Let's just see if it fits you.'

I sighed in defeat, praying it wouldn't fit. I desperately wanted to be perceived as fashionable.

I put my arms through the short, puffy sleeves and let the straight silk skirt fall down around my ankles. The waist was ridiculously high, resting just under my bosom. Unfortunately, the ancient monstrosity fit me perfectly.

Once Mother fastened the hooks and eyes on the back of

the bodice, Mother beamed at me. I wanted to vomit. The dress was hideous. 'My, how you've grown into a woman,' she said, 'Now curtsy.'

I wanted to argue over the dress, but I was afraid Mother would change her mind and not let me attend the ball. So, I curtsied as quickly as possible, saying, 'Your Highness.'

Mother shook her head in disapproval. 'Lower. You must grovel with humility.'

I curtsied again, only this time, I bent down so low, I lost my balance and tumbled to the floor. Mother groaned.

It was a two-hour carriage ride to Windsor Castle, and with my corset so tightly fastened, every bump and ditch in the road felt like a knife jabbing my ribs. I tried not to worry about my dress. I figured there would be so many guests, it's likely to not even be noticed.

Finally, the chariot of torture made a sharp turn and Mother and I were at last travelling up the long road that led to the entrance of the castle.

10

Windsor Castle was stunning – the stuff of dreams. And enormous! Its bricks were a soft, sand-coloured stone that seemed to reach up into the sky. William the Conqueror had constructed it shortly after the Norman Conquest in 1066. Nearly eight hundred years later, it was still standing, stronger and larger than ever. The Round Tower, added by King Henry II, was undergoing renovations, but it still stood proud and strong like a noble knight. Windsor Castle was perhaps the largest structure I had ever seen, sprawling over thirteen acres. I calculated that all the structures would equal the size of 200 houses had they been connected together, and that didn't include St. George's Chapel with its perpendicular gothic architecture.

The stretch of manicured, green-blue grass leading up to the castle walls was adorned by giant topiaries, carefully trimmed to look like dragons. They were beautifully fearsome.

As our carriage approached, I saw a fountain in the court-yard that was filled with red wine. Several male guests put their glasses under a spout and collected the ruby-coloured liquid. Only the King of England would have such a fountain, I thought to myself. Mother espied the fountain, too, but didn't seem nearly as impressed as I was.

The carriage stopped abruptly. Two footmen opened the door, reached for our hands and helped us onto the ground.

Mother and I then made our way into the castle for my very first ball.

As we entered through the large wood and iron doors, I immediately saw a dozen or so aristocrats playfully mingling, drinking and holding French half-masks, the ladies with their pinkies sticking out. It was something out of a fairy tale. I thought to myself: tonight, I will be one of them -- my glorious life has finally begun.

'Where do we go first?' I asked.

'Just follow me,' said Mother.

My heart pounded as we passed Lords and Ladies in half-masks, all in dazzling gowns that made mine look like a table dressing. On the wall hung more half-masks, reserved for arriving guests. Mother handed me one that was pink with gold lace around the edges. She chose not to hold one.

We eventually made our way into a large room where musicians were playing waltzes and people were dancing. Oh, how easy the dancers made it look! Ladies glided effortlessly across the floor, flirting with their partners through their half-masks.

As the song ended, so did the dance. The crowd of people applauded as the musicians put down their instruments and exited the stage. Across the room were King William IV and Queen Adelaide, seated on their thrones, also applauding.

Mother took me by the elbow and we joined a group of guests who were queuing up in front of His and Her Royal Majesty. Could we really be waiting to be introduced to Royalty? Suddenly, the room felt very small and very warm. As the number of guests dwindled in front of us and our turn grew closer, I could feel my face getting red. I tried to cover it with my mask, but Mother pulled it out of my hand. I guessed one didn't wear a mask when meeting the King and Queen.

Mother fidgeted with my dress then noticed a drop of sweat on my forehead.

'Wipe your brow or his Highness may mistake you for a cod,' she said as she handed me a handkerchief.

As we were about to step forward in the queue, a man with a notebook most rudely cut into the queue saying, 'Evening ladies, I'm Mr. Quincy, reporter and sketch artist for *The Times*. Do you mind if I get a sketch of the famous Byron lady for the paper?'

Mother replied, 'I don't mind being sketched.'

Quincy cracked half a smile and said, 'It's your daughter I'm interested in, if it's all the same to you.'

Flustered, Mother said, 'It's not the same to me,' and shuffled the reporter away.

He wanted to sketch *me*? Why on earth would he want to sketch me? I'm not anybody.

I was about to ask Mother what that was all about when I noticed two male guests speaking just in earshot of me. I heard the man in a black mask lean over to his companion and say, 'That Byron girl is lovely as a peach.'

His friend replied, 'And I'd wager she's mad as a herring. Just like her father.'

The black mask continued, 'I heard Lord Byron didn't actually die but went to try his luck in America.'

His friend asked, 'Which do you reckon is worse?' To which both men laughed heartily.

I found this behaviour outrageous and had no choice but to address the men. I marched up to them.

'Do not speak about my father as if I'm not here.' The men

looked at me, more shocked than embarrassed. But before the men could reply, Mother intervened.

'We beg your pardon,' she said, wrangling me away from them. She whispered to me in a low voice, 'The last thing I need is your temper-tantrum on the front of tomorrow's newspaper.' Mother gestured with her eyes to another reporter standing directly behind us. It was clear he was writing down our every word.

Just then, the King's Attendant called out, 'Lady Annabella Byron and Miss Augusta Ada Byron.' A trumpet flourished. Mother escorted me over to meet the King and Queen of England.

In his sixties, King William had a kind face, a receding grey hairline and pink, round cheeks. He was married to Adelaide of Saxe Meiningen, who was shockingly half his age.

To me, Queen Adelaide seemed so very young compared to the King. The Queen had a robust appearance and wore a beautiful, cobalt-blue velvet gown with ivory lace sleeves that came to a point just above her delicate fingers. Her gold crown was decorated with seven stunning rubies the colour of ox blood.

I began to tremble – ah, my nerves again! All eyes were on me and the room quieted. Mother curtsied, grovelling nice and low, but I found myself frozen in terror. The King's brow furrowed.

That's when Mother elbowed me in the calf. It was now or never. I managed to curtsy, though not my best go at it. My voice quivered as I said, 'Your Hi-i-ighness.'

The King and Queen then smiled. Queen Adelaide spoke to me first, 'I knew your father, girl.' The King looked over at the Queen, a bit surprised.

'Yes, your Highness?' I asked, hoping her words would not

be too harsh.

'Lord Byron was the greatest talent England has ever known,' she said with a determined nod.

King William interjected, 'Other than Shakespeare, of course.'

I lifted my face, raising my eyes to meet his. As I was about to argue that my father was the far superior writer, Mother chimed in.

'His Highness is most gracious and most kind,' she said and shepherded me away to the other side of the grand room.

Having persevered through the introduction to the King and Queen, I let out a big sigh of relief.

'Well, we survived at least,' I said, trying to find out what Mother thought of the whole event, but that nosey Mr. Quincy approached us again.

'Lady Byron, it seems I made a great mistake. It is you I truly desire to sketch. Could I trouble you? It will only take a few minutes.'

'Very well,' said Mother. Mr. Quincy escorted her over to a table with a candelabra. She posed next to it.

As I watched Quincy work, a man with a tray of drinks offered me a glass of apple nectar, which I accepted though gulped down too quickly.

Shortly, the musicians returned and began to play. Dancing once again commenced. I watched the men and women, praying no one would ask me, when a man in an emerald-coloured half-mask approached me.

'My Lady, may I have this dance?' he asked. He was much older than me, but had beautiful brown and green eyes that appeared mostly green against the emerald mask. With Mother still occupied, I wasn't quite sure how to politely decline.

'I…' but before I could construct an answer, several pushy reporters forced their way in front of the man in the emerald half-mask.

One shouted, 'Miss Byron! What do you make of the rumours that your father may still be alive?'

Another inquired, 'Will you live at Newstead Abbey upon your inheritance?'

And the questions exploded from there, each newspaper man was getting more aggressive. One even tugged on my arm. I didn't know how to respond. They began closing in on me until I was backed up against the wall. Without Mother, I felt I had no choice but to run.

I elbowed my way past the newspaper men, past the man in the green mask and raced past men and women of influence. I had no idea where I was going as I weaved in and around servants, nearly causing one to drop a tray of prawns. Finally, I saw a group of girls my own age. Refuge, at last! Or so I thought.

As I tried to catch my breath joining the circle of girls, one of the girls, looked me up and down. I noticed she was wearing a dress adorned with fairies. I thought a complement was a good way to start a conversation. 'Good evening. Such a lovely dress.'

The girl in the fairy dress flapped her lace fan and replied, 'Are you somebody famous?'

Another girl with numerous fairy pins in her hair, butted in, 'Fannie! Don't pretend you don't know.'

'Of course!' said Fannie. 'You're the daughter of that poet… what's his name? Oh, Lord Bunion.' The other girls giggled. Fannie didn't stop there. 'Or was it Lord Baboon?'

That's when one girl with a very round and stout build, wearing long gloves beaded with fairies, spoke in a pretend deep, raspy voice, 'Lord Byron. The one who was mad, bad and dangerous to know.' The girls laughed.

'How does that stupid poem go?' asked Fannie. Then the incorrigible girls had a field day mocking the poem.

The larger girl began reciting a line, 'She walks in beauty like the night of cloudless climbs and starry skies.'

Then Fannie delivered the stinger to my face, 'Clearly, the poem wasn't about your gown.'

The girls laughed heartily, barely able to console themselves. They then began to roughly pull and poke at my dress. They tugged at the lace flower stitched onto the waist until it hung by a single thread. I knew I must run away. As I pushed through the girls, breaking free from them, my small, silk satchel was torn from my hand and fell to the ground. I stopped, about to retrieve it, but Fannie kicked it into the crowd. What a horrible girl!

I left the satchel, for now, knowing it would turn up sooner or later. I began to experience vertigo and felt as if my heart was going to pound out of my rib cage.

The man in the emerald half-mask approached me. 'My lady, please allow me to retrieve your satchel for you.'

But I couldn't stop for the stranger, who could possibly have ill intensions. I kept running. I knew Mother would be beside herself not knowing where I was, but I felt like a trapped animal and had to escape. I saw a marble staircase and decided to see where it led.

As I ran up the black and grey stone stairs, attempting to get away from all the reporters and spiteful girls, I found a landing and hallway that led to an empty outdoor terrace, overlooking the Thames. I thought this would be a perfect place to hide myself. At least until I caught my breath. I pushed open the door and walked out onto the terrace in the moonlight. The stars were twinkling and the breeze chilly. Then I heard an unfamiliar woman's voice say, 'Like a lion's den down there, wouldn't you say?'

So much for being alone. I turned around to see a woman in her fifties with chestnut-coloured curls pinned neatly all around her face. Her blue silk dress had a white lace collar and a Russian mink stole rested gently on her shoulders.

'I'm lucky to have my hide,' I said cautiously.

'Don't you know you're the sport for the evening?'

I'm the sport? Me? I thought. I still couldn't tell if the woman had good or ill intentions.

'Are you here to pick at my carcass as well?'

'No,' she said with a kind smile then opened a tiny tortoise-shell box with a hinged lid and held it out to me.

'Snuff?'

I didn't want to be impolite so I reached into the box and took a tiny bit between my forefinger and thumb, unsure exactly what to do next. She also took a pinch of the stuff then quickly inhaled it into her nostril with a sharp sniff. I followed suit, also taking a sharp sniff. Did I ever regret that! It suddenly felt as if I had inhaled fire. The tobacco burned the lining inside my nose, sending me into a sneezing fit. I was incredibly embarrassed, but the woman didn't seem to mind that I lacked the ability to inhale snuff properly.

Once I finally stopped sneezing, the woman said, 'I'm here to ask his Highness if he would consider allowing women to study at our great universities alongside men.'

Women studying at a university? 'That's a grand idea. I

should like to study at one myself,' I said, trying to wipe the mucus that was now running from my inflamed nostril. 'What are your interests?'

'Astronomy, geography and mathematics.'

'I also like mathematics. The only other lady mathematician I know is--'

'Lady Byron!'

'How did you–?'

She smiled and motioned with her eyes for me to turn around. I looked over my shoulder and saw Mother making her way onto the terrace. She was carrying my silk satchel in her hands.

'You'll catch your death out here,' said Mother.

'Poor girl had no choice,' said the woman, 'the reporters closed in like wolves on a wounded lamb. I'm attempting to calm her nerves.'

'Thank you, Mrs. Somerville. It is a pleasure to see you again,' said Mother as she handed me my satchel, 'Seems you dropped this.'

I paid no mind to my satchel – I was standing before Mary Somerville, the famous female published scientist. This was incredibly exciting, much more so than meeting the King.

'You're Mrs. Somerville? Mother has mentioned you many times and I've recently read *On the Connexion of the Physical Sciences*. It is masterpiece.'

'You're very kind, Miss Byron,' said Mary, before turning to Mother. 'You're daughter is quite bright. No doubt due to your diligent care and education.'

'The Lord knows I have tried my very best,' she said as her eyes motioned up to the heavens. 'This is Ada's first introduction to society.'

'I see. Are you familiar with Charles Babbage, the inventor?' asked Mary.

'I have read some of his electromagnetic theory, but I don't know him personally,' said Mother.

'He often throws these delightful soirees at his home with the most fascinating people of science and art in attendance. You both should accompany me to the one he's hosting next week. I'm sure your daughter will find it intellectually stimulating.'

'I'd like that very much,' I said, then looked to Mother, eyes pleading.

'Thank you for the invitation,' said Mother politely, 'it is possible we should like to attend one but in due time. Ada has special requirements forcing me to introduce her to society slowly. Perhaps we could instead invite you to our home for lunch?'

What 'special requirements' was she referring to? She made it sound as if I had some nasty disease of the mind and must only be brought out of the attic on rare occasions. I was furious but knew better than to contradict her in public.

'Ah, that sounds absolutely perfect. How about Tuesday next?'

'We'd be most delighted to have you.'

With that, Mother smiled and escorted me down the marble staircase and out of the party. I hoped Mother was serious about lunching with Mary and wouldn't get some kind of dreary headache and need to cancel. I had so many questions to ask the lady scientist.

Outside the castle, as we waited for our carriage to be brought round, I noticed something that struck me as unusual. The man in the emerald mask seemed to follow us out of the castle and head down the long walkway in our direction. He walked at first, then picked up speed as he saw our carriage approach where we were standing.

'Mother, is that man coming toward us?' I asked.

Mother looked, 'Probably another bloody reporter.'

'He asked me to dance,' I said.

'Of course he did,' she said as she helped me into the carriage. With the crack of a whip, we started moving.

I looked out the carriage window to see the man stopped in his tracks, trying to catch his breath, but still carefully watching us as we rode away. Was he really just a reporter? Why did he offer to retrieve my satchel? I supposed I would never know.

As the coach bumped up and down, I longed to remove my corset. The pain was just another reminder that the night had gone far worse than any possible scenario I could have predicted. My nostril still burned.

'Did you enjoy yourself?' Mother asked, as if to taunt me.

'Not sure which part of the evening was most amusing. Let's see, there were the girls who made fun of this hideous dress, there were the reporters who nearly skinned me alive, but, oh, having you tell Mrs. Somerville I wasn't fit for society may have been the enjoyable moment of all. How could you?'

'Stop your grumbling. Now you know what it's like to be a Byron. You should thank me that the evening wasn't any worse.'

'*Thank* you? This was supposed to be the most exciting night of my life. Instead, you embarrassed me and I think you enjoyed it,' I said as the fatigue and frustration oozed out of me along with a stream of tears. I tried to wipe them away quickly, but they just kept coming.

'My nerves, Ada. If you continue to carry on this way, I'm

likely to have an attack,' said Mother as she rubbed the crook of her right arm.

I opened my satchel to get my handkerchief. As I put it up to my nose, I noticed a small envelope pinned to it. It read *To Ada from Lord Byron.* I gasped.

'Mother! Look at this!' I showed her the envelope. 'Father's alive, I knew it. This note is from him.'

Nonchalantly, Mother said, 'They're writing to you now, are they?'

I tore open the letter and read it aloud, 'Dearest, I am in fact alive but hiding from my enemies. It breaks my heart that we have been apart for what seems like an eternity. A daughter is a thing to be cherished, but my circumstances are--'

Without even looking at the letter, Mother finished my sentence, 'Desperate. Please send one thousand pounds right away, Lord Byron.'

I looked at Mother, 'How do you know what it says?' Then Mother opened her own satchel and dumped out another letter from 'Lord Byron'.

'I've been getting them for the past year.'

'Then they must be real! Did you write him back?'

'No, but I had them investigated,' said Mother, 'Lord Byron didn't turn up. However, several well-known con artists did.'

'But what about the man who asked me to dance, then watched us as we rode away. I'm certain he's the man who gave me this letter. You don't know with confidence that he wasn't Lord Byron.'

Mother picked up the letter, 'What I do know, is that we must get you married before every ne'er-do-well in England tries to make a meal of your inheritance.' With that, she ripped the letter to shreds.

11

The day after the ball, Mother started dedicating her life to finding me a husband. With adopting this new focus, she began to fill our schedule with dances, dinners and parties, but only with London's most elite. Luckily, Mary Somerville was part of the elite and she came for lunch on Tuesday as planned.

The early morning rains cleared by noon, the time at which we were expecting Mary. The lunch menu at Fordhook consisted of quail, devilled kidneys, asparagus and pear tarts. Since this was intended to be a ladies' lunch, Dr. Poole did not join us in the garden as we ate.

Mary was dressed in a white blouse with leg of mutton-style sleeves. The fabric of her floor-length skirt was printed with beige and yellow flowers on a brown background.

I wore a taupe-coloured dress adorned with green stitching and lace trimmings. I also wore my favourite emerald drop earrings. Though I know Mary cared little for fashion, I wanted to appear somewhat au courant considering she'd only ever seen me in Mother's horrid wedding dress and I didn't want her to think I made a habit of wearing embarrassing gowns.

General pleasantries were exchanged as we enjoyed our meal with glasses of rum punch. Mary was kind and always careful with her words. She spoke of meeting so many great scientists, some more interested in seeing women enter their field than others. She told a humourous story about Pierre-Simon

Laplace, whose five-volume work, *Celestial Mechanics*, was translated into English by Mary.

'My husband William and I were on holiday, staying with Laplace at his family chateau in Saint-Julien de Mailloc in France. We were discussing the prospects of encouraging more women to contribute to the sciences. His face grew rumpled, as if the idea made him displeased. He then said, "In all my life, there have only been three women who have understood me. You, Caroline Herschel, of course, and a mysterious Mrs. Greig. Do you know of this woman? I believe she is British. " Of course, William and I started laughing.'

'But why?' I asked.

Mother interjected, 'Mary's first husband, God rest his soul, was the Captain, Samuel Greig. Mary was actually two of the three women he was referring to.'

I understood and also laughed.

After lunch, we took tea in the parlor. Mary offered both Mother and I snuff, but this time, I declined, as did Mother. As we drank our tea, Mary noticed a kaleidoscope sitting on an end table.

'May I?' she asked referring to the kaleidoscope.

'Please,' said mother, 'but it is only a trinket I picked up in Bath and probably not as interesting as others you've seen.'

She looked through the eye-hole as she held the wooden tube up toward the window for light. She smiled as she rotated the front lens to make colourful shapes and patterns appear inside.

'It's like looking deep inside a volcano. I can see an entire world raging, bursting and forming before me. It is as terrifying as it is beautiful.'

'Is that what you see when you look through a telescope

– terror and beauty?' I asked.

'Very much so. Do you know of the Hindu god, Shiva?'

Both Mother and I shook our heads.

'Shiva is both the destroyer and the creator.'

'I don't understand,' I said.

'Like Shiva, destruction and creation is the business of the universe. It is an endless cycle of birth, death and rebirth. That is what the telescope reveals.'

'I would very much like to learn about the planets and their order. I often wonder if there is a mathematical equation or algorithm that explains what you see in the night sky,' I said.

'I would be more than happy to tutor you,' said Mary, putting down the kaleidoscope.

'Mother, do think I could set aside time for some studies with Mary?'

'That is quite an imposition, Ada. Besides, I'm sure Mary would agree that a head full of astronomy is unlikely to help attract a husband.'

'On the contrary, Annabella. How do you think I met Mr. Somerville?'

We all smiled, even mother, who said, '*Touché*.'

'If I may be so bold as to give some advice to Ada as she searches for a husband?'

'Please,' said Mother.

'Find a man who understands your appetite for knowledge. If he is intimidated by your intellect and puts limits on your mind, it will be a very unhappy marriage, indeed.'

Mother sighed. Finding a husband was far more complicated than I had ever imagined.

Over the next year, Mother continued to parade me around London in what felt more like a fishing expedition than a search for an eligible bachelor. I was growing weary and thought I might never find someone suitable. In general, the men Mother preferred for me were older, around her own age. Many were kind, but most seemed better suited for her, not me. I knew it was likely I would not marry a man as young as me, but I was certainly hoping we'd find someone who was at least close.

There was a period of three months where Mother tried to convince me to marry Dr. Poole's cousin Algernon, who was fifty-two. He and I exchanged a few letters, but when he arrived from America, where he had started a shipping business in New Orleans, he never took his eyes off Mother. Because neither of us had husbands, he presumed he could choose either of us. When Mother made it clear that I was the one on the marriage block, he could only make suggestions of friends back in the States who might be interested. The whole thing was a fiasco.

I did begin to spend one afternoon a week studying with Mary and it was truly exhilarating. To have three hours each week to forget about marriage and focus on something I loved, meant so much. Mary's knowledge was endless so we chose to start with our own moon. I wanted to learn everything there was to know. Mary even gave me one of her telescopes to use at home.

It was also because of Mary that Mother finally agreed to allow us to accompany her to one of Charles Babbage's soirees. Little did I know how one evening would change the course of my entire life!

The following Sunday, Mother and I journeyed to Babbage's home in London, where we were to meet Mary. I was cautiously optimistic about the evening. But, given that I had been so excited about the King's ball and what an ignominious failure that turned out to be, I tempered my enthusiasm. At least Mother allowed me to wear my fairy dress. Though I didn't anticipate running into another pack of beastly young women, if I did, at least they couldn't torture me about my dress. Or, so I hoped, on the long carriage ride over.

One Dorset Street featured a row of sturdy, three-story brick homes, each one with its own crow-stepped gable and rectangular fireplace. Our carriage stopped directly in front of Babbage's home, but there was no doorman to greet us, making Mother question whether or not we should enter. I convinced her to go inside with me, if only for a short while, considering we didn't want to disappoint Mary.

Mother and I let ourselves into the party, and from the entrance hall I could hear some foreign-sounding music and people chatting and laughing. Just from the sound of things, it seemed the mood of the soiree was very different than that of the ball, much to my relief.

As we entered the parlor I noticed the walls were covered in red velvet wallpaper with a floral pattern in black that repeated from the floor to the ceiling. The inverse of the same floral pattern repeated next to each row, as if mirrors lined the walls. Fringed velvet curtains hung over the large windows that looked out onto the street. The ceilings were low but not stifling. A portrait of a plump, beautiful woman hung over the fireplace. I assumed it was Babbage's wife in the picture, but I did not see the woman at the party.

While there were also new, dazzling sights that I had never before witnessed, no one conversed in an impolite or condescending way. Luckily, there were no reporters there and the guests appeared to be enjoying themselves. Could I possibly enjoy myself, too?

We did not immediately find Mary, but I did count not three, not four, but seven animal skulls hanging in the parlor alone. Two of the larger ones seemed bovine in origin and one may have even been from the ancient aurochs that was now extinct. The five smaller ones were difficult to determine. I was pretty sure at least one of them came from a fox.

On the far end of the room, a woman with a green scarf tied neatly around her head pounded on a pianoforte with vigour, forming a lively tune unfamiliar to my ears. An African man with skin as dark and beautiful as ebony timber beat a drum with his hands next to the pianoforte, setting the brisk rhythm. Peeking into the dining room, I could see several women hovering over a spirit board, attempting to make contact with the dead. Their fingers rested gently on top of a heart-shaped planchette that glided over the mysterious wooden board filled with letters and numbers. I couldn't believe my good fortune in being in this exciting place, amongst such interesting and intriguing people. If there was a man suited for me, I knew he must be here.

Mother did not share my sentiments, however. The party was far too informal for her.

'This soiree has a wretched bohemian taint. I don't think I've ever been to a party with so many eccentric guests. Hold onto your satchel this time. I fear if you lose it, there's little chance it will be returned,' she whispered into my ear.

'Just because these people appear different than us doesn't make them thieves. They are likely artists and musicians, even writers.'

'Exactly. Thieves. If you're not careful, they'll steal your *soul*.'

We walked past the entrance to the dining room, where Mother saw the women at the spirit board.

'There's already three souls lost in the night,' she said, shaking her head. Then, with a spark in her eye, she said, 'Ah! Now, there's a proper gentleman.' I turned to see a well-dressed man in his fifties leaning against the doorframe. The man had a very serious look on his face as he spoke to another guest. When his jaw moved, so did his ginger side-whiskers, giving his face a cat-like appearance. His cravat was made from an ornate, and no doubt, very expensive silk lace. That's when Mother took my hand and led me to an empty hallway, where she instructed me to flip my head upside down for twenty seconds. I told her didn't want any part of her ridiculous beauty tricks. That's when she pinched my cheeks. Hard.

'Ow! Mother, stop!' I said as I batted her hands away.

'I'm trying to make them rosy. You're so pale, you look ill.'

Why was it that all her efforts to encourage me only left me feeling frustrated? I spun round and led myself into the crowded parlor, away from the ladies at the spirit board, away from the wealthy cat-looking man.

Looking around the crowded room, I felt much more comfortable in this crowd of misfits than I did in high society. This soiree would have been my father's kind of party, I'm certain of it.

After a few minutes of taking in the guests, I noticed Mother had struck up a conversation with another man. He was also well-dressed in a suit, wore a plain cravat and his greying moustache led me to believe he was in his late forties. Mother caught sight of me out of the corner of her eye and waved me over. I had no choice but to oblige.

'Darling,' she said, 'meet Mr. Ragsdale. He is a surgeon at the Royal Hospital.' I curtsied, but did not smile. Mother continued, 'You should see Ada's needlework. Her stitches are immaculate. I'm sure a surgeon such as yourself could appreciate them.' I hated being spoken about as if I were a child. I had a purpose of my own that was far more important than the spacing of my stitches.

As Mother prattled on, I managed to slip a few feet away. In addition to all the animal skulls, the walls of Babbage's home were lined with wooden shelves that held the most interesting mechanical items, most of which I had no idea what their purpose might be. As my eyes scanned the shelves, they stopped to focus on a row of mechanical clocks. All different sizes, one clock was built inside a violin case; another was set inside clear glass, making it possible to see every cog and wheel. Another had several intricate mirrored panels. I carefully picked it up to examine it, holding it by the edges as to not smudge the mirrors. That's when I heard a familiar voice behind me. I positioned the clock to see Mary speaking to two men. I know it's not polite to eavesdrop, but I so wanted to hear the discussion so I did it anyway.

One of the men was in his twenties, with long tufts of russet brown-coloured hair on each side of his face, speaking to Mary. Tonight, she wore a braided bun on the top of her head and a beaded grey dress. Another man, about the same age, with dark, curly hair and a clean-shaven face, interrupted the younger man to speak to Mary.

'Forgive Darwin's stench, Mary. Four years on a ship and all he brought back was that stink,' said the man with curly hair, pinching his nose.

Darwin, the other man, replied, 'You've been making the same joke for the last three years, Dickens. You might want to add another to your repertoire.'

Dickens thought for a moment then quipped, 'He developed such a fear of the sea, he's now too scared to even bathe. How's that?'

Mary then opened her fan and waved it in the air, saying, 'Tis not the smell I mind Charles, but rather its strong gravitational pull toward my celestial body.' She and Dickens laughed.

Then Darwin said, 'No wonder you're paid only a penny a word, Dickens. Everything you say sounds cheap.'

I giggled to myself. Mary was able to be regal yet flippantly bold at the same time. I was about to approach Mary and greet her, but when I went to put the clock back on the shelf, someone behind me bumped into me, causing it to slip from my fingers. Before I could pick it up a man intervened.

'Allow me,' said a man's voice. I turned around to find an earnest looking man with pale blue eyes in his early thirties retrieve the clock from the ground. Thanks to the thick rug, it didn't appear to be broken. Before I could thank the man, he spoke to me.

'You should see the rarity Babbage has over there,' he said to me without an ounce of superiority. No introduction, no apology for the bump. Instead, he spoke to me as if he'd known me for years. While many women would take offence to such a casual meeting, I admired it. It felt very modern to me, not at all like the priggish introductions I was forced to make in high society. And it made me feel as if I belonged with this group of sensational minds. These people were the new order of things to come and I longed to share my ideas of Poetical Science with them.

Curious to see this rarity the man mentioned, I followed him over to a table with a silver, mechanical doll that was in the form of a ballerina. A delicate little bird sat on her finger. With lips puckered, she looked as if she were about to kiss the creature.

As the man knelt down next to the doll, I did the same. 'Look closely, now,' he said as he wound up the knob. It went 'zip, zip, zip' as he spun tension into the gear, creating stored energy.

As he let go, the doll's eyes suddenly opened and it began to pirouette round and round. I watched with rapt attention. It was so beautiful and of such distinguished quality — I had never seen anything so intricate yet so functional. I was transfixed as I watched it spin. After a moment, however, I noticed that as the doll spun around, its ballet skirt twirled up, revealing her nude bottom. Though shocking, I had to admit this was the funniest thing I had ever seen. I looked at the man with the pale blue eyes and we both started laughing.

Mr. Babbage then rushed over to us and whispered, 'Now you've seen Giselle in all her glory,' and he pushed the doll's skirt back down.

'Babb, the doll could use some knickers,' said the man I was beginning to find quite handsome despite not knowing his name.

'Perhaps you've a pair to spare?' I said to the man. Other party-goers, who had also watched the doll, laughed at my comment. This made me feel elated. People here thought I was clever and I liked it.

Mother's eagle eyes found me and the man kneeling together,

laughing. I stood up, so did the man as she walked over to us.

'I don't believe I've made myself acquainted. I am Lady Byron.'

'Forgive me. I'm William King, Baron of Ockham. How do you do?'

He kissed Mother's hand, causing her to perk up.

'Baron, did you say?' asked Mother, embarrassing me. I did not care that he was a Baron. I only cared that, of all the ladies at the party, he had spoken to me.

'This is my daughter, Ada Byron,' Mother said, 'you'd be astounded by her needlepoint. Her specialty is embroidering Bible verses. If only you could see the eiderdown pillow that beautifully displays John 3:16.'

Again with my needlepoint. Can't she understand men aren't interested in such things?

'I'd bet all my horses that it's as grand and enlightening as the Rosetta Stone itself,' he gave me a little wink before kissing my hand, indicating he was just playing along with Mother's silly attempt to impress him. Upon hearing this of course, Mother beamed with pride, not detecting his jovial, if not somewhat patronizing tone.

I was impressed by William's ability to fully charm and impress my haughty mother as well as connect with me in a youthful, unassuming way. I hadn't encountered a man who could engage both the older, more traditional generation, yet also seem boyish and relatively uninhibited. I wondered if I should try to be more like him.

Mary made her way over to us. 'Ada, Lady Byron! I see you've met Mr. Babbage and Mr. King.'

'It is a privilege to have both of you as guests at my soirée,' said Babbage, 'You've come on an exciting evening,' he said as he climbed up onto a wooden chair. He whistled loudly to get the crowd's attention. Everyone hushed.

'Everyone, come with me now to marvel the Difference Engine. This machine will change your life,' he announced.

A machine? This was marvellous!

I headed over to Mr. Babbage, desperately wanting my own life to change. I pushed my way through the crowd, finally gazing into Mr. Babbage's eyes and said, 'Take me to the engine.'

Mr. Babbage's workshop had the minty scent of freshly shaved cedar wood. William helped Babbage light some lamps, softly illuminating the dusty but neatly organised workspace. The walls had been painted white some number of years ago and were greying now. Several wooden tables with stone countertops rested against the wall. Carpentry tools of all kinds hung on a hundred hooks. Mother came up beside me and whispered, 'Stay close, you never know what kind of odd device he could unveil.'

'Ladies and gentlemen, behold the Difference Engine,' said Mr. Babbage as he removed a drop cloth from the three-foot tall machine. I gasped. This engine was nothing like anything I had ever seen or even dreamed of.

Three rows of numbered brass cogwheels were configured on a wooden base. The wheels were all connected by brass rods, and similar to gears, the wheels meshed perfectly with each other. A lever with a black plaster handle jutted out to the side. A roll of parchment was also connected to the contraption.

'I should tell you this isn't the full-sized version of the calculating machine I'm intending to build. This is merely a demonstration model, small enough to be shuffled about to lectures or scientific societies. The full-sized Difference Engine is to be ten times the size of this model,' he said.

Ten times the size? It had dozens of intricate brass wheels and adding ten times the number of wheels would certainly cost a fortune.

'As you can see, this working model is comprised of three tiers of wheels, gears and cranks. The wheels rotate when acted upon by these rods which are arranged in the shape of a helix, causing these shiny brass number disks to spin,' he said as he pointed to them.

I just had to get a closer look, so I wriggled away from Mother to get nearer to this wondrous invention. I could smell the tinny, fishy scent of the oil that had been applied to the cogs and gears. William lit another lamp and held it above my face to help me see it better.

Babbage continued in his best showman's voice, 'Watch closely as the Difference Engine shall perform a miracle!'

Of course Mother had to interrupt him. 'Surely you're exaggerating. Only the Lord may perform miracles.'

'Judge for yourself. William, choose a number on the first dial,' said Babbage as he waved him over.

That's when William looked straight at me with a smile and said, 'Miss Byron, you choose.'

I could barely contain my excitement. I knew I had to choose carefully, so I reached over to the machine and rotated the dial to the number three. My gold and ivory bracelet slid down my arm as I stretched out my hand.

Babbage explained, 'The engine will perform a series of mathematical equations to the power of three,' and he used the lever to crank the machine, setting the cogs and wheel in motion. Then, the row of number dials began to rotate on their own. In sequence, the numbers read three, nine, eighty-one, 6561.

I watched with intense focus and delight. Even Mother was so curious, she stepped closer. The tiny clinks of the metal parts moving together made an unlikely symphony. Then, the number dials suddenly jumped sequence, calculating three to the third power, startling us. It went three, twenty-seven, 19,683.

Mother stared at the beautiful instrument, the way a savage person might if seeing a compass or a rifle for the first time. She was thoroughly bewildered.

'My God,' said Mother, 'surely there must be some trickery involved.'

'The only trick is that it calculates correctly, every time,' said Babbage.

Just like that, my mind began to think of a dozen uses for such a machine.

'I once read about a sea captain who unfortunately used incorrect tables to make his calculations and he shipwrecked. Calculations are also important in the construction of flying machines,' I said, prompting Mother to elbow me.

'Calculations are equally as important in my architecture. I could benefit greatly from such a machine,' said William.

Mother seemed relieved to hear William had a respectable vocation.

'Think of artillery officers who calculate trajectories --' said Babbage.

'Or bankers who calculate interest!' I said.

'All this and more will happen once the expanded version gets funded,' said Babbage.

Mother looked at him suspiciously, 'I thought the Royal Science Society was funding your work.'

'Not since they've decided to build a bloody zoological garden,' said Babbage.

'Surely, there must be other ways to raise the money,' I said as I looked at Mother with pleading eyes. Babbage took my lead and looked at her, curious to know if she might want to invest a sum of money.

'Good luck in your efforts, Mr. Babbage,' she said, 'It's getting late and we must return home.'

'But, Mother, we've only just arrived,' I said. I would have stayed all night if I could.

Before she could reply, Babbage said, 'Yes, I understand. Well, I do hope you'll return very soon. Just one more thing.' Babbage went back to the machine and ripped a piece of paper off the paper roll connected to it.

'A souvenir for the lovely lady,' he said as he handed the paper to Mother.

'What's this?' she asked.

'The results of the calculations, of course,' he replied. But Mother still didn't understand.

I leaned over to her and said, 'The machine prints the results of the calculations so a ledger is kept.'

Mother was rendered speechless by this mechanical feat. I took the paper from her and marveled at the wondrous thing.

William set down the lantern he was holding and said, 'May I escort you out?'

As William accompanied Mother and me outside, walking with us to our carriage that was waiting nearby, I couldn't stop talking about the machine. 'A mere nine seconds is all it took to calculate to the second and third powers – nine seconds!' I practically hopped up the steps into the carriage, needing no assistance.

That's when Mother said, 'Please excuse her excitability.'

'Your daughter is wonderfully inquisitive,' said William. He then said, 'Lady Byron, may I ask your permission to court her?'

What did he just say? Immediately, I poked my head out of the carriage. My panicked eyes met Mother's, wondering what she would say. Part of me hoped she would say yes, another part of me was terrified at the prospect. My heart pounded like a timpani. The Baron of Ockham *was* quite charming. And handsome.

Mother's face grew very serious. Finally, she said, 'Lord King, should you wish to court my most virtuous and obedient daughter, I would be most pleased.' And that was all that was said on the matter. I was officially being courted by a man. This made me excited in a way that was both thrilling and frightening. I could almost feel the blood as it pulsed through my veins, the saliva in my mouth nearly drowning my tongue. I swallowed hard, understanding that I was a woman now, and lots of new opportunities and relationships would be available to me. I leaned back into the carriage and grinned slightly. My life was about to change immensely; I could feel it in my bones.

12

The following Saturday afternoon, William called at Fordhook. I was nervous to see him again. I honestly didn't know if I would fancy him or not, given our encounter was so brief. When I saw him however, he appeared like an old friend and was far more handsome than I had remembered.

He was dressed in what must have been his best brown suit with a red silk waistcoat that peaked out underneath his jacket. His silk paisley-patterned cravat was loosely tied, creating just the slightest touch of bohemian flair. I wore a plum-coloured pinstriped dress – one of my favourites. My hat was adorned with fresh lilacs that I attached to the brim with a needle and thread earlier that morning. This was just after I hid the pillow embroidered with John 3:16 under my bed. I was learning I needed to be more zealous in my efforts to avoid embarrassment.

Mother, along with Dr. Poole and I, guided William on a tour of the grounds. Mother laughed giddily, the way she often did in front of strangers to make them think she was light-hearted. With each coy giggle at William's witty remarks, I looked at William's face to see if he detected any insincerity. But when Mother looked at William, his eyes just seemed to fixate on me, as if he and I were the only ones in the garden. Those moments felt very special.

Then Dr. Poole asked William questions about his position

on the fate of post-revolutionary France and if there would be another war. William looked a bit embarrassed and confessed he didn't really follow politics on the continent. His work designing and building homes kept him busy most of the time.

I was quite happy not to speak about politics and grew more embarrassed by my jailers every moment. Finally, Mother asked if we should take a break for biscuits and tea.

'Sounds delightful, Lady Byron. But first, would you mind terribly if Miss Byron showed me her tulip garden,' William said.

Mother nearly choked. 'That is my garden. It is I who cultivates those flowers, not Ada.'

'Tis a pity,' said William. 'There's nothing more sublime than the vision of a pretty young woman in a garden of flowers.'

I'm sure I blushed. Mother was at a loss for words. Before she could think of what to say, Dr. Poole piped in:

'Ada, I think it would be grand if you showed your mother's tulips to Lord King. Lady Byron and I will take a seat and rest a spell.'

Fast as lightening, William took my arm and we were on our way to the tulips. I clutched William's arm as we walked, thinking he must be terribly strong.

As we strolled in the sunlight, we spoke not of flowers or bulbs or weeds. Instead, we spoke only about Babbage's machine.

'You seemed quite impressed by Babbage's Difference Engine. It's rare for a woman to take such an interest in machinery,' said William.

'As a young girl, I used to build all sorts of machines, much to Mother's chagrin,' I said.

'What kind of machines did the young, adventurous Miss Byron build?'

'Please, call me Ada.' He nodded. I'm sure I blushed again.

It was difficult for me to imagine that William was truly interested in my childhood experiments, but he seemed earnest enough.

'If you must know, I was trying to achieve human flight.'

He laughed, 'Well, did you?'

'Yes. For exactly 3.5 seconds. Then I achieved what most would call human folly.'

We both laughed. 'It may sound silly, but I truly wanted to be the first person to soar across the English Channel, high in the sky in a winged glider. Unfortunately, none of my machines achieved much success.'

We looked over at Mother and Dr. Poole, seated off in the distance. Mother gave a frantic, girlish wave, making it seem as if her arm were having a spasm. She was constantly inventing new ways to embarrass me.

William turned from them and took a step closer to me.

'Machines or not, your mother is quite proud of you.'

'Can't say that it feels as such. Her constant nagging and sheltering make me feel as if she'd preferred a son.'

'I'd bet she sees a lot of herself in you.'

'Herself in me? We are nothing alike, I've made certain if it.'

'Let's see. You're both smart, curious. And of course, beautiful.'

I had never been told I was beautiful before. It made me feel uneasy. It was most likely nothing but flattery, I thought.

'I'm hardly beautiful. I suppose Mother was in her youth. I'm more…gawky than anything else.'

William laughed. 'And I see you're humble as well. Surely you learned that from your mother, too,' he said.

I couldn't help but smile. Maybe William was right, perhaps

Mother did have the best intentions. But I couldn't believe I was greatly influenced by her. I felt as if I were more like my father in a hundred ways. But I didn't tell this to William. The last time I revealed my true feelings to a man about the topic of Lord Byron, it didn't end well.

'Care for some tea, Miss Byron?'

'Sounds marvellous.'

William called on me the next eleven Saturdays in a row. He even visited one Saturday, despite having a cold. He was terribly embarrassed by his sneezing and runny nose, but I found it endearing and felt the urge to comfort him, freshen up his tea and the like. Is this what love was like? I didn't know, but each visit was like a breath of fresh air for me, despite Mother's overbearing presence. Fortunately, she was growing very fond of William and on his seventh visit, she allowed us to take a short walk on the grounds without a chaperone, as long as we stayed within her visual range. It felt like absolute freedom!

I enjoyed William's company, particularly holding onto his burly arm as we walked round the grounds. He was much less irksome than Stephen and didn't waste his time making silly sketches in the French or any other style. William was a professional person who envisioned large structures for people to inhabit and then built them – often with his own hands. He was a true man.

As we were walking unchaperoned through the garden that was in the shape of a large parabola, William grew quiet for a moment as a pair of grey squirrels ran up a nearby tree, one chasing the other. His pale blue eyes met mine and he said, 'Ada, if you could have anything in the world, what would it be?'

I had never been asked this question. I was about to blurt out how much I wanted to be released from my mother's talons, but I stopped myself. I knew this was the answer a mere girl would give. William was asking Ada the woman. I took a deep breath.

'More than anything,' I said carefully, 'I would like to contribute something meaningful to science through my mathematical endeavours. I know I'm a woman, but I feel very strongly that it's possible for me to add something novel to the field of mathematics – I've been developing something I call Poetical Science that uses mathematical principals to uncover a higher truth.'

William smiled. 'A most noble aspiration. One, I'm sure you'll achieve tenfold. No, a hundred fold.'

I looked at him. Was he mocking me? I had never heard such encouragement from a man before. I shuddered at the thought he was simply placating me. I had to ask, 'William, are you patronizing me?'

He looked at me, shocked by the question.

'Ada,' he said, 'I'm being most sincere. I believe you have the mind and will to accomplish anything you set your heart to. And if being a woman makes it more challenging, I believe your clever wits will find a way to use your womanhood to your advantage.'

I looked at him, sceptically. Though I didn't fully realise it then, it was in that moment I had to decide whether or not to trust William. If I believed he was capable of supporting my aspirations in this way, I knew I could love him – really and truly love him in the way the night sky loves the moon. But only if he was genuine. Such a big decision! I had no geometric proof or algebraic equation to guide me. In the end, my heart made the decision for me. I took a deep breath before humbly saying, 'Then, thank you.'

We walked in a relaxed silence after that. Finally! I felt like someone understood not only who I was, but who I was to become.

On the twelfth Saturday, William brought Mother, Dr. Poole and I out for a picnic near a new railroad that was recently constructed to connect our village all the way to London. Railroads were being constructed all over England and travelling to other cities would take just a blink of time. If only they could build a railway that stretches to the continent, perhaps a floating one that could support of the weight of a stream engine, now that would be exciting, I thought.

But here, in the English countryside, the hills were carpeted in thick, emerald clover, the scenery was lush and moist. Clouds scattered over the glorious rolling slopes, like clotted cream floating in green coffee. Lilacs grew sporadically in the grass and I could just make out the steeple of a church off the distance. The sun was overhead, warming the earth. It was the loveliest of sunny days, a day made for being out in the open air.

It was summertime now and while Mother wore her typical black dress with a high neck, I wore a dress made of summer white linen, accented with only an orange sash. My hat was made of flax that I embroidered with fuzzy little starbursts and I added an orange rosebud I had picked yesterday, praying it wouldn't shrivel before visiting with William.

Sitting on a blanket, we crunched cucumber-walnut sandwiches and apple slices with cheddar cheese. After about forty minutes of light conversation, I saw William glance at his pocket watch.

'If it's on time, we should expect a steam engine at a quarter past,' said William.

'I've never heard of an English train being on time,' said Mother.

'Well, there's one way to tell. Ada, may I?' said William as he stood and held out his arm to me. Quickly, I hopped up, took his arm and we headed off toward the iron rails before Mother could protest.

Once at the train tracks, I stepped up onto the rail and tried to balance.

'Watch your ankle!' Mother yelled from the hillside.

'Her eyes must have been fitted with tiny telescopes. She sees everything,' I said to William as I hopped off the rail.

William knelt next to the tracks. 'They say you can hear the train coming if you listen very closely to the rails.'

Curious, I knelt down next to William and put my ear on the rail. I almost thought he was teasing me, thinking how foolish I must look until, after a moment, I heard what sounded like a hundred bees buzzing.

'I hear it!' I screamed, then turned around to see a brilliant black steam train racing down the tracks. Giant plumes of white-hot steam billowed into the air against the most vibrant of countryside – it was a breathtaking sight. It was a vision of progress, of modernity.

'Over here,' said William, smiling as he ran towards the train. I followed him as he crossed over the tracks.

A whistle blew loudly as the train passed by us, making the loudest rattling sound I had ever heard. The train continued passing, creating a barrier between us and the picnickers on the hill.

In this brief moment of privacy, behind the moving train, William took my hand. 'Marry me,' he said.

I looked at him, stunned. I had no idea what to say, so I pulled away. It's not that I didn't want to marry William; it was just all happening so fast. Once I had come of age, it was as if I climbed onto that grinding, churning locomotive, increasing speed each day. For the very first time I wanted my life to move just a little more slowly. The only thing I could do was be honest with him.

'I know nothing of being a wife,' I finally said as the train was still churning by us.

'You'll learn,' he said, with a smile.

I was dumbfounded that William wanted to marry me. Then I realised, I shouldn't be. Of course, all these Saturdays spent together added up to a marriage proposal. Was this Mother's doing? Or did he really love me? I thought about Mary's advice about choosing a husband who appreciated my intellect.

'Mathematics is the only thing at which I'm… I'm proficient,' I said, a little embarrassed. 'I have a very large appetite when it comes to numbers.'

'Then you shall have your numbers. Just marry me,' he said.

Again, there were no equations or proofs to help me decide. This was a matter of the heart. In that moment, every part of my body and soul wanted William, yearned for him. I wanted to touch him, to love him. I smiled and nodded excitedly and said, 'Yes!'

William drew me close to him and kissed me on the mouth. My blood raced as his lips touched mine. I could feel the tiniest amount of stubble on his jaw, as his faced brushed my cheek. I kissed him back eagerly, purposefully, drinking in his passion, until the end of the train passed by.

As the end of the train rolled by, we both instinctively stepped back from each other, no doubt wearing guilty smiles on our faces.

That night, William asked Mother and Dr. Poole for my hand in marriage. Without showing any emotion or surprise, Mother calmly agreed. It was as if she had been expecting it all along. And just like that, the matter was settled. In a few months, I would become Mrs. Augusta Ada Byron King. Mother couldn't wait to plan my wedding, but as focused as she became on the event, I knew there was a lot more to nuptials than walking down the aisle of a church in a pretty gown.

13

It was to be a simple, yet sophisticated wedding, per Mother's wishes, but it took six months of planning. If there were one thing Mother would never do, it would be to parade her wealth in an ostentatious or garish way. But it was still important to create a ceremony on par with the daughters of her aristocratic friends. One matter we both agreed on was that only the finest of British cuisine would be served and the fewer the guests, the finer the cuisine could be. She also thought a very large affair would attract newspapermen and other riffraff and Mother didn't want any of that. An Anglican minister would marry William and me, binding us together for eternity.

Being a wife was going to be a whole new parametric equation, with its curved trajectory unknown to me. I was telling the truth when I told William I knew nothing of being married. Mother was a divorcée by the time I was a year old and she didn't have a husband to obey or dote on. How could I know how to behave? And then there was the bedchamber. I only knew that the husband and wife must be naked to conceive a child, at least that's what Miss Stamp told me, but I didn't understand the mechanics of it. The Bible mentioned men and women 'lying' together, so it made sense that baby-making would happen in bed. Could it possibly take place while we slept, like in some kind of dream-state? There was much I needed to learn.

I didn't want to ask Mother to explain it, but I didn't want to look like a fool on my wedding night, either. Then again, if I seemed too knowledgeable on the subject, that could be problematic in its own way. A virgin-bride shouldn't be skilled in these matters. Marriage was already so complicated and it hadn't even happened yet.

I would have asked Mary, but she was away at a scientific conference in Vienna. I thought about writing to her, but if the letter were read by anyone else, it would be very embarrassing. I now regretted all the hours we spent talking about the moon and the stars. Why didn't she tutor me in more important things like life?

I thought the best way to educate myself on the topic was to steal one of Dr. Poole's medical books. While he was stabling the horses and Mother was napping, I snuck into his room and found a book labeled 'Human Anatomy.' I took the book into the library. At least there, if anyone entered, I could quickly hide it amongst the many others.

Flipping through the pages, I found a diagram of the anatomical male. The chest and arms looked perfectly reasonable, but when my eyes travelled downwards, to the drawing's groin area, I was a bit baffled. A tube-like appendage protruded from between the legs, called a 'penis.' I searched for a Latin dictionary. After a moment, I was able to discern the Latin root of the word 'penis' meant 'tail.' Men have tails? This was shocking! How could I not have known this? Did Dr. Poole have one, too? And, goodness, did that mean William also had a tail between his legs?

I flipped the page to find a close-up drawing labeled 'The Male Sexual Organs.' Here was a larger drawing of the penis that revealed two small sacks just below it labeled 'Testes.' I looked up the Latin root for testes, which meant 'to witness.' I scratched my head, more confused than ever. Perhaps the testes were like two eyes that watched the tail? My heart sank – these were discoveries I was not pleased to make. I prayed William would show little interest in creating babies anytime soon. Why hadn't Miss Stamp told me any of this?

As the days grew closer to our nuptials, Mother's nerves became more and more on edge. The pressure of providing the church and the reception fell onto the bride's family, so Mother had to make the arrangements on her own. William offered to help, of course, but Mother would have none of it. The Anglican wedding ceremony would be conducted at a tiny country church walking distance from William's estate, Ashley Combe in Porlock Weir, Somerset, which was right on the coast. The wedding party would be held in the church's garden. On my wedding day, I would take up residence with my husband at his estate. Mother and Dr. Poole would also be residing there temporarily to help me get the household in a working order that pleased both me and William. Mother said she would also take it upon herself to set up a nursery and find a suitable governess. Of course, I had no plans to have children anytime soon, but it would give Mother something to do when she wasn't getting her leech treatments from Dr. Poole.

Mother was a lot less controlling than usual when it came to picking out the pattern for my wedding dress. Though I didn't get my first or second choice, I was very confident in my third choice and the seamstress, an Irish woman named Claude, vigourously agreed. Claude, a stout woman with black hair, blue eyes and a lilt in her voice, also suggested a soft primrose-coloured silk chiffon with sleeves that would puff out at the shoulders and gather just above my elbows where they were synched with a long ribbon. The hemline of the skirt was to be decorated with tiny glass beads to create a floral pattern that shimmered in the light. A fur-lined stole would rest on my shoulders when I was outdoors.

Claude seemed to sew very slowly and it took nearly a dozen fittings before the dress fit me properly. But when it did, I thought it looked stunning. As I modelled the dress for Mother, I couldn't help but grin at my own image as I stood in front of a full-length mirror. It was then, as I stood there smiling like the cat that ate the canary, I realised Mother and I had hardly quarreled since my engagement. William was proving to be good for me in more ways than I'd realised.

Just then, Mother rose to join me at the mirror to hold my long tresses up on top of my head to see what I'd look like with my hair coiffed, but she appeared to get lost in thought at the sight of me. I wondered if she was thinking back to her own wedding day, a day full of excitement and hope. Then her face grew melancholy.

'What is it, Mother? You seem sad.'

'I was just thinking how much more successful your marriage will be than mine. William is a good man, remember that when the sea grows turbulent.'

When the sea grows turbulent? I felt my mind racing. Was she using some sort of euphemism for the wedding night? I felt my cheeks grow warm.

'What are you trying to suggest?' I asked, my voice wavering. Maybe it wasn't to do with the bedchamber... maybe Mother was alluding to something deeper, having to do with my rebellious nature.

'Trouble finds us all. But you can trust William to guide you. You must obey him in all matters and make his needs your priority.'

'But William has made it very clear to me that I am his priority. He values me and my desires.'

'Courtship and marriage are two very different things,' she said still looking at me in the mirror. Her eyes were still sad, but appeared to me in a way I'd never before seen. She looked like she was about to say something else… something important. I looked at her, wanting to understand. Was she going to tell me something about Father? About their life together? I held my breath, waiting for her to continue, but then, suddenly, the moment was over.

'Stand tall,' she said, all business once again. 'Like nobility. Shoulders back, you don't want to walk through the church like a hunchback.' I followed her orders, further exposing my long neck, all traces of tenderness between us gone.

'Now suck in that atrocious gut, you look like you've swallowed an entire goose,' she said. I took a long, deep breath in and Mother buttoned up the last few buttons on the back of my dress.

Normally, Mother's hurtful comments would make me flustered, but today was different. Knowing that I would be leaving her care, moving on with my life, I was able to let her nastiness wash away, like water being poured from a gourd. I could still see a shadow of vulnerability in Mother's eyes, though. Here was a woman letting go of her only child; a woman who'd had to raise that child on her own and who'd fought hard to make sure I turned into the kind of woman who would one day marry a Baron. I felt my skin grow hot as I realised how difficult I had often made things for her. And now she was getting older. For the first time, I felt empathy for her, and could actually understand where Mother's motivations came from. My whole life, she was simply a mother protecting the only child she had in the best way she could. I couldn't quite forgive her for the hurt she had caused me as a girl, but I finally had enough maturity to see Mother for who she was – a flawed, frightened human being, just like everyone else. I felt a tear trace its way down my cheek as I thought of her, of how strong she was, and how much she must have protected me from. It was in that moment I knew that I had truly reached womanhood and I felt a swelling of pride. I was no longer afraid of my mother, of getting married, or that my husband-to-be may have a tail between his legs.

I finally let out my breath only to hear several buttons pop off the back of my dress and hit the tiled floor. Mother simply called out, 'Claude?'

14

The morning of the wedding was bright and crisp, the sun lustrous, shining like a giant yellow pearl as it rose out of the east. It was May and the lowlands were just starting to warm up from their spring chill. I could just barely smell the fruity scent from the rows of bearded irises growing nearby.

Hoping to fit perfectly into my wedding dress, I declined a large breakfast, taking only tea and a lemon scone around seven o'clock a.m. Once I was dressed, I adorned my hair with *Peigne d'Alger* hair combs that had finely cut crystals attached to delicate chains that would swing ever so slightly as I walked.

I checked my image in the mirror at least ten times. I don't know what I thought would change with each new glance, but perhaps I just wanted to make sure I was still me and this wedding was actually about to take place. Once I convinced myself it was, Mother and I headed to the church. The wedding was to begin precisely at ten o'clock a.m., as was the typical time for most English weddings.

As Mother led me into the church filled with about forty or so guests, I felt an enormous adrenaline rush. My heart started pounding as all eyes in the church turned to look at me. The light shining through the church windows was blinding, and I hoped that the crystals in my hair were sparkling like daytime stars as I walked towards my groom.

William's eyes captured me in his gaze. He gave me a soft,

tender smile that made him look so happy. I couldn't help but wonder if Father looked at Mother that way on their wedding day. It is terribly sad if he didn't. I dispensed with any melancholy thoughts and focused on the handsome man standing before me.

As the vows began, I felt excited and proud to offer myself to my husband before God. I didn't realise how much William meant to me until the pastor pronounced us man and wife. Tears welled-up in my eyes. I knew Mother loved me, but I was her own flesh and blood. William *chose* me to love, not because he had to or felt obligated to, but because he wanted to. I now felt a part of something bigger than myself; like I had a duty to my husband, a duty to love him.

As William leaned down and kissed me, I grinned with happiness. I couldn't remember a more blissful moment. It was like the whole universe had disappeared and William and I were floating somewhere very far away, in our own delightful time and sky.

Our reception was small by society's standards, which was fine by me. The church garden was decorated with ribbons and fresh cut dahlias in vibrant apricot and magenta. Six tables were set to provide the guests a hearty breakfast of goose liver sausage with mint and mustard, lava bread with cockles, and stargazy pie – a fish pie where the actual fish heads poke out of the pastry as if gazing at the stars above.

Despite Mother's hope for an unostentatious event, the newspaper reporter Mr. Quincy, the man she and I met at the King's ball, made an appearance. With everyone in a good mood, William and I agreed to be sketched for the paper. Mother was not asked.

Instead, she spent much of her time dancing with Dr. Poole and seemed quite content. I could see them whispering into each other's ears and smiling. Mother even laughed a time or two. I wasn't used to seeing her so happy. I couldn't tell if she was happy because the wedding was a success or because I was finally married off. Or was something more going on? It was then that it dawned on me – could Mother and Dr. Poole be in love? I felt a fool to not have thought of it sooner. Dr. Poole spent so much time with us... and Mother, though older, was still quite beautiful, and yet I'd never seen her even consider taking a suitor. But if they were in love, why weren't they married?

I watched as Mother rested her head on Dr. Poole's shoulders while he tenderly stroked her hair. I'd never seen such warmth between them before though, I was sure of it. Perhaps his affection for her was new? Or had I simply been too focused on girlish things to notice? I was certain I had never seen Dr. Poole behave with such a sweet air around her.

But before I could decide on what was brewing between them, I heard Charles Babbage call my name from the other side of the garden.

'Ada! Come for a toast!' he said as he popped the cork from a bottle of fine French champagne. I smiled and headed over to his table, where William handed me a fluted glass of sparkling, Dionysian goodness.

Babbage raised his glass and said, 'A toast to a romance that began over my calculating machine. William and Ada, in Euclidean geometry two parallel lines never touch. I sincerely hope your wedding night is spent exploring non-Euclidean geometry and that it goes on longer than Abel's impossibility theorem.'

Mary and her husband laughed and applauded. After a moment, others began to follow likely not knowing that the theorem Mr. Babbage mentioned was 500 pages long.

'And to celebrate your nuptials, I bestow on you a Leyden jar,' said Babbage as he presented William and me with a large, water-filled clay jug with a copper wire protruding from the opening that boasted a copper cylinder at the very top.

William looked at the contraption curiously, saying, 'What on earth is this, Babb?'

'Lightening in a bottle!' said Babbage.

'I don't understand,' said William.

'The latest craze,' said Babbage, 'electricity.' William just shook his and laughed, but I was entranced. Many scientists were beginning to experiment with electrostatic energy and I was thrilled to own such an intriguing contraption.

'Babb, you must demonstrate this electricity for me. It looks--' But I was interrupted by Mother, who rushed up to William. Her demeanour was no longer calm.

'Another newspaperman has tried to enter the reception. Dr. Poole tried to remove him, but they had a scuffle. He's bleeding,' said Mother.

That's when I looked up to see the two men grappling with each other in the distance.

'One sketch! I'll pay twenty quid,' yelled the excited man.

Who knew the newspapers were so eager for our wedding portraits?

William, Babb and Mother hurried over to the brawling men.

I took my glass of champagne and went to my dining table, which was decorated with dahlias.

When I pulled out my chair, I saw a small envelope resting

on the seat. It read 'For Ada to read with a slice of venison pie.' I shook my head as I opened it, certain it was another con man hoping to abscond with my money, only this weasel had a fondness for pie. William would get a good laugh when he saw this, I thought!

To my absolute shock, however, the thin letter inside was a jumble of numbers. Their order didn't make any sense– at least the integers weren't in any immediately identifiable sequence. I wondered if it were some kind of joke left by the angry news-paperman, but I didn't think the man made it past the garden gates. I read the envelope again. 'For Ada to read with a slice of venison pie.' But we weren't serving venison pie today, so why did the author mention it? Could this be a note from William? It didn't seem likely. Savoury pie wasn't a favourite of mine, nor did I believe William had ever expressed a particular fondness for such a dish, and he had never written to me in any type of code. Then I thought, perhaps I shouldn't interpret the note quite so literally. Venison is the meat from a deer, a very timid creature. I was not timid, however. A play on words could mean dear, as in someone who's dearest. As I looked at the numbers again, a hot shiver ran up my spine; a play on the word pie could be the mathematical constant *pi*. Yes, it had to be! But who would write to me in numbers? That's when I gasped. Suddenly, I knew in my bones that this letter was a reply to the note I wrote to my father, years ago. The letter that Miss Stamp gave to Mr. Hobhouse, for which Miss Stamp was terminated as my housemaid. I had asked my father to write back in code, which he did. Now, I had to decipher it. I looked around for a pencil, or fountain pen, but who would have such a thing at a wedding?

William was still arguing with the newspaperman at the edge of the road. I could just make out that the newspaperman was gesturing with a pencil in his fist, but of course I couldn't walk up and ask him for it. Mother, the newspaperman and my new husband would all think I was mad! My eyes made their way across the rest of the guests, but I quickly realised even if someone in attendance did have a pencil on their person, it would surely strike them odd that the bride wanted to borrow it. Never mind, I thought, I would just have to concentrate very hard and work out the code in my head. The first two lines of the code read:

3-15-3, 27-841-3-84 62-2 23-69 27-62-0-93, 95-5-35-27 35-27 69-62-0-83 95-83-0-9 2-3-95-5-9-83.

My heart hammered against my ribcage at the idea that this letter could actually be from my father, which made deciphering the numbers quite difficult. The first part of the code read 3-15-3, which I suspected to be code for Ada, my middle name, by which only a family member would address me. It was a good start.

I looked at the rest of the numbers and felt the hammering in my chest start to quiet; math was taking over. The first twenty-six decimal digits of pi were 3.14159265358979932384626433. If I substituted the numbers for letters in the alphabet, three would correspond with 'A', but 'D' would be four, not fifteen, as the fifteenth letter of the alphabet is 'O', which didn't bode well for my initial guess. Then it dawned on me—since some digits repeat in pi's long sequence, it would be necessary to combine digits within the strain or else the code would be messy and confusing.

So, if I combined two consecutive numbers after one repeated itself, that would make fifteen represent 'D', while nine alone would represent 'E' since it hadn't yet repeated, and so forth. I felt a rush of excitement fill my entire body as I realised I had solved the code! After that, I plugged the 'A's and 'D's into the equation, and soon was able to decipher the first line:

Ada, swan of my soul, this is your true father.

Could it really be him? But how could he have delivered the letter to my table? Perhaps he did it when we were distracted by the reporters' scuffle. I scanned the party with my eyes. I watched the musicians playing their instruments. I turned to see a servant carving the goose. William was off in the distance. I felt lightheaded. Could this coded letter really be from Lord Byron?

My eyes snapped back to the letter, working out the last line which translated to:

I will come to you at a discreet hour, my pippin, but rest assured, I am here. Lord Byron.

I drew a deep breath and thought to myself, my father, at last!

After all the guests had left, William and I, along with Mother and Dr. Poole, took a carriage to Ashley Combe. This large and beautiful home was built to emulate an Italian villa and I was quite fond of its romantic styling. It was nestled into the hillside which created an air of mystery since much of the home was hidden by large trees. William, it turned out, was incredibly keen on adding to this feeling of mystery about the place, and had created several tunnels on the property. I don't believe these tunnels served any practical purpose, I think they just made him feel clever, which was fine by me as I enjoyed their mystique immensely. It turned out my husband also enjoyed cultivating exotic gardens decorated with turrets and towers, which brought a sense of adventure to evening walks.

Fourteen Roman-styled arches lined the many walkways that were connected with an outdoor spiral staircase that led to the top. Peacocks and peahens roamed freely, along with swans that preferred to stay near the pond that was nestled next to the hothouse. On clear mornings, you could hear the peacocks calling to one another all the way up to the main house.

I didn't notice any of the estate's intricacies on my wedding night though. I was too anxious and excited about what was next to come.

Inside Ashley Combe, the décor was sophisticated and a bit over-decorated in some rooms, in my opinion. But those matters could be addressed later. Exhausted from the day's events, Mother retired to her temporary bedchamber early. Dr. Poole drank a whisky alone by the fire, which seemed odd since he usually retired at the same hour as Mother. I wondered if it had something do with the way they were dancing and carrying on. Did one of them say something to irk the other?

As much as I wanted to know the answer, my thoughts wandered straight back to the letter and whether or not I would see my father tonight. That's when William took my hand and led me to the bottom of the staircase.

'I have a gift waiting for you in our bedchamber,' he said with a coy look. Normally, I loved presents - but on this night, I was entirely distracted, wondering when and if Lord Byron would pay me a visit. And tonight, on what may be a father and babe reunion, William may ask me to make a baby of my own. Oh, goodness, the irony of the situation unsettled me as I followed William up the stairs, my hand still in his.

My wedding gift was a beautiful oil painting entitled *Cock Robin Defending his Nest*. Resting on the chaise lounge, it depicted a dozen or so little magical fairies attempting to steal the robin's eggs with the robin hovering over the nest. The fairy queen had mustard-coloured gossamer wings and seemed fearless as she faced the powerful, hungry bird.

'Well,' asked William, 'what do you think?'

'It's beautiful,' I said, 'how thoughtful of you to remember my love for fairies.'

'I shall hang it over the bureau so that happy, little fairies will be the first thing you see when you wake in the morning,' he said as he went to gather a hammer and nail.

But it wasn't fairies I wanted to see right now, it was my father and I was starting to grow nervous I would miss his visit.

'It is so lovely, but shouldn't we wait till morning?' I said. 'The pounding on the wall will certainly wake Mother.'

'Oh, how insensitive of me. Forgive me, I'm just so eager to please you,' he said.

'I couldn't be more pleased,' I said as I embraced my husband.

With our arms around each other, I knew William could feel me quivering ever so slightly. So much was happening so fast, I was a bit overwhelmed but couldn't tell William any of it. 'You're trembling, my love.' He paused, took a breath, then said, 'I must confess, I know why.'

I looked at him in shock. How could he know? Did he already discover my father? What if William sent him away?

William looked me in the eyes and said, 'I won't take advantage of you the way your tutor did.'

'What?' I asked, confused.

'Your mother told me all about the scoundrel and how he tried to sully your innocence in your garden,' he said.

'She told you about Stephen?' I said in disbelief.

'Yes, but don't worry. Tonight won't be anything like that, I promise,' he said.

'How dare she stick her nose into my bed,' I said.

'There's only room for you and me in this bed,' he said and he pulled me to him, kissing me on the lips. Tasting his mouth felt strange, but wonderful. Almost like eating a juicy, savoury fruit.

I felt my resolve to chastise my mother and my preoccupation with my father lessening with each sweet kiss. I was relieved to know William wasn't aware of Lord Byron's possible visit, but his knowledge of the incident with Stephen had added a whole new level of worry to tonight's impending physical congress. But as William continued to kiss me, thoughts of my father, and of Stephen, drifted away. My body began to respond to William's in an unfamiliar way. I became less fearful about what might happen next.

William's neck had a peppery, citrus scent; a little sweet, a little woodsy. The more we kissed, the more my body became alive. I decided I liked this strange new feeling.

William stopped kissing me and just looked at me for a moment.

'Have I done something wrong?' I asked in a panic. 'Because, despite what my mother told you, I really don't know anything about the machinations of marital bedding.'

William smiled, 'I was just going to blow out a few candles.'

'Oh, of course,' I said with relief.

He extinguished several flames and the light got very low. We could still see each other but the shadowy room now had a more intimate ambiance.

William seemed to have everything under control. His confidence combined with his concern for me, made me more curious about our coupling. I watched in anticipation as William began to remove his suspenders, his shirt, then his trousers. Now it was my turn. Kissing the back of my neck, he undid the tiny buttons that went down my back. My silk dress made a whoosh sound as it hit the floor. There, I stood by candlelight, in only my corset and petticoat.

'Take the combs out of your hair,' he whispered, 'I want to see it spill onto your gorgeous shoulders.'

'Like this?' I said as I removed the silver combs and let my silky chestnut locks tumble down to the middle of my back.

'Yes. There is no wrong way to do any of this. You are most lovely and eager, like a beautiful bird ready to take its first flight. I am the luckiest man alive,' he said – it was a wonderful feeling to know he was so fond of me.

He unlaced my corset and unhooked my skirt, his hands surprisingly deft with my undergarments' complex machinations. I sat on the bed as he slowly slid off my silk stockings, kissing my knees and then my toes. He removed his undergarments and gently laid his body on top of mine, in a parallel position on the bed. His muscled chest brushed against my bare breasts. I took a deep breath. His body next to mine felt perfectly warm and wonderful. I couldn't believe I had been so fearful of bestowing my virginity on him.

'Are you ready, my little bird?' he whispered as he ran his fingers through my hair.

I wasn't sure what he could possibly be talking about. Then I remembered. 'You mean, you're going to poke me with your tail, now?'

'My what?'

'Your... penis tail. I read about it in one of Dr. Poole's medical books.'

William broke out laughing. This made me worried, 'What is it?'

'I don't have a tail, silly!' he said.

Then I started laughing as well, feeling much relieved.

'It's generally not nice for a wife to laugh at her husband on his wedding night,' he said, feigning humiliation.

'No, I'm sorry! I'm not laughing at you, but at me. I fear I got the male anatomy terribly wrong. The Latin root for penis is—well, never mind. Please, let's carry on. I mean, if you'd like to. I don't actually have any idea what's coming--'

He abruptly put his lips to mine and gently showed me a closeness like no other. Our bodies fit together in the most surprising way – a way I never would have imagined.

When our coupling was finished, William kissed me, deeply, passionately. Then he rolled over and, within seconds, fell asleep.

And just like that, I had truly become a married woman. Though I tried to fight my exhaustion, wanting to relive every moment before it faded into yesterday, I also quickly fell to sleep.

Sometime in the middle of the night, I awoke to feel something brushing against my bare back. I opened my eyes. The light of one single candle stump burned on the nightstand, but it wasn't enough light to see much. I rolled over to see my dressing gown dangling over me. At first, I thought it was William holding it, but my husband was snoring soundly next to me. My eyes adjusted to the dark a bit more and I could see a man put his index finger to his lips to shush me. He dropped the gown onto the bed and left the room.

Then I remembered – my father was coming to see me at a *discreet hour*, which he must have meant to be very late in the night, when everyone would be sleeping. How did he get into the house? I worried this could all be a dream as I quickly wrapped the gown around me.

15

As I tiptoed into the hallway, anxiety seized hold of my body. Sneaking into one's bedchamber was a mighty strange way to make one's acquaintance. But, I had been warned my whole life that my father was a peculiar individual. I thought perhaps I should be stern with him, lest he think such behaviour okay and make a habit of sneaking in during the wee hours of the night.

Now, at the end of the hallway, I stopped in my tracks and said, 'I'm not going one more step until I know for certain who you are.'

'A poison long already mixed, a blade between your fingers fixed,' the man said and kept walking.

Cautiously, I followed him down the staircase and almost let out a shriek as I felt something brush against my leg. Looking down, I let out a sigh. It was only Puff, who Mother had made sure to deliver to Ashley Combe the week before. I gave him a frown for scaring me so, but he only swished his tail playfully, as though he knew we were on an adventure.

Puff and I continued to follow the man, who led us out of the servant's entrance and into the garden. Suddenly, I wasn't sure this was the best decision to meet him alone. Perhaps I should have woken William, or at least alerted him that my father might visit, but now it was too late. As we walked past the brick arches and into one of the secret tunnels, it struck me that this man seemed quite familiar with the grounds. I looked back, suddenly aware of how far from human ears we had wandered. The tunnel let out onto a small clearing where an unfamiliar black horse was tied to a birch. It must belong to him, I thought.

'Show me proof you're really my father,' I said, surprised at the force of my own voice.

He turned to look at me in the moonlight. His wide, masculine face had been beaten and bruised, his lower lip cut and bleeding. I gasped. His eyes were brooding with flecks of both green and brown I could just make out in the moonlight.

'Do you know what I've been through to get to you?' he said, almost angrily.

I felt my temper flare. Why should he be angry with me? I had every right to demand he explain himself.

'I want to believe you...' I said as he pulled a medallion-sized locket from his jacket. He dangled the locket before me, as though to offer it to me, but as I reached for it, he snatched it back.

'Careful what you wish for,' he said. I narrowed my eyes at him, and he dangled the locket again, only this time, he allowed me to grasp the locket with my hand. I quickly opened it to find two portraits inside. One was of me - but so young, I could only have been a toddler; the other portrait was of an unfamiliar woman.

'This one is me, but the other is not Mother,' I said defiantly.

'Do you think I'd take a picture of Medusa onto the battle-field? It's my sister, for whom you're named,' he spit back.

'My aunt Augusta?' I asked.

'She walks in beauty like the night, of cloudless climbs—'

I interrupted him, 'They say you have a deformity. A clubfoot.'

'Ay,' he said.

'Show it to me, then.'

He unlaced his right boot and carefully extracted his stocking-clad, misshaped foot. On the side of the stocking was a bulge that oozed with blood, turning the white silk a dark reddish-brown. As ugly as it might be, I wanted to see his foot without the stocking. As I reached down and attempted to remove it, he howled in pain. I'd never heard a grown man wail so miserably before and it scared me.

'I've seen enough,' I said motioning for him to put his stockinged-foot back into his boot.

I then locked my eyes onto his. 'Father, it's really you,' I rushed into his arms.

'My child, my soul,' he squeezed me tightly.

'My worst fear was that you were dead and I'd never know you,' I said, so many emotions running through me.

'I'm alive like fire,' he replied with a wicked smile, his teeth glowing in the moonlight.

'What happened? I want to know everything,' I said as we heard a rooster crow.

Lord Byron pursed his lips. 'There's time enough,' and he turned to go.

'Wait! I must see you again. Please, return here tomorrow night and bring me some of your poetry. I'll be waiting in the stable,' I said, and without a farewell, Lord Byron climbed onto his horse with ease, paying his clubfoot no mind. Then my father clicked his tongue twice to signal to the horse. He galloped off into the night.

I ambled ever so carefully and quietly through the secret

tunnel, suddenly noticing the brisk air and cold stones under my bare toes. I picked up my pace as I scuttled back into the home I now shared with my husband. What a day I had had, what a strange, wonderful, auspicious day. I couldn't wait to see what tomorrow would bring!

Two new servants had been added to Ashley Combe to coincide with my arrival. Kate and Mack were individually acquired, both with outstanding recommendations. Now that I was married, it seemed quite acceptable to Mother to have a young manservant in the home, though William had neglected to ask her opinion. At just twenty-years-old, Kate was a simple-minded, thin, freckled girl, who wore her ginger hair in a braid that she looped into a bun on the back of her square-shaped head. Mack, just four years older, had sandy-brown hair and dark brown eyes emphasised by thick, bushy eyebrows. His oily, boyish face had an ever-changing constellation of pimples – one day Cassiopeia, the next, Orion.

On the first morning of my married life, both of our new servants stood quietly at attention at the breakfast table as I entered to find William, Mother and Dr. Poole already seated. Mother appeared irritated as William and Dr. Poole stood.

'Finally. I thought I might faint from hunger,' said Mother.

'Ada was no doubt exhausted from all the rigorous events of her wedding day and surely needed a little extra sleep,' said Dr. Poole, making me blush. At Mother's stern gaze, he quickly retreated with his words, saying, 'I merely meant, with enter-taining so many guests and the large meal—'

William gallantly interrupted them to greet me, 'Good morning, Lady King.'

'Good morning, happy husband,' I said with a big smile. 'I'll take my tea extra strong,' I kissed Mother on her cheek, 'and extra sweet,' and kissed William on his cheek and then sat at my place at the table.

Mother bit her lip as she resisted the temptation to critique my bold display of physical affection. But everyone in the room knew William and I were married now, why pretend otherwise?

Kate began to serve breakfast, which consisted of collared tongue, pig's cheek, stewed figs and bread with apple marmalade and butter.

'I take it you slept well,' William said to me.

'And woke up well. I may need another fairy painting for my study,' I said. From what I could tell, it seemed no one knew of Father's visit and I was quite relieved.

'Your study?' Mother asked.

'Ada shall be carrying on with mathematics as she pleases,' said William as he added sugar to his tea.

'Babbage agreed to oversee my tutoring,' I said, just in case Mother wanted to volunteer for the job.

'It takes a great deal of time to manage and run a proper home,' Mother warned.

'If we need to hire more servants, so be it,' said William. The tone of his voice was kind, but I got the distinct impression he was trying to let Mother know that she no longer ruled the roost.

Mother, ever the contrarian, was about to reply when Dr. Poole offered, 'Lovely figs this time of year.' To which we all agreed.

The rest of the day passed in relaxed leisure since the wedding left everyone a bit fatigued, but Mother was right; running a home was not an easy task, and as William's wife, I had duties to attend to. Of utmost importance, it seemed, was laundering the prior day's linens before stains set in to the beautiful lace tablecloths and napkins that had decorated our wedding tables.

Behind the house, Mother and I supervised as Kate pinned the clean wash onto laundry lines. I looked up as low, formless clouds began to roll in to blanket the heavens, slowly turning the blue sky a shade of unpolished pewter. Rain would be coming soon, but not today.

Mother inspected a lace tablecloth as she spoke. 'I've never seen a man so willing to squander money,' she said before telling Kate to add more pins to the tablecloth on the line. Pockets empty, Kate went back into the house to retrieve them. Mother continued, 'Had I known he would cater to your every whim, I wouldn't have handed over such a large marriage settlement. At least Newstead Abbey is in your name and he can't squander that,' she said.

At that moment, a gust of wind blew the tablecloth off the line and onto the ground. The white cloth was now soiled with earth and would need another washing.

'Where is that girl?' Mother shrieked and took off back to the house.

I reached down to pick up the grounded tablecloth. When my eyes returned to the clothesline, I saw a book pinned to it entitled *Don Juan by Lord Byron*. I snatched the book then spun in a circle where I stood, taking in all 360 degrees of my surroundings, but seeing no one. Quickly, I made my way behind some hanging sheets where I saw a pair of familiar boots. As I swept the sheet up and over the clothesline, I was quite shocked to find Lord Byron standing in front of me in broad daylight.

I spoke in a hushed, panicked tone, 'You shouldn't be here!'

'Old crow's still squawking over money, eh? Someone ought

to poison her porridge,' he said.

'You should heed my warning quite seriously. If she or William catches you—'

'Ada?' called Mother.

'Meet me in the stable after midnight. Bring wine,' he said and scurried off. Mother pushed the sheet aside to find me, alone with my father's book.

'Where did you get that?' she asked.

'A wedding gift,' I lied. She tore it from my hands.

'You know I disapprove. It is a blatant mockery full of foul lies,' said Mother.

'I'm a married woman now, with thoughts and ideas of my own,' I retorted, as I retrieved the book from her. Though I was enjoying my new status as head of my own household, I was terribly relieved she didn't see Father.

Mother looked down at the dirt for moment, scratching the crook of her left arm before looking me squarely in the eyes.

'Just how long do you think William will tolerate such a headstrong wife?' she asked, pointedly.

'He loves me the way I am,' I replied.

'So do I,' said Mother, 'But in marriage, it's important not to be yourself too much.'

As she went back to surveying the laundry, I realised I had no idea what she meant. Was she suggesting I create some type of charade to make William think I was someone other than my true self? Or pretend I'm dull-witted? Suddenly become a meek little mouse? I was beginning to fear I'd never catch on to being a wife.

later that evening, I retired with William to his bedchamber at ten o'clock. After our physical congress, he again promptly fell into a deep sleep. It was as if finishing the act used every last ounce of his energy, rendering him utterly useless. This worked out perfectly for me since I was planning to meet Father at midnight, but first, I crept out of bed to retrieve the book he'd so blatantly clipped to the laundry line earlier that day.

I spent the next hour reading all sixteen shocking cantos from *Don Juan* by candlelight. They told the story of an incredibly unhappy marriage between Don Juan and Donna Inez, presumably inspired by he and Mother's brief time together. He wrote that Donna Inez's *Thoughts were theorems, her words a problem*, and that ...*she was a walking calculation*. Yes! That described Mother perfectly! She was always calculating and trying to solve me as if I were a mathematical problem. Father saw her the same way I did. It was as if all my feelings of childhood frustration were suddenly validated.

When the hallway's grandfather clock finally struck midnight, I crept out of bed as quietly as I could, collected a sweater and my boots from my bedchamber, and began my escape down the hall.

The dark house was silent. I lit a candle in the kitchen and shone it over the bottles of wine resting on their sides in the pantry. I hadn't been instructed on how to choose wine, so I picked a bottle at random, hoping it would be to Father's liking. Alone and excited, I made my way out of the back of the house and headed toward the stable looking forward to a long discussion of *Don Juan*.

16

The night air was chilly but at least there was no rain as of yet. The moon waxed as it dangled in the sky behind some clouds, emanating less light than the previous night, making it difficult to follow the path to the stable. Once I passed through the west tunnel and could feel the stone bricks under my boots, I knew I was almost there.

The stable was now home to four horses, Voltigeur, Dubby, Cymbeline and the sturdy Sylph. Sylph was my horse, a Friesian with a coat so black, it had a blue hue in the sunlight. She perked up as soon as I entered the pitch-black stable. My candle illuminated Sylph ever so slightly as I brushed her nose with a shaking hand. Would Lord Byron keep his word? Or was I a fool to walk all the way out here in the night? My stomach twisted slightly as I called out in a low whisper, 'Father?'

I felt a hand on my shoulder, startling me, and I stifled a scream as I spun around to find him.

'You're here!' I said and embraced him, burying my face in his chest.

'Ah, my daughter. My love will always find a way, even through paths wolves fear to prey. Did you bring wine?'

'Yes, but I must admit, I'm not a connoisseur,' I said.

'Is it red?' Father asked.

'Yes,' I replied.

'My girl, that's all there is to know,' he said as he took

the bottle from me. With his thumb, he pushed the cork down into the bottle, causing a bit of wine to splash out. After licking off the drops that splashed onto his hand, he took a big swig from the bottle, then handed it to me. I had never drunk anything directly out of a bottle before - the act seemed terribly crude. But this was Father's way and I decided it would be mine, too—at least when I was with him. Repeating the gesture in my mother's company, or William's even, would no doubt elicit a scolding. I put the bottle to my mouth, and took a dainty swig. The wine was warm and pungent on my tongue, and I welcomed the calm it brought to my nerves.

Father gestured for me to take a seat next to him on some bales of hay, but we'd hardly even been settled before I began to ask Father questions. Most curious to me was how he was able to fake his own death and why anyone would choose such a fate. I could see the reflection of the candle flame in Lord Byron's eyes as he spoke.

'I had had enough of England. This wretched country doesn't deserve a great poet like myself. I wanted respect, not servitude to the deranged men calling themselves my debtors. I went to Greece and was embraced by rebel soldiers fighting for their freedom. Freedom is all there is to a man. To oppress him is to castrate him, like a bloody animal. Battling for freedom awoke a great passion in me, but war is a dangerous mistress. When my battalion was taken hostage by the Ottoman army, they put us on a boat and set it ablaze. I was the only one who could swim,' he said.

'The other men drowned?' I asked.

'Or worse,' he said, taking another swig of wine.

I considered what a death worse than drowning would be like, and shivered at the thought.

'How brave you are,' I said. Father didn't respond, but took another swig of wine. I couldn't stop myself from adding, 'But they said they recovered your body.'

At this, he set down the bottle and looked at me with great seriousness.

'I traded uniforms and identification with one of the dead soldiers. I now had a new identity, a rebirth if you will. A resurrection,' he said with a laugh, toasting himself it seemed with another drink.

'Thank God you're back in England,' I said with relief.

'Bloody hell. If I'm caught, I'll be beaten and thrown into debtor's prison. I risk it all to be near you,' he said.

I took his hand and squeezed it, hoping to reassure him that he had done the right thing. Then, he asked, 'Did you read *Don Juan*?'

'Yes, it is a masterpiece. Now I know why Mother kept it from me all my life. The first canto is about her, isn't it?' I asked, carefully.

Father quoted from his book, 'Don Jose and Donna Inez led for some time an unhappy sort of life, wishing each other not divorced, but...' he stopped speaking and looked to me to finish his line.

Which I did, reciting, 'Wishing each other not divorced, but dead.' Silence filled the air. I had never really considered father's point of view on my parents' marriage. Until tonight, I had only ever heard mother's side of the story.

'Mother says you were divorced not five weeks after I was born,' I said. 'So, were neither of you happy in marriage?'

143

'I'd prefer a sinking ship on the river Styx,' he said and nearly finished off the bottle of wine. 'She kept a notebook of what she perceived to be all my faults, as if she could cure me. I had no choice but leave and get as far away from her as possible.'

'Why did you not ever try to see me?' I asked.

Lord Byron got fired up, raising his voice, 'I tried all the time!' Voltigeur neighed upon hearing this stranger's voice. The sound made me remember the late hour and suddenly I realised how terrible it would be not only for Father to be found in the stables, but for me as well. I hadn't been married long, but I was fairly certain getting caught in the stables with a dead poet in the middle of the night wouldn't be a good way to begin our marriage.

'Please, lower your voice,' I pleaded. 'The horses.'

'I wrote you volumes of letters, sent you precious dolls from Greece.'

'Mother never spoke of such letters or gifts.'

'Annabella is most secretive and cunning. Have you not learned this?'

I nodded, yes. He then put his face very close to mine. I could smell the acidic wine on his breath and his lips were stained slightly redder in colour. He said, 'You must never tell her or anyone else that I'm here. Not even your husband. Do you understand? My mortal safety is in your hands.'

I nodded again, only more vigorously this time, adding, 'It pains me greatly to know you've been wronged.'

'Sometimes it takes great pain to know we are truly alive. You see, the great object of life is sensation,' he said.

I thought about his words, trying to understand their meaning. What exactly was a sensation, I wondered. Was it something only great poets or artists experienced?

'I'm not sure I've had a sensation yet,' I said.

'Well, recite me some of your poetry,' said Father.

'I don't write poems. My passion is machines,' I replied.

'Your mother has ruined you,' he said as he rolled the empty wine bottle across the stable. It clank loudly at it hit the stone wall, spooking the horses.

'Please!' I whispered, resolving not to bring wine to our next meeting. He was staring at me with such intensity, I knew I had to reply.

'Machines aren't so awful,' I said.

'Sooner or later, they'll destroy the world if the Luddite society doesn't stop them. Humanity cannot be reproduced and it is a travesty, an insult to the creator to attempt to do so. Ada, it is time for you to do something.'

'What?' I asked. I was quite overwhelmed by our midnight meetings already, and yet he had more for me to do? I felt a flush creep up my neck, fearful but excited that he had a plan for me. He was being fatherly and I loved it. But then he did the strangest thing. Lord Byron put his hands around my head and squeezed it.

'Discover what's in here, my girl. Grab hold of your imagination. Squeeze it with your fingers, clench it in your teeth, suck it into your lungs and never, never let it go,' he said, before cupping my face with his hands. I looked up at him in awe. Mother had always discouraged me from being inventive and following my fancy, and now here was Father asking me to do just that. It was almost too much to bear. I felt like I was being cleaved in two. Then, still holding my face in his hands, he leaned down and kissed my forehead, his wine-stained lips lingering several seconds.

I felt entranced by him. I was completely under his spell, despite his noisy ramblings. I didn't share his primitive notions about machines, but I did happily drink in my father's attention, relishing each and every moment with him. I felt my shoulders squaring; I was determined to change his mind about the future and the machines that would soon find their rightful place amongst people.

'Is there any more wine?' he asked, licking his lips.

'I dare not go back for another bottle.'

'The hour has grown too late anyway, and I must be off.'

'But we haven't even discussed the other fifteen cantos of *Don Juan*.'

'Something to look forward to,' he said with a devilish grin.

I smiled too, though I felt truly sad as he walked out of the stable. I followed him out. With ease, he hopped into the saddle and again, with a double cluck of his tongue, he and his black horse rode off into the night.

I quickly made my way back through the tunnels, back toward William's bedchamber, not feeling the cold air on my face, only feeling as if I had witnessed a new colour for the first time. My father's affection was like a new, wondrous burst of light that was as bright and clear as the North Star – such a shame this father and daughter can only visit in secret. If only I could stand under his light in the daytime, too, and not be confined by the shadows of night.

17

Three months had passed since I last met Father in the stable and I was beginning to think I may never see him again. Between Babbage's tutoring sessions, studying, overseeing the servants, providing a daily shopping list and menu, searching the tunnels for Puff when he failed to return for three days (seems he met a female stray and spent the time having adventures with her), and rearranging the rooms to accommodate my furniture and artwork, my days were dizzying. I was happy to feel needed and to have a clearly defined place at Ashley Combe, but each day I looked for some type of clue that my father would be returning for another visit. Each moment not knowing when or if I would see him again was excruciating. During his absence however, I thought a lot about trying to employ my imagination in new ways. My studies with Babbage were advancing to a much higher level and I was mindful to search for other perspectives when considering engines and their functions and how they could fit into Poetical Science.

I grew to adore Babbage, even if he could be cranky, if not downright gloomy at times. On those days, when he appeared sombre, we didn't bother with calculus; instead we talked of all the exciting things the future might bring. On a day when Babb seemed terribly distraught over the idea he may never be able to prove the existence of ghosts – he so dearly wanted to communicate with his deceased wife, Georgiana, whom he missed terribly – I could see a melancholy mood coming over him. To take his mind off the matter, I asked him if we should take a train and research some mathematical applications to machinery in the field.

Babbage's eyes quickly turned from sorrowful to cheerful as an idea suddenly washed over his face.

'What a grand idea, my dear! There is something spectacular I want to show you.'

I was breathless with anticipation. 'Well, what is it?'

'A new type of weaving loom.'

'Whatever could be so exciting about a weaving loom?'

'You're about to find out.'

With William's permission and some quick planning, Babb and I were able to board a steam train within an hour. We were heading to Kidderminster, where the exalted weaving loom was located.

Train rides were such excitement. Though being on a train wasn't as physically vigourous as riding Sylph, I enjoyed watching the rolling emerald countryside from the train's window as Babb and I rode in a first-class car.

'Please tell me more about this loom. What makes it so extraordinary?' I said to Babbage as a man brought us tea service. My tea cup rattled softly in its saucer from the motion of the train.

'Unlike looms of the past, this loom automatically weaves patterns into fabric without needing a man's hand to guide the thread.'

'Without a man's hand? How is that possible?'

'Through a clever mechanism invented by a Frenchman

named Joseph Jacquard. He has one factory in England and we are on our way to visit it.'

I sipped my tea with anticipation as the train trotted on. If what Babb said is correct, Mr. Jacquard's loom is a remarkable invention. I looked out the train window and noticed the lines of the trees and flowers appeared just slightly fuzzy from the motion of the racing train. It was as if an oil painting hadn't quite dried and the oil was slightly smeared to delightful effect on the canvas – one colour bled into the next. It was fascinating to witness the world at such a high rate of speed and was much faster than anyone could ever have achieved on a horse. Travelling this fast felt like something out of a dream. The ride was also fairly smooth, unlike a bumpy carriage ride that pained my ribs when my corset was affixed too tightly. I imagined the entire world organised by trains. Since William liked building tunnels, I thought I should approach him with the idea of building a train tunnel all the way to the continent, so anyone could visit Spain or France without the care or fuss of taking a ship.

As I looked over at Babb, it seemed as if the train's vibrations and rhythmic rattling had lulled him to sleep. Perhaps trains could be the perfect tool to help infants suffering from colic to fall asleep. I would ask Babbage's opinion when he awoke. I liked that Babbage took my ideas seriously and liked to hear my opinion on matters. It made me feel intelligent, as if I had the potential to contribute great ideas to the world some day.

As we neared the end of the train ride, excitement coursed through my body. When the train's engineer finally blew the loud whistle, indicating we were about to arrive at our destination, Babb sat straight up, wide awake. He looked around, realizing he had slept most of the journey.

'That was one fast train, if I dare say so myself.'

I laughed to myself.

'I am terribly eager to make Monsieur Jacquard's acquaintance,' I said, 'I think it polite to bring him a small gift of appreciation when we arrive. Any ideas of what he would like?'

Babb rubbed his eyes before he spoke.

'A gift would not be appropriate due to the fact that Jacquard is not expecting us,' he said matter-of-factly.

'Surely he'll be thrilled you took him up on his invitation to visit his factory, even if the visit is a spontaneous one.'

'There has been no invitation, quite the opposite, really. Jacquard's not terribly fond of sharing his ideas. The man is selfish and petty.'

I looked at Babb in disbelief. 'How on earth shall we gain entrance into his factory if he doesn't want us in there?'

'That is a task that will take some creativity,' smiled Babbage just as the train-whistle blew again. The train came to a halt. We had finally arrived in Kidderminster but without an invitation.

Jacquard's factory was called the Second Rusty Cross Weaving Factory; the First Rusty Cross Weaving Factory was in France. It was easy to locate it in town due to its large red cross that sat on top of the factory's roof. If I didn't know better, I would have thought the building to be a place of worship.

Babb thought it would be best for us to enter the factory from the rear of the building, and so we made our way there with cautious anticipation. Suddenly, I grew nervous.

'I think we should simply knock on the front door instead of skulking about. It's beneath us.'

'Nothing is beneath us if it's done in the name of scientific discovery,' he said. I sighed and continued to follow him.

Once we walked around to the back of the large brick structure, we schemed on how best to get inside. I felt terribly uncomfortable sneaking into the factory to the point where I almost refused. Then I thought, what would father do? He'd use his imagination. So I decided to pretend I was a detective and needed to solve the mystery of the loom. With this mindset, I began to grow excited.

We searched for open windows or a door with a lock that could easily be picked, but the place seemed as fortified as Dover Castle. Just as we were sure there was no way to break in, however, a factory worker exited out the back door and propped it open with a bolt of fabric giving us a break in the case. The man headed to a nearby tree where he began to relieve himself. I was shocked to see this man behaving so crudely, but Babb simply whispered, 'One man's call to nature is another man's opportunity,' and quickly scuttled me into the back of the factory through the open door. I had to admit, this sneaking around was thrilling, I just hoped we didn't get caught.

Once inside the factory, the first thing I noticed was the thundering drumming sound coming from all the weaving looms -- there must have been a hundred of them. I could smell a slight fishy odour from the looms, which told me they must have been lubricated with whale oil to diminish friction between the moving parts. The looms themselves were the size of a small horse, constructed with a solid pine frame that held large spools of thread.

Babb and I crouched behind one of the looms, hoping not to be seen by any of the workers. Babb whispered, 'That's

Monsieur Jacquard, there,' and he pointed to the other side of the factory, where Jacquard, a tall, lean man with shoulder-length gray hair and black moustache, was arguing with a worker.

While Jacquard was occupied, I began to examine one of the looms more carefully. Without any human assistance, a piece of brocaded fabric emerged from the machine, displaying the image of a fox hunt in bold reds, greens and browns. I marveled at the fabric and asked, 'But how does the loom know which colour thread to use?'

'By reading those,' said Babbage, pointing to a dozen or so white cards attached to the loom. The cards each had a specific sequence of holes.

'Punched cards guide the loom's rods, which are threaded with different coloured silks,' he said. We both sat in awe, watching the rods move over the punched cards, determining which colours would be woven into the fabric. There was a beauty to it; it was almost as if the rods were dancing in a choreographed dance to an unknown symphony.

'The holes in the cards are punched into a pattern, thereby instructing the threads,' he said.

I looked to the loom next to the one we were crouching behind. It was also weaving fabric with an identical fox hunting scene. 'So, by using replicas of the punched cards, each machine may create the same exact pattern?' I asked.

'Genius isn't it?' said Babb as I began sketching the cards in my notebook. 'If only I'd thought of it.'

'But you did not, Monsieur Babbage!' said Jacquard, in his thick French accent, standing behind us, fuming. I continued to sketch the machine while Babb engaged him.

'Monsieur Jacquard, lovely to see you,' said Babbage, politely, as he turned to greet him.

'First the Luddites, now you! I will not tolerate you spying on me,' said Jacquard.

'I'm not spying on you, I merely wanted to invite you to my soiree this Saturday,' said Babbage.

'*Sacré bleu*, get out! And take Madame d'Éon with you!' yelled Jacquard and picked Babbage up by the collar. I shrieked. Jacquard then shoved Babbage down the row of looms. Babb could barely maintain his footing. Jacquard had a wild look in his eyes; he seemed a very unreasonable man. I worried the situation might come to blows. Babbage kept trying to calmly engage him, but it was no use. As Babbage neared the front door, Jacquard forcefully shoved him out of the factory. I cowered as I ran after him. As we exited the Second Rusty Cross, Jacquard slammed the door behind us.

But there was no time to let our guard down, as we suddenly noticed we were surrounded by a group of Luddites, protesting the mechanized weaving looms Jacquard used. We hadn't noticed the Luddites earlier, since we entered through the back of the factory.

The Luddites carried signs, one read 'Machines are the Devil's Business' and another read, 'Jobs for Men, Not Machines.'

I had heard about these roving bands of factory workers – they were men who hated any type of machine because they knew these new methods of industry would replace human workers – which they did in droves. These men were left without any chance of an education and needed to support their families by working with their hands. Unfortunately for them, the industrial revolution was taking over England and they would need to learn how to adapt to the new order of things if they wanted to survive.

While I felt a great sympathy for their plight, I also didn't want to endure any physical harm by their strong, calloused hands. Babb and I tried to quickly run past the mob of angry men, when one of them shouted, 'God created men, not machines!' and he pelted Babb with a rotten tomato. It exploded all over Babbage's jacket. The other Luddites followed suit and several squishy tomatoes landed on me, squashing in my hair and on my dress. As we both ran down the street, away from the Second Rusty Cross, away from the Luddites, I couldn't help but laugh at the adventure of it all. To think of all that had transpired just because of a loom.

Once we were back on the train, after having cleaned ourselves up as best we could in the train station's privy, I embellished my sketch of the punched card from Jacquard's loom. In the background, I added the fox hunting scene that was woven into the fabric. My mind was focused on figuring out a way for Babb to incorporate the punched cards into the design of his Difference Engine.

In my mind's eye, I pictured myself standing inside a cotton mill. Through a window, I could see the circular, rotunda-like storehouse where all the raw cotton was stored. A worker carried the cotton in a wheelbarrow into the mill and began feeding card-shaped pieces of cotton into the spinning mule. The mule spat out long strings of cotton numbers.

'Think of the number wheels on the Difference Engine as a *storehouse*. By adding these punched cards, they could work as the *mill*,' I said to Babb as I then sketched a storehouse filled with integers and a mill filled with algebraic command symbols.

Babb studied my sketch carefully, trying to understand my meaning. 'If the *mill* could instruct the number wheels to follow a sequence of commands—'

Babbage interrupted me with, 'All sorts of possibilities exist!' as he pulled a chunk of tomato from his ear. Then he gave me a serious look. 'My dear, I've had similar ideas. Instead of weaving threads, I have also conceived of a machine that would use punched cards to calculate numbers, the cards would be the equation.'

'Yes!' I said, 'Do you think it's possible to create such a machine?'

'I think we must try.'

I shook my head. Did he just say 'We'?

'It seems as if today's outing has inspired in me an idea for a business proposition that I'd very much like you to consider.'

'Business?' I asked.

'I would like for you to endeavour to help me find the funds to build a machine that will change the world.'

I felt my jaw drop in the most unlady-like of ways, but I didn't care. I couldn't believe that Charles Babbage wanted to create a partnership with me! It was the most exciting endeavour I could think of. My dream was to have a profession of my own – to contribute something to the world of science – and here it was, actually happening, on a steam train no less! All I could think about was whether or not my father would be proud of me. I sincerely hoped he would.

18

That evening, I returned from Kidderminster, still wearing the tomato-stained dress, but rather than admonish me for my recklessness, William was eager to hear all about my journey. Alone in my study, William helped me out of the dress and into a dressing gown, while I told him all about getting caught by the angry Frenchman.

'Jacquard threw dear old Babb out on his rear!'

'Was that before or after your tomato bath? Your dress is ruined,' William said, but I didn't care about the silly dress. I showed him my sketch of the punched card and tried to explain the idea of using the cards to make a calculating machine.

'That all sounds very interesting, indeed. Do you really think Babbage can pull it off?' he asked.

'Here's the exciting part,' I said as I stepped into my silk dressing gown, 'Babb has offered to make me his business partner in the venture. To work side-by-side with him to obtain funding to build a new machine using Jacquard's technology!'

But instead of excitement, William's face filled with worry. I could see him trying to take in all this new information and make sense of it.

'Another machine?' He sighed. 'Our lives are beginning to move at such a fast pace. Steam engines whizzing by at every turn. Soon, there may not be a need for thinking at all. We'll have machines to do it for us,' he said.

'A thinking-machine! Won't it be wonderful?' I said, taking William's hands into mine. He couldn't help but laugh at my enthusiasm, even if he didn't share it.

'Please, I want this so, so very much.'

William was quiet for a moment. Then, he said, 'Birdie, grab hold of your senses. It's wonderful to be excited about new ideas, but let's be practical for a moment. Soon, you'll have children to attend to. Their welfare would be put in jeopardy if your focus lied in a business,' he said, adding, 'I never realised what a lovely nursery this room would make.'

I was appalled. This was my study. 'You agreed to let me study as I wish,' I said, not understanding his reversal in thought.

'Studying is one thing. Business is another.' I was shocked at his rigidity. The kindness on his face didn't waiver, but I felt cold nonetheless. 'I cannot allow it,' said William. He kissed my cheek and walked out of the room.

I was stunned – he had always been supportive of me. I was used to hearing 'no' from Mother, but from William? He'd been my champion since the day we met. I felt there must be some way to work out a solution that would make both of us happy. I knew far too well that opportunities like this rarely came to anyone, let alone a woman. I felt strongly that Babbage and I could forever change the world by improving upon it.

That night, as I retired to my bedchamber alone, Kate came to collect my clothes to launder. I paid no attention to her until she pulled something from her pocket that froze the blood inside my veins: it was a coded letter from my father. She handed it to me as if it were a shortbread biscuit. Quickly, I closed the door to my bedchamber and looked Kate square in the eyes.

'Where did you get this?' I demanded.

'I swore on the Virgin, I wouldn't say,' she said, her eyes averting mine.

I grabbed the girl firmly by the shoulders, 'This must never, never be spoken about. Do you understand? Not to William, not to anyone.'

Her eyes filled with fear. I had never been coarse with her before and it seemed to really startle her. I eyed her up and down, wondering if I could trust her.

'I understand, my lady.'

I took a coin from my purse and gave it to her.

'This shall forever remain our secret,' I said.

Kate took the coin, quickly curtsied and shot out of my room. Lord Byron, with all his charm, must have secretly befriended Kate without my knowledge. Now I understood how the letter had made its way to my bridal table. But why didn't he tell me?

I felt wary about entrusting a servant with such a big secret, but hopefully, Kate could see the value in receiving some extra coins. My surreptitious relationship with my father had gone undetected so far, and perhaps having her as an emissary would actually be more helpful than anything. I sighed, determined not to worry anymore on it that night, and then ripped open the letter and translated the code. It read:

My dearest Pippin,

I should like to visit tonight. Please do not disappoint me. My clandestine travels have been torturous. My soul longs for the comfort of my dearest daughter, you are the closest thing I have to a home. Bring food and wine.

Your doting father
Lord Byron

My mood instantly lifted. I may not yet know the magic words to convince William to agree to enter a business arrangement with Babbage, but surely my father would be on my side. I couldn't wait to see him as I felt certain Father would know what to do.

Later that night, as William slept in his own room, I quietly got out of bed and wrapped myself in a blanket to protect myself from the cold night air. I looked down each hall, all the doors were shut. I walked to William's bedchamber and put my ear to the door. I could hear him snoring softly.

As I descended the stairs, the blanket wrapped around me accidentally brushed up against a small portrait hanging on the wall, catching its edge and pulling it off its nail. I held my breath as it tumbled down the stairs, and prayed I didn't wake anyone. I padded down the steps as quietly as I could, retrieved the portrait, and put the picture of William's aunt Theodosia back on the wall. Then I tiptoed back to William's bedchamber door and pressed my ear against it again. It was silent, then after a moment, I heard William return to snoring. All's good, I thought, and I made my way down the stairs more carefully this time.

In the kitchen, I gathered some chicken and potatoes for Father to eat, and a bottle of wine, of course. I made my way through the tunnels quickly but when I approached the stable, I could hear voices coming from inside. Who could Father possibly be talking to? I didn't know if I should enter or return to the house immediately. I decided to enter.

That's when I saw Kate giggling as Lord Byron engaged her in flirtatious conversation.

Eyes on each other, they did not notice my silent approach.

'Is it true ginger-haired lasses feel pain more strongly?' he asked Kate as he pinched her arse.

'Ay. Pleasure, too,' she taunted back. I did not like the coquettish behaviour I saw before me.

'That will be all, Kate,' I said. Kate and Lord Byron looked up at me, startled. Kate curtseyed, but failed to exit, clearly waiting to be tipped a pence. I had no coins with me, so I shot her a stern look. Kate finally exited the stable.

'You could have told me you made yourself acquainted with my servant,' I said, as I laid the meal out for Father.

'I've got the girl wrapped around my finger. I have a way with women.'

'I don't like it. It puts us in peril.'

'On the contrary, it ensures the safety of our secrets,' he said, stuffing the chicken into his mouth with his fingers.

While I preferred he'd use the knife and fork I brought him, the truth was, I couldn't stay mad at him for not telling me about Kate. I was just happy to be near him.

While he ate, I told him about Babbage and the Luddites and how Babb and I wanted to work together on a new machine, but that William said no. I was careful to emphasize all the good this new machine would bring about, considering Father sympathized with the Luddites. But more importantly, I pointed out that I would be employing my imagination, just as he suggested.

'Father, I know it's foolish for a woman to dream of having her own profession. But that's what I want most. To feel that my ideas are as important as any man's with a similar intellect,' I said, glancing at him, trying to determine if he agreed. He nodded, so I continued, 'I hate that my sex is looked down upon as inferior. They say men are more intelligent than women because their brains are larger. I don't believe it is the size of a person's brain that matters, but how they use it. How they think with it. Do you agree? Or is this a witless notion? Please, tell me your thoughts. You are my sole advisor in this matter,' I said with desperation.

Lord Byron took his time before answering, rubbing his jaw with the palm of his hand. His greenish-brown eyes blinked several times.

'More than a woman, you are a Byron. The world is your birthright – you must take it,' he replied, casually.

'But how?'

'How? The only way a Byron knows how. You must imagine it.'

'But William is imagining children. Lots of them,' I said, wincing.

He took a drink of wine, again out of the bottle, then wiped his face on his sleeve. 'There are ways around that, girl. In fact, I once knew a French courtesan who conducted all her business in a bath of peppermint oil. She never conceived a child and every part of her tasted like candy. Ah!' he said.

'Father, please,' I said, embarrassed.

Lord Byron then wiped his hands on his trousers and pulled a rag doll from his pocket. He handed it to me and said, 'This little trinket is childish, I know. But I've kept it for you all these years.'

The doll was just larger than the palm of my hand. Its hair was made from yellow yarn that was braided into two braids that were each tied with pink ribbons. The tiny dress was made from a pink and white floral fabric that included lace around the trim of the skirt. Her eyes were made from two buttons that were a littler larger than was proportional to the size of her face, giving the doll a sweet, doe-eyed countenance. Her mouth was stitched with red yarn, no smile, just a thin red line. She was a bit tattered and dusty, but I saw only the years it had weathered, waiting for my Father to find me and place it in my hands himself. It was the most beautiful thing I had ever seen.

I took the doll and pressed it against my heart, 'I love it. Thank you.' I took Father's hand and squeezed it tightly. He kissed my cheek before he said goodnight, leaving me with a new type of joy in my heart, and I realised, as I watched him walk away, that whatever holy silk our souls were spun from, they were indeed from the same silkworm.

The next day, I decided I had not tried hard enough to convince William to let me work with Babbage. I was encouraged that Father felt it was my birthright, but I also knew I couldn't argue that point to William, for fear he would think me too emboldened. I knew that William loved me ever so deeply and perhaps the idea would just need time to take root in his mind.

I prepared a special evening for my husband, based on Father's advice. I put fresh roses in a vase, then I drew a bath for William from water I heated on the stove to ensure it was very hot. I lit the bathing room with two dozen candles, creating a path to the washtub. Then I made sure to pour a few ounces of peppermint oil into the hot water.

At around nine o'clock, I led William into the bathing room which was now prepared for a romantic holiday. Each candle flame sent shadows frolicking along the walls. The aroma of sweet mint filled the air.

'What's all this?' he asked, pleasantly surprised.

'Just a little bath for my husband to show him how much I love and appreciate him,' I said coyly as I began undressing him.

'Well, how fortunate for me,' he said as I undid the buttons on his shirt, kissing his chest with each one. After I had removed all his garments from his body, he slowly stepped into the bath water, which was so hot, he had to submerge his legs just a few inches at a time. When he was finally sitting, I knelt next to the bathtub. I took a bar of bergamot-scented soap and began lathering up his shoulders and chest. I was surprised by how much I enjoyed watching my hands slide over his firm pectoral muscles.

William began to relax and enjoy the pampering. His head tilted to one side as he watched me lather up his feet.

'You're beautiful in sunlight, but by candlelight, you're absolutely ravishing,' he said, pulling his foot out of my hands and placing it back into the water. 'Come here and kiss me,' he whispered. I did. The steam from the hot water made my face moist, and the room appeared to be enveloped in a candle-lit fog. The sound of splashing water serenaded us as we kissed. William's tongue brushed against my own ever so softly. I realised I was also enjoying this seduction, and was excited to explore these new ways of being intimate. They also seemed to please William quite a bit.

I whispered to him, 'I want to give you a baby.' He smiled and as he started to stand, water dripped from his naked, excited body. 'Stay in the water,' I said as I dropped my white silk robe to the floor. The candlelight flickered on my naked body as I stepped into the bath, displacing some of the sudsy, minty liquid over the sides of the tub. I climbed on top of William, kissing him.

'Can a baby be made this way -- with me on top of you? Or is it necessary for me to be on my back?' I asked, genuinely curious.

William was so aroused, he had trouble answering the question. 'I, uh...believe so. In fact, I'm pretty certain there are many ways to make a baby,' he said.

'I should like to learn each and every one,' I cooed into his ear. 'But...' I paused a moment to make sure he was listening. The water became still.

'But what?' he whispered back.

'I must be allowed to work on the machine,' I said with a kittenish smile.

He gazed into my eyes, 'You don't give up.'

'That's why you love me,' I said as our bodies came together in the peppermint-scented water.

'Damn it. I do. I love you. You may have the machine,' he said as we kissed again. My love for him deepened that night, but little did I know at the time, that decision would forever change my life.

19

Over the next few months, I continued to visit with Father in secret. I was beginning to feel that by knowing him, I better understood myself, as we were alike in so many ways. I often wondered if perhaps a day would come when he could live safely out in the open. If only I could find a way to clear his name and resolve his debts.

Mother and Dr. Poole went to southern Spain for a change of air, hoping the warmer climate would alleviate Mother's headaches.

Babbage had been on the continent for a month, looking for funding sources for the new machine, but had recently returned. William and I received an invitation to dinner at Mary's home, and I was pleased to hear that Babbage would also attend.

I was excited for William to get to know Mary and her husband better. She was so smart and fascinating – she even had an island in the Arctic named for her when explorer Edward Parry made one of the first expeditions to the frozen landscape. Since Mary lived some distance from Ashley Combe, we would stay overnight as guests.

The rain hammered our carriage so heavily as we made the trip to Hampstead Heath, that I wondered if we'd develop webbed feet by the time we arrived. I wore a simple oak-coloured silk dress, with sleeves that were cut into a bell shape, with black lace peeking out of them. By the time we arrived, I couldn't tell which I was happier about: finally escaping the carriage or seeing Mary. I took a deep breath of the rain-dampened air and felt a thrill, like a wave of electricity, go through me. I was elated to have finally arrived, despite having to stomp through rain puddles to get to the front door.

Once inside, Mary and her husband, also named William – Dr. William Somerville, greeted us warmly. The Somerville home had a comfortable, lived-in feel to it. The drawing room had yellow striped wallpaper and a canary yellow Borne settee at its center. The two yellow sofas were a bit worn and threadbare in a few spots. A Grecian urn rested on top of a pianoforte, where a calico cat named Persephone sat, curious to see who just arrived. Above the fireplace was a beautiful rococo portrait of Mary from when she was perhaps seventeen or eighteen. In it, she wears a mustard-yellow dress with a lace collar. Her expression is wistfully pensive.

Babbage was running late it seemed, so while the two Williams discussed business, Mary and I discussed the stars. During my tutoring with her, she explained how the universe is so much bigger than our minds may conceive, which of course only sparked in me a desire to conceive the impossible.

Tonight, however, she asserted that the Earth was much older than the 6,000 years the Bible claimed, which would have elicited the greatest of ire from Mother. Mary was ever so provocative in her conversation, and I ate it up like cake.

'But how do you know the Earth is so old? Isn't the Bible the best historical document we have?' I asked.

'The answers are in the mountains. Let me show you something.'

Mary fetched a box and brought it to me.

'Tell me what's inside.'

I opened the box to find a dozen or so seashells. Some were clamshells, some were nautilus shaped.

'These are shells from the ocean, once the homes of crustaceans.'

'Yes, very good. But what if I told you they were found on top of a mountain in South America?

The question was intriguing enough to get the attention of both Williams.

'A mountain top? How did they get there?' I asked.

'It is somewhat of a mystery,' Mary's eyes twinkled as she spoke. I could tell she was enjoying the instructional moment. 'There are different hypotheses.'

'Could they possibly be left over from when Noah's flood covered the Earth?' my husband asked.

'It would have taken much longer than forty days of rain to cover this towering mountain range. Rather than the brief flood, I think there may have been a time on Earth, many thousands, perhaps hundreds of thousands of years ago, where much of the land we walk on today, would have been covered in water. A very different Earth. I believe only time and a great deal of research will yield the answer.'

My William raised an eyebrow, and I knew that he found the thought more amusing than anything else. That was one of the things I loved about being married to him; where Mother had been angry and skeptical, William was mirth and possibility.

'Fascinating ideas, Mary. I've never heard these expressed before. I—,' my sentence was interrupted by a knock on the door.

'Must be Babbage,' said Mary.

Indeed it was him, about forty-five minutes late. He arrived, very disheveled in appearance, complaining there had been an overturned carriage blocking the road. The streets were flooded and his carriage could not immediately get around the mess. Mary got him a sherry to calm his nerves.

By dinner, Babb seemed more relaxed and we all enjoyed our pheasant and mash. I thought the evening was going wonderfully and felt very inspired by Mary. She had accomplished so much, and still had so many adventures ahead of her, I couldn't help but believe that one day I would host a dinner and regale an audience with tales of how Poetical Science came to be.

After the main meal, a servant appeared with a cutting board on which he cored and sliced a pineapple before our very eyes. I loved exotic fruits and relished my serving with gusto. The pineapple had come all the way from Bermuda!

The dinner conversation covered most of William and my recent events. We spoke about the move to Ashley Combe and how happy we were they had come to the wedding, of course. But after the tropical dessert, the conversation turned back to the heavens.

'I'm fairly certain,' said Mary, 'that another planet lies beyond Uranus. I've been studying it though my telescope and I can see something, the tiniest of specs, just beyond it.'

I was astonished by her insight, 'A ninth planet in our solar system? Imagine that!'

'Have you thought of teaching at the University, Mary?' asked my husband. 'So many young minds could benefit from your vast knowledge.'

'Of course I've thought about teaching,' she replied, 'but that would require me to have a degree of some kind.'

'Oxford uses the textbook you wrote to teach astronomy. Surely they would grant you a degree,' said Babbage.

'Women aren't allowed to teach or study there. Whether they've written the textbook, or not,' she said.

'That's madness,' I said, feeling sincerely frustrated for her and for all women. Mary was just as smart as any man. Possibly smarter than most. I couldn't stand that women were treated as second-class citizens – even in England. But before I could speak on the topic further, a terrible clap of thunder broke the mood and the rain outside began to pick up.

'Bloody weather,' mumbled Babb. 'I should invent a machine to parcel out the rain in small portions instead of it coming all at once. Near flood waters out there.'

'You'll have plenty of time after you've constructed your current machine,' I said.

'Charles,' said Dr. Somerville, 'Which machine is this?'

My William replied, 'The one he and Ada are conceiving together.'

William smiled at me and I couldn't help but beam back at him. It was official: I had a profession of my own.

'This is wonderful news!' said Mary.

'William, I am most grateful for your willingness to allow Ada this opportunity,' said Babbage.

'She's a hard woman to say no to,' said William.

'I certainly know what that's like,' joked Dr. Somerville. Mary and I exchanged a grin.

'Once the plans are finished,' said Mary, 'a patron will most surely turn up. What is this miraculous invention called?'

'The Analytical Engine,' said Babbage. And just then, lightening struck outside, filling the rainy sky with white-hot light, followed by an ear-shattering CRACK! We all looked at each other.

'And the gods are already angry,' I said. The table laughed.

After dinner, we retired to the parlor, where Dr. Somerville smoked a pipe, Mary dipped her snuff and my husband and I drank port wine from tiny little glasses that looked like they were stolen from a dollhouse. A fire crackled in the fireplace, making the room quite cosy, despite the foul weather. The only wrinkle was a leak in the thatched roof, but Dr. Somerville had placed a bucket on the floor to catch the rainwater and I decided the constant drip, drip, drip echoing in the bucket was actually rather soothing.

I had hoped Mary would allow William to peer through one of her powerful new telescopes, but the weather made it impossible. Instead, we spoke of whether or not we thought God had filled the other planets with strange and complicated creatures, like those found on Earth. Mary felt certain that other creatures existed, but where and what kind she declined to predict. She said with so many worlds in the universe, it would be selfish to think we were all alone and that perhaps some of these beings had already visited Earth.

Babbage snorted at this, and said, 'Any unearthly life form that thought it wise to visit our world would be sadly disappointed.' He then said something disparaging about the Royal Science Society, hoping they'd all get sent to Uranus.

As the evening went on, Dr. Somerville excused himself to attend to more leaks. Though he seemed quite embarrassed, he allowed William to help him.

Mary grew sleepy and began to nod off in her chair, while Babb drew illustrations of his Analytical Engine. As I listened to the scratching of Babb's pencil, I fidgeted with an actual copper number wheel he had brought with him – it was just like the ones used for the Difference Engine demonstration model. These number wheels were precisely designed, painstakingly cut and polished, costing a good deal of money to manufacture. The brass was cold on my fingertips as I touched the engraved numbers.

'Will the Analytical Engine also add and subtract numbers?' I asked.

'Yes, but now that I've added the punched cards, I'm able to command operations to be applied to the numbers. It then analyses the results of those operations,' he said as rainwater began to drip onto the sketch.

'A new leak,' I said before moving the papers out of the way. I put one of the tiny port glasses under it to catch the water. It did little good.

I then studied the number wheel in my hand. 'These number wheels, could they have other values assigned to them?' I asked.

'Any polynomial or square root would work,' said Babbage.

'I mean, other than numbers,' I said.

'*Other* than numbers? I don't understand,' he said as he scratched his neck.

Suddenly, my mind was buzzing with new ideas. I held up the number wheel, 'Say instead of numbers, the wheels had letters of the alphabet?

'But I don't see the need. We have a printing press to create books,' he said.

'Not to simply print books, but create stories, ideas or to share theories with other people -- other machines even,' I said.

'I'm afraid I don't understand your meaning.'

I closed my eyes in thought and tried to describe what I was seeing. In my mind's eye, I was standing in a room with two large machines. Each had a mouth that could speak, but instead of English words coming out, each machine spoke an entirely unknown language.

'I'm thinking ahead to the future. I'm trying to consider all the things machines could be capable of. What I'm suggesting is the possibility of creating a language specifically for machines to communicate with each other, the way the punched cards communicate with the weaving looms. Perhaps one day we could even connect a machine to a telegraph line and send messages over the wire using the lettered wheels. One could send a message to the next town, order a fancy luncheon perhaps, then get on a train and have it waiting for him when they arrived!'

Babb just looked at me as if I told him the sky was pink, not blue, or that the King of England was in fact an eggplant. I knew I needed to use a different metaphor to make my point clear.

'Forget letters and messages for now. What about adding colours, or musical notes to the number wheels. You could programme the machine to compose elaborate pieces of music, create works of art,' I said.

He seemed like he was slowly grasping the concept I was so eagerly trying to express.

'So, you're suggesting a machine that could be programmed to create. Organically. To think all on its own?'

'It seems quite impossible that a machine will ever be able to think or create anything new entirely on its own. But if programmed with the proper punched cards, armed with wheels that contained words we created, could it not be capable of a type of poetry?'

'Poetry from a machine. Surely your father would be outraged,' he said.

'He's certain machines will destroy the world any day now,' I said.

'Did your mother tell you that?' he asked.

I then realised my slip by speaking about him in the present tense. I tried to cover by saying, 'Yes, she must have.'

'Well, he was wrong. These analytical machines will create a whole new world,' he said with a gleam of hope in his eyes.

Rain then began to leak onto Babbage's head. I laughed, stirring Mary. Mary opened her eyes and said, 'Snuff, anyone?' But it was clear, it was time for all of us to retire to bed. A new day of poetical science awaited me.

Inspired by Mary Somerville's intellect, I vowed to work day and night on helping Babbage with his Analytical Engine, even designing my own machines that used punched cards, including a steam-powered oven that, when connected to a clock, that could be programmed to turn on and off by itself. For me, the world was opening up and the future looked so incredibly wonderful, I barely wanted to sleep for fear of missing some exciting part of it. The only thing bothering me in my life was the limited ability I had to see Father. It just seemed wrong that our relationship needed to be kept secret. I thought a lot about telling William the situation. Wouldn't he take pity on me?

20

On a cold Thursday in December, a week before my twenty-seventh birthday, Babbage arrived to Ashley Combe with some exciting news. Seated on a leather chair inside my study, he told me there was to be a grand science expedition in London to be held in a 'Crystal Palace'. I was puzzled by this; the only palaces I had seen were made of stone.

'This will be a giant palace constructed entirely of cast iron fittings that hold together plate glass walls and ceilings. There is even to be a glass fountain,' he said.

I tried to picture it in my mind's eye. 'It sounds quite lovely. It is to house an expedition of scientific endeavours?' I asked.

'Exactly! It will be a showcase of England's greatest scientific and technological achievements. Scientists and factories seeking new industrial machinery from all over the globe will attend,' he said.

'And so must we,' I said.

'Ada, we must do more than attend The Great Exhibition, we must also be a part of it,' he said.

'In what way?'

'This is our opportunity to present the Analytical Engine to the world,' he smiled.

I looked at him, confused, 'But the engine hasn't been built yet.'

'Precisely why we need to get cracking!' We have less than three years until the exhibition.'

If he was serious, we had a lot of work to do.

That night, I crawled into bed with William, eager to feel his arms around me. He embraced me, but not as eagerly as usual.

'How are your studies going with Babb?'

'Excellent, though slow. There's to be a grand scientific exhibition two years from now. It is imperative the Analytical Engine be ready in time. We are planning to double our weekly hours of research and experimentation.'

'Double? I barely see you as it is.'

'Don't worry, my love, I will always have time for you,' I said as I kissed him.

But something about the dullness in the way he kissed me back had me worried. Could he be jealous of the time I spend with Babb? I would have to work harder to reassure him that the machine was worth our sacrifice. I thought about revealing that I'd been visiting Father, but decided against it. No need to stir up the pot even more.

December tenth was my twenty-seventh birthday. I woke up early, sat at my desk alone, writing letters to various scientific journals, trying to solicit interest in the Analytical Engine. I barely paid notice to the ants crawling over a rotting apple core left from the previous week. My mind was focused on finding at least one institution, one person, who would support our endeavour. William entered the room carrying a new painting.

'Happy Birthday, Birdie. Look, your new painting arrived,' he said.

I looked up to see it was another fairy scene, presumably by the same artist.

'Thank you, my darling. How very sweet. You may leave it,'

I replied with a smile before returning to work.

'I'm happy to hang it for you,' he said and he looked for some empty wall space. Illustrations of the Analytical Engine and other machines crowded the walls. He began to remove one to make space for the painting.

'Please don't touch those,' I said, having painstakingly put them in order of prototypes.

'I was merely going to move them,' he said.

'Don't. Everything is exactly where it needs to be,' I said. To be honest, I was eager for him to leave, just so I could more fully concentrate. But William stood in silence for some time. I finally looked up at him.

'Is it?' he asked. 'Tell me, where do I fit in all this?'

'You know how much I love you. There's no need for such questions.'

William softened, saying, 'Then come with me now. We'll take the afternoon and walk down to the railroad tracks and picnic like we used to. We had such fun back then.'

'Darling, I would, but I am to accompany Babbage to the Royal Science Society this afternoon. We cannot miss our appointment.'

'I see,' said William as he set the painting on the floor and left the room.

'William, wait,' I called after him. But he had gone. I had the instinct to go follow him, to explain why I needed to focus on my work today, but it was already after nine o'clock a.m., and Babbage was already late fetching me.

At a quarter passed ten o'clock a.m., Babbage and I hopped into a carriage heading to London to meet with the Royal Science Society. Babb polished the number wheels on his demonstration model of the Difference Engine on the ride over. The demonstration model would be shown to the scientists as a visual aid to help them understand what the new machine would be capable of. The machine would have thousands of intricate parts that would need to be precisely designed by highly skilled brass workers. A team of engineers would need to be consulted and paid for their work. No machine of this grandeur had ever been built. I hoped the Royal Science Society would be as enchanted by the Analytical Engine as I was.

We finally reached Somerset House, which is located on the south side of the Strand in central London, overlooking the Thames River, and just a stone's throw from Waterloo Bridge. Once a Tudor palace, this majestic building is where the Royal Science Society made its home.

As our carriage pulled up to the front of the building, Babbage began to yell at the driver, 'Behind the building, Sir, behind!'

Right away, I worried something was wrong. Why couldn't we enter through the front? Was it because I was a woman? The carriage driver obliged Babbage and took us round to the alley in back of the building. Then I wondered if this was going to be a repeat of our day at the Second Rusty Cross factory and sighed.

In back of Somerset House, we exited the carriage and carefully rested the model of the Difference Engine on the ground.

Babbage spied a broken window on the building's second floor. 'How good are you at scaling walls?' he asked.

I looked at Babb incredulously, saying, 'Babb! Why can't we enter through the front door like everyone else? Are you embarrassed because I'm a woman?'

'Goodness, no. We can't enter through the front entrance because, well, I've been banned from the building.'

'You told me we had an appointment.'

'We do – with fate!' he then walked up and down the back of the building. After nearly a quarter of an hour, he found a wooden ladder lying near a dock on the river. He carried it to the rear of Somerset House and rested it underneath the broken window.

'Ladies first?' he said before realizing how improper it would be for me to climb a ladder ahead of him, considering I was wearing a dress. 'No, terrible idea. I shall go first. Hold the ladder still?'

I held my breath as Babb carefully made his way up the rickety ladder. The wood creaked with each step he took. Finally, at the top, he managed to slide the broken window open and stuff himself through. He then took a rope and tossed one end of it down to me.

I tied my end of the rope around the Difference Engine model and Babb precariously hoisted it upward. I couldn't watch as the precious, one-of-a-kind machine banged against the stone wall with each tug.

When Babb finally had the model at the window, he wrapped the rope tightly around his arm to hold it in place while he reached for it with his hands. Carefully, he pulled it through the window.

Now it was my turn to climb up. I took a deep breath as I tucked the rolled-up illustrations under my arm and headed up the ladder. I was not afraid of heights, but the pathetic state of this ladder gave me butterflies in my stomach. I was a little wobbly at first, then grew more steady at about the forth rung. About the twelfth rung up, the wood suddenly snapped, causing my foot to land on the rung beneath. The ladder shook, nearly causing me to fall.

'Steady now, go slowly,' called Babb.

I wanted to shout at him that I *was* going slowly, but instead I focused on the task at hand. Finally making it to the window, Babb pulled me into an empty laboratory -- we were in.

'Well done!' said Babb, and patted my head like a puppy. I groaned. When I had pictured our day with the Royal Science Society, I certainly hadn't pictured it beginning like this.

Stealthily, Babb peeked out of the laboratory and looked down the hallway. The path seemed clear, but as we started into the hallway, we saw a clerk rolling a cart of books in our direction. We hid until the clerk passed then rolled the demonstration model down the hall in the opposite direction. As we quickly rounded a corner, we crashed into a man with a monocle, holding a tray of beakers filled with fluid. The Difference Engine tumbled over as the beakers crashed and spilled onto the marble floor.

'My life's work!' shouted the man with the monocle, 'Everything shattered on the floor!'

'Truly sorry,' I began, but before I could finish my sentence, Babb had righted his machine and had pulled me half-way down the hall.

We continued on before stopping at a double doorway. Both doors were closed. The sign on the door read, 'Royal Science Society Fellows ONLY'.

Babb looked me straight in the eye and spoke in a very serious tone, 'Now, when you speak in front of the committee—'

'When *I* speak?' I said, absolutely aghast. I was under the impression that I was there solely for moral support, not to address the Society. That would be outrageous.

'Don't take no for an answer!' he said. But before I could protest, Babbage threw open one of the large wooden doors to reveal a dozen men of science engaged in a heated debate. Babbage pushed me into the room, then ducked into the hallway. The men stopped speaking when they saw me. I stood there nervously, my knees shaking a bit, not sure what to say. Sweat began to drip from my forehead.

'Uh... Good afternoon, gentlemen.'

The man in charge barked at me, 'Kitchen is in the basement.' The men resumed their debate. But I corrected him.

'I am no kitchen maid, I am Lady Byron King,' I said, but they weren't paying attention. I looked at Babbage in the hallway and mouthed the words, 'Now what?' He motioned for me to keep going. I hesitated, then cleared my throat.

'Gentlemen!' I said in my loudest voice, 'I'm here to speak to you about a new machine. One that will change the world.'

I could tell the men were surprised by my nerve. One of the fellows, a man who spoke with a lisp said, 'Thend her away.'

A large, rotund man in his fifties, said, 'Let her stay, I could use an amusement.' Some of the men of science laughed.

Another, who wore a hairpiece on top of his mostly bald head, attempted to toy with me, 'Very well, then. What, my dear, do you know about machines?'

'A great deal,' I said, trying to exude confidence. Two scientists exchanged dubious looks. 'You see, I'm in possession of plans for... ' I paused, looking around for my papers.

After what felt like the longest moment of my life, the rolled-up plans, along with the now dented Difference Engine demonstration model, rolled into the room. I knew it was Babbage who pushed it in, but he remained hidden. I winced when I noticed that one of the number wheels was hanging askew.

'Ah, here are the plans,' I said, as the scientists chuckled.

I cleared my throat again as I unrolled a large illustration of the Analytical Engine and placed it before the man with the hairpiece I could now tell was crooked.

'The Analytical Engine will perform mathematical equations entirely on its own with 100 percent accuracy. This would eliminate costly, even dangerous miscalculations often made by humans,' I said.

The room went quiet. The man in charge held up the detailed illustration. Other scientists began to examine it.

Out of the corner of my eye, I could see Babbage in the hallway, silently cheering me on.

Inside the room, a few of the scientists started whispering to each other.

'Once programmed, the Analytical Engine will solve complex calculations, without the assistance of human intellect or hand,' I said, trying to reiterate my point.

Now, with very serious expressions on their faces, the scientists started whispering again, exchanging glances with each other until the one with the lisp stood up, 'Are you thuggesting thuch a mathine can think?'

'I'm suggesting—' but I was cut off.

'Machines that can think?' said the man in charge, 'Blasphemy, I say!'

I panicked, trying to clarify, 'It reads punched cards—'

'Now it can read!' scoffed the large man.

I was struggling to explain myself when I saw a tapestry

hanging on the wall that depicted the solar system.

'The Analytical Engine would use the same principals of Monsieur Jacquard's weaving loom,' I said as I pointed to the tapestry, 'Is that tapestry also blasphemy?'

'There is a big difference between weaving and thinking,' said the man in charge.

'Not to a woman,' said the man with the crooked hairpiece. The men all snorted as the leader tried to regain order.

'Composure!' he said.

'How dare she interrupt our colloquium on the geology of Noah's Flood with this poppycock,' said a man with a large, bulbous nose.

Then it happened – the most humiliating moment of the afternoon.

'The Analytical Engine is real science, conceived by me!' said Babbage as he stomped his way into the room.

Upon seeing Babbage, the scientists groaned. The man with the lisp dropped his head into his hands. 'Thould have known you were behind thith,' he said.

'Mr. Babbage, shame on you for sending this poor girl here to do your dirty work,' said the large-nosed man.

'I'm forbidden from entering the building, what am I to do?' Babbage asked.

'Stay out!' said the large man.

'But this machine will alter the course of human history,' pleaded Babbage.

'Mr. Babbage, even if we were to conclude that your Analytical Engine adheres to Christian principles, I don't see it having any practical purpose,' said the leader.

I pulled on Babbage's arm, trying to keep him from further

embarrassment. But Babbage wouldn't give up.

'You're not grasping its full potential,' said Babbage.

'Good day, Mr. Babbage,' said the leader, and with that, I shuffled Babb and the Difference Engine model out of the room.

As we walked down the hallway, Babb cursed the men of science.

'Damned, bloody cockchafers – bootlickers, all of them!' he said.

'Babbage, control yourself,' I said.

'I feel like the wretched Cassandra. The more I speak the truth, the less I'm believed. Why won't they listen?' he said with a tinge of sorrow in his voice.

I stopped walking and put my hand on his shoulder to reassure him, saying, 'We'll get the funding. I promise.'

But Babbage continued to tread heavily down the hall, dragging the damaged Difference Engine demonstration model, wheels squeaking, behind him. I had no idea what to do next.

21

As I arrived back at Ashley Combe, a dusting of feathery ice crystals that displayed a six-fold symmetry, known also as snowflakes, had just covered the roof. Given my experience at the Royal Science Society, my spirit was feeling as cold as the snow.

William had left me a note saying his grandfather had suddenly passed away and he had to attend to family business. Surely he was still cross with me for not spending the day with him and now he had to handle these matters alone. I felt terrible, especially since nothing had come of our visit to the Royal Science Society. Maybe William was right in that I should focus more on the home and his affairs, but I felt quite deeply that the work Babbage and I were doing would be the most significant thing I'd accomplish in my life.

Mother and Dr. Poole had returned this afternoon from visiting my elderly great-aunt Beranice whom she reported was in much better health than when they first arrived. But the trip had taken a toll on Mother and she missed taking her water cures administered by Dr. Gulley.

Water cures were a type of hydrotherapy that were becoming very popular throughout England and Europe. The patient would be doused with a shower of very cold water in an effort to stimulate the nervous system. Mother had begun taking these treatments on Wednesdays but had missed the last six.

She approached me in my study, seeming quite agitated.

'My nerves are a wreck. Would you mind administering my leech therapy to me tonight?'

'Me? Doesn't Dr. Poole know your regimen much better than myself?'

'Dr. Poole is no longer under my employ.'

This was shocking news. He had been with us ever since I could remember. I knew something was amiss between them, but I had been so focused on my work, I neglected to fully grasp the full situation.

'He is not ill, I hope,' I said, fishing for some explanation.

'No, he's decided to go work for a large family in Coventry.'

'Coventry? Won't you miss him, Mother? He's been with us for so long. I recently even wondered if there might be a spark of romance between you two.'

'Yes, well, I suppose there was on his part.'

I knew it!

'But another marriage is out of the question,' she said matter-of-factly.

'Why, Mother? Now that I'm grown and married, why not try to gain some happiness for yourself.'

'Happiness?' she scoffed, 'Nothing about marriage is happy. It is only indentured servitude. I will never give my power to another man, as long as I live. Now, might you stop with the questions and administer my therapy?'

Stunned by her revelation, I followed her upstairs. Surely, marriage must lead to some happiness I thought, but judging from my own marriage, it does seem difficult for both husband and wife to feel joyful all the time.

As I entered Mother's bedroom, my eyes fixed on a single

jar of leeches that rested on her nightstand.

'My head is simply pounding, Ada. There's a ringing in my ears.'

To be honest, I still found these creatures disgusting. But having to listen to Mother complain about her ailments was even more unsettling. I helped her undress and she laid on the bed.

'Three at a time on my shoulders until they are engorged and release from my flesh on their own.'

I opened the jar and reached for the slimy little bugger. It slipped between my fingers, falling back into the jar. I finally managed to get two and placed them on Mother's back. They wriggled until their suckers clamped down on her skin. Mother gave a tiny moan. I picked up a third, but before I could put it on her back, its sucker clamped down on my index finger. I was repulsed by it.

'Mother, one has bitten me, how do I get it off?' I said in a panicked voice.

'Rip it off and stop being so damn squeamish. I raised you better than that.'

With my left hand, I tore it off and flung it onto Mother's shoulder. There was a tiny trail of blood on my finger where it had been feeding.

Once the three leeches detached from Mother's flesh, I returned them to the jar. She had me administer three more, then three more. Finally, she asked me to put one in the crook of her arm.

'You may go,' she said.

As I closed her door behind me, I walked into Dr. Poole's now former room. All his personal belongings had indeed, been removed. He must have done so this afternoon while I was gone. I wondered if he'd write me a letter to say goodbye. He was always kind to me and tempered Mother. His heart must be broken. Poor soul.

I waited up until after midnight to tell William the news about Dr. Poole. But I was feeling sleepy and decided to retire to bed. I would have to make up with him in the morning.

The next morning, I woke up alone and went down to breakfast only to find that William had already eaten. I went up to his bedchamber to find him preparing to go on an overnight trip.

'Is it more family business that takes you away?' I asked.

'It is work. One of my client's home is in shambles from a recent fire. I need to oversee the repairs. Surely, you of all people understand the need to attend to business matters,' he said as a verbal jab.

'I'm sorry for the other day. I was being selfish and I didn't mean to hurt you, honestly.'

'I'm not hurt. Far too busy to be hurt, I shan't give it another thought,' he said as he exited the room. I followed him.

'I'm very sorry to hear of your grandfather's passing. When is the funeral?'

William stopped walking, but did not turn around.

'In three days.'

'I should like to attend. Also, Dr. Poole has left Mother. Permanently.'

As he headed toward the stairs, he said casually, 'I'm surprised he didn't leave sooner.'

I let out a sigh. William was clearly still cross with me and it was a problem I had created. I had not the slightest idea how to resolve it. As a child, I had nothing but time. Now, between being a wife, my work with Babbage and finally getting to know my father, there was very little time for anything else.

As I worked inside my study, Mother entered holding a letter. She wore a worried look on her face.

'I have received a most distressing letter,' she said.

I looked at her face and felt a cold chill prick the back of my neck. I prayed Mother hadn't intercepted a letter from Father. If she did, I would just have to play innocent, but I was never confident of my deceptive skills when Mother's intuition was involved.

'What is the matter?' I carefully asked, trying not to show my panic.

'Someone has made a claim on Newstead Abbey.'

I was relieved it wasn't a letter from Father that she was speaking of, but this created a whole new set of concerns.

'But who could claim the property?' I asked.

'Apparently, a man says your father owed him a large sum of money and is declaring himself the rightful owner,' she said.

'For what reason could my father owe someone such a large amount of money?' I asked, my head swimming.

'Oh, Ada, you've no idea the trouble your father could cause.'

'But I'm the rightful owner of Newstead. Soon as I turn twenty-eight,' I said.

'Let us keep hope alive,' said Mother, as she the rubbed the crook of her left arm.

The next evening, after William had returned from his trip, we dined on fried skate fish and poached eggs. I suppose Mother decided it best not to mention the claim on Newstead Abbey until it was investigated more thoroughly. In truth, I think that minding the issue on her own made her feel in charge of my welfare once again and so she preferred to handle the matter personally.

William was exhausted from his trip and retired to his bedchamber after dinner without saying a word to me. I thought about asking him if we could talk about how he's feeling but I decided to give him some privacy. I hoped he would come around in a few days.

William said very little to me over the next few days. Tomorrow, he would travel to Oxford to receive an architectural award. He didn't ask me to go with him, which I knew was out of anger, but I didn't want to stop working either. It's much easier to concentrate when he is not looking over my shoulder. One morning, after I began work in my study very early, William entered around half-past six.

'Ada, there is a matter I must broach with you,' he said.

I met his blue eyes that looked as if they had not slept well. 'Yes, my love?'

I went to check on Voltigeur last night, his front left leg seemed to be troubling him.'

'I hope it's nothing serious.'

'The horse will recover, that's not the matter. When I opened the stable door, I found Kate. She was with Mack. They were indisposed, clearly enjoying the effects of drinking an entire bottle of our finest wine,' he said as he held up the bottle.

My heart skipped a beat. The wine bottle was one I had brought for Father. I had neglected to dispose of it.

'You're in your study all day, you come down here after I've gone to sleep. Who knows what they could be getting away with.'

'Indeed. I will keep a closer eye.'

'I told them they will be reprimanded. It is up to you to determine the punishment and administer it. You must be firm with them. You need to set a precedent.'

'Of course. I will do it this afternoon. Please, my dear, don't let a couple of servants sour your journey.'

'I'm not going.'

'But you must. The architectural society will think you ungrateful.'

William looked at me carefully, studying my face as if it may reveal some wary secret thought. He grew suspicious.

'Why are you so eager to get rid of me?' he asked.

'I'm not,' I said with frustration. 'Nothing I say pleases you.'

We looked at each other for a long moment. He finally broke the silence.

'I realise now how sheltered you've been. Running a home is a big adjustment and it's my duty to guide you. We must work together until things are running smoothly.'

'Very well, I only want to please you.'

He paused and looked at the floor. 'I suppose I will go to the award ceremony. I just wish you were coming with me,' he said.

'If I stay and work while you're away, it will free up some time for us to spend together when you return.'

William nodded and paused. I stood and kissed him on the cheek, saying, 'Thank you for allowing me this time, it is quite generous of you,' But it didn't seem to please him. He began to exit but stopped and pulled a book from his pocket.

'I almost forgot,' he said, as he set a book onto my desk. It was the copy of *Don Juan* that my father gave me. Chills ran up my spine. 'Apparently Kate and the kitchen boy are fond of your father's poetry. Didn't think Kate could read.' And with that, he left my study. I took a deep breath. I needed to be much more cautious.

That afternoon, Mother and I took the carriage to the lawyer's office in London.

22

Mr. Lushington had been Mother's lawyer ever since she sought to divorce Father. It was customary for the husband to gain custody of the children in a divorce, not the wife. For the wife to retain custody of her own flesh and blood, she would need to demonstrate that her husband was financially or mentally unfit to care for them. For better or worse, Mr. Lushington was successfully able to convince the court that I would be better off with Mother.

Once we arrived at the law office, Mr. Lushington's secretary brought us straight into his office. Mr. Lushington wore an expensive hound's-tooth suit and shiny new crocodile shoes, probably trying to impress Mother. This was the first time I had met the man who secured my place at Mother's breast all those years ago. I hadn't heard many details of the trial and for the first time, I wondered what would have happened if Mr. Lushington had lost his case and I was sent to live in Father's care. Part of me thought it would have been wonderfully exciting. But another part of me knew how much effort Mother put into protecting me. If only they could have reconciled their differences and stayed together, but it was never to be.

On the wall behind Mr. Lushington's desk was a portrait of him. It must have been painted many years ago, because it depicted him as a young, wiry man with thick dark hair. Lushington was now in his sixties, well-groomed and thin, except for his belly that protruded over his trousers. His hair was nearly white. I couldn't help but be distracted by the difference between the portrait and the man in front of me. It disturbed me for some reason, as if it were hanging on the wall to create the illusion that Mr. Lushington was still young and spry. I wondered if he thought he still looked like the portrait or maybe he just admired himself more as a younger man. It would be highly inappropriate to point out the differences between the smooth visage of the subject in the painting verses the wrinkled, puffy skin of the man sitting at the desk, yet those vast differences were all I could think of. I decided it best not to look at the painting at all, if possible. Instead, I stared into his narrow-set brown eyes as he spoke.

'I'm so grateful you could visit in person, Lady Byron. Your very presence illuminates this cluttered and lowly office most splendidly.' Mother blushed. I rolled my eyes.

'Why, thank you Mr. Lushington,' said Mother.

'And Ada, what a pleasure to meet you. You are every bit as beautiful as your mother,' he said.

'You are most kind,' I said politely, hoping to quickly get to the matter at hand. 'Please do tell us about this claim on Newstead Abbey, Mr. Lushington.'

'Yes, the claim. I have a man investigating it, but I'm almost certain it will turn out to be superfluous. Lord Byron did owe several of his compatriots upwards of £30,000, but I think this particular claim is merely a scare tactic to frighten you into settling Byron's debt with the man, which he claims is £28,000. I'm assuming you have no interest in paying this…' he looked through his papers, 'this Mr. Davies for Byron's recklessness?'

Mother's face grew severe, 'Pay that scoundrel? Not even if Jesus himself commanded it,' she said with vitriol.

'Who is he, Mother?' I asked.

'A bootlicking gambler and drunkard,' she said with disdain, having used the harsh words typically reserved for my father.

Lushington patted my hand, 'Miss Byron, please do not worry. When pressed, he couldn't produce any evidence of this debt, so as it stands now, you will inherit the estate as planned,' he said, then looked back at Mother.

'Ada was recently married,' said Mother. 'I'd like to confirm that her husband, though gracious, will not also be named owner of the estate.'

'He bequeathed it solely to her. Newstead Abbey is Ada's to inhabit, manage or sell as she sees fit,' he said.

'How much do you think it's worth?' I asked.

'It hasn't been appraised in years. I've been told it's in quite a state of disrepair. Perhaps two hundred thousand pounds?'

My jaw dropped. That was a lot of money.

'Now Ada,' said Mr. Lushington, finally looking at me, 'would you mind giving your mother and I a moment alone?'

'I'll wait for you outside,' I said and exited his office.

As I made my way to the hallway, my head was spinning. I leaned against the wall just outside his office, trying to take it all in, when I realised I could hear Mr. Lushington through the wall. It was terribly rude to eavesdrop, but I was so curious to know what matter they needed to discuss.

'Dearest Annabella,' he said in a sincere tone, 'it is truly lovely to see you again. I often reminisce about the time we spent together, so long ago. Us, working together for justice, side by side. It was you and me against the world.'

I was shocked to hear him call her by her first name. Even Dr. Poole only did that in privacy.

'I am forever grateful for your assistance, Mr. Lushington,' Mother replied, 'If there is another matter pertaining to my daughter, please make it known.'

'I have thought about you so many times over the years, always knowing that after the divorce, it would not have been proper for me to ask to court you.'

'Court me?'

'Yes, I had a true fondness for you, I must confess. Then I met my Fanny and we married. We had three boys, but Fanny is no longer with us. Annabella, my heavenly angel. May I have your hand in marriage?' he asked.

Marriage? He hasn't seen her in over two decades and he wants to marry her? This is the reason we had to meet on the matter in person, I was sure of it.

'You are most kind,' said Mother, 'But I shall never give my power to another man. Good day, Mr. Lushington.'

I quickly trotted down the hallway and exited the building.

On the carriage ride home, I let my thoughts drift to imagining what a grand and wonderful place Newstead Abbey must be. My ancestors had lived there and surely I too would feel at home there. I thought Father would be thrilled to know the inheritance was moving according to plan – surely he'd hate the idea that one of his friends was trying to steal it from me, or actually him, since he's still alive. Considering Mr. Lushington didn't seem terribly concerned, I thought it best not to tell Father and worry him. I suddenly understood why I must not tell William – or anyone – about Father's survival. So many legal matters would be put into question. This meeting solidified to me why I must tell no one of his return. At least for now.

The next day, I invited Babb to spend the afternoon with me to run electrical experiments with the Leyden jar he had given William and me as a wedding present. If there were a way to electrify the Analytical Engine, all the better!

We sat outside on the balcony that overlooked the terraces that were covered in ivy. It was a brisk, but sunny day.

The Leyden Jar consisted of a gallon-sized glass jar filled about halfway with water. The jar was lined with thin metallic sheets. In the middle of the jar sat a metal rod. Half of the rod was inside the jar, touching the water, the other half of the rod protruded out of the neck of the jar.

'This capacitor stores static electricity. Many scientists in Germany and Holland are conducting experiments with these,' said Babbage.

'How exciting!'

'Shall we give it a whirl?'

'Sure,' I said, reaching my fingertip to the rod that was protruding from the top of the jar.

'No,' said Babb as he stopped me from touching it. 'You'll likely get a painful jolt. That's what these are for,' he said as he dug to the bottom of a sack of potatoes. He pulled out a rotting potato to find a cockroach crawling on it. 'Let's see what this little devil thinks of electricity.'

He held up the beetle that was nearly the size of Babbage's pinky finger, and said, 'I fear you've met your end, old boy.'

He dangled the cockroach over the Leyden jar then dropped it onto the spherical conductor. Sparks shot off the jar as the cockroach made a hissing sound, similar to the sound of a rasher in a frying pan. I watched aghast as the bug was destroyed by electricity.

'Absolutely gruesome,' I howled, then begged him, 'Do it again!'

Babbage searched through the potatoes for another cockroach, finding another that was a bit smaller. It also fried on the spherical conductor.

As Babbage pulled another roach out of the bag, I decided I felt brave and held out my hand. He placed the beetle in my palm and I quickly tossed it onto the Leyden jar itself. Large sparks flew this time, causing me to shriek. We did this for over an hour, until we could find no more roaches.

'Well then, I think we've done enough murdering for the afternoon,' I said giggling. Then Babbage's tone grew more serious.

'I sent the plans for the Analytical Engine to the French Scientific Commission,' he said.

'And how was it received?' I asked.

'Not well, unfortunately. However a Monsieur Menabrea did write a paper on it,' he said.

'That should stir some new interest,' I said with a wisp of hope in my voice.

'Hardly. It's in French.'

'*Je parle Francais, mon ami*,' I said in nearly perfect French. 'Send me the notes and I'll make a translation straight away.'

'Really? That's brilliant news. If we could get your translation printed, we could spread the word quickly and not have to rely on the bloody Royal Science Society, those --'

'Don't get worked up, Babb,' I said calmly.

'If this doesn't work, I...' he paused, then said sadly, 'I think I should give up on this endeavour for good.'

'Don't say such a thing!'

'My dear, every day that goes by, my heart gets broken into more and more pieces.'

'But this is my dream, too,' I said looking him straight in the eyes. That's when the idea hit me like a ton of bricks. Before considering whether or not I should speak my idea, I looked around to be sure no servants were listening. I spoke in a hushed tone. 'Babb, I stand to inherit a large property. If I decided to sell it, the money could fund the construction of the machine.'

'Heaven's no,' he said, 'Ada, I could never take your money. Never. Do not speak of such foolishness again.'

'It may be our only way to get the Analytical Engine built in time for the Royal exhibition in the Crystal Palace.'

Babbage shook his head. 'We must get the scientific community behind us or we'll look like fools. Translate those notes. It is our best hope.'

'I agree,' I said as I spied another cockroach crawling out of the potato sack. I caught it and dropped it onto the Leyden jar. The roach sparked, then caught on fire as it fell to the ground.

'Goodness,' I shouted. Babbage stomped on the burning roach until the fire was out.

After Babbage had left, Kate delivered me a coded letter from my father. I still hadn't punished her or Mack for being in the stable. I spoke quickly to her in a hushed tone.

'If Mr. King asks if I administered punishment for your indiscretion with Mack in the stable, tell him I withheld two week's worth of both your salaries.'

'But will you, Miss?'

'No. He just needs to believe that I am a firm mistress. Take this,' I said, handing her the gold and ivory bracelet from my wrist. I thought the trinket would ensure her fidelity to me. 'Do not wear it in the house, understand?'

She nodded and ewent back into the house. Finally, I could read the note from Father.

Dearest Pippin,

I should like to take you out tomorrow for a lovely afternoon at the horse races. Please join me for a day of excitement. Meet me at Epsom downs at high noon.

Your loving father,
LB

I read the note with excitement, and felt relieved that William was still away at his architectural event. Masking an afternoon at the races would be a difficult ruse to pull off even without William's recent suspicions about how I was spending my time. Fortunately for me, I wouldn't have to worry without William here to mind my absence.

I arrived to the racing grounds wearing a blue hat and that matched my organdy frock with blue satin sashes. This was my first time at the horse races and I was thrilled by the possibility of actually betting on a horse. I had no previous gambling experience but was excited to learn.

In order to conceal his identity, Father wore a blond wig under his hat, which he held with his hand every time the wind gusted up.

Father led me to the paddock to watch the jockeys saddle and mount their lean, powerful horses. He pointed to a young jockey dressed in purple and gold on a brown Thoroughbred.

The horse wore a banner with the number five embroidered on it.

'Five is my lucky number,' he said.

'What's its name?' I asked.

Father referred to his race card, 'Devil's Fire.'

'Considering it's your lucky number *and* my favourite prime number, I should like to bet on him,' I said.

'Devil's Fire it is,' he said and led me to the bet-maker's window. Father laid down a pence, to which I added five more.

'Someone's feeling *very* lucky,' said Father.

'Simply spending the day with you makes me terribly lucky,' I said as I wrapped my arm around his. I squeezed it tightly.

From the stands, we prepared to watch the horses gallop. A gunshot signaled the start of the race and the stallions took off like wildfire. The sound of the hooves pounding on the grass was as loud as thunder. I had never imagined any horse could run so fast, let alone seven at once and not run into each other.

Devil's Fire stayed in the middle of the pack for most of the race, but as the hot-blooded horses neared the end, it remarkably pulled ahead.

I gasped, 'Look! He's speeding up!'

'We may be winners yet,' said Father as he grasped my hand tightly.

We watched transfixed as Devil's Fire took the lead. My blood was racing through my veins. For a single moment, my mind was totally encompassed with the hope of our horse winning this race. Fate was on our side when Devil's Fire managed to cross the finish line first. The crowd cheered as Father wrapped his arms around me, picking me up off the ground and spinning me around. It was a terrific thrill.

In total, we bet on six races. Though our bets didn't pay out on four of them, we came out ahead overall.

We went to collect our winnings, which turned out to be a total of one shilling.

'Not bad for a day's work,' said Father as he handed me the winnings.

'The power of those Thoroughbreds! My heart is still pounding,' I said.

'Now I know what excites you,' he replied.

'I'm afraid you know far too well,' I said blissfully. Being around Father had awakened something in me. For the first time, I felt possessed by a wild spirit and no longer feared things as I had in the past. I felt powerful in ways I had not felt before. I knew I had Father to thank for this new state of mind. I was finally coming into my own as a Byron.

As we drank a cup of tea and shared a bag of peanuts, Lord Byron's face grew serious.

'Pippin, I'm afraid I won't be seeing you for a while.'

'But why not?'

'A business venture fell through. I'm out of money.'

I couldn't bear the thought of him no longer around.

'I'll get you money. I'll get you anything you need,' I said as I pulled the winnings from my satchel.

'I refuse to take money from you,' he said, pushing the cash away.

'Please, take it. It will allow us to continue to spend time together,' I said.

Reluctantly, he took the money from me and tucked it into his jacket pocket.

'You are my angel,' he said and kissed my cheek. 'Now. Shall we get drunk?'

23

Though I thought Father was joking about getting drunk, it soon became quite clear he was not. We headed down the road, arm in arm, to a public house called the Stag's Head. Over the entrance hung a real deer's head that had massive antlers but was missing one of its porcelain eyes. I could hear lively music from a concertina wafting out of the tavern windows.

Before we entered, the shrill cries from a woman, likely a prostitute I'd bet, caught my attention. She was arguing with a man who seemed entirely out of his wits.

'You stole me coin purse. Hand it over,' said the woman to the drunken man.

'Or what? You'll send the Chaplain after me?' he said.

'You *are* the Chaplain!' she yelled. He laughed as she beat him with her hands.

Father approached the Chaplain, saying, 'Say a prayer for me, sir,' as he pickpocketed the woman's purse from him. Father then tossed it to the woman.

'Bless you!' she said to him as she caught it in her hands. It took a moment for the Chaplain to figure out what had just happened. The intoxicated Chaplain got right up in Father's face, which frightened me. I had never seen someone so inebriated before.

'That harlot promised to save me soul. She couldn't even wake it up,' the Chaplain slurred.

Father just pushed the man aside. He stumbled off. Much to my shock, the woman sidled up next to Father and purred, 'For fifty shillings, I can save your soul.'

'If only I had one,' he replied and slapped her on the rear.

I intervened, 'I'm quite thirsty. Perhaps we might discuss theology inside?' Father held out his arm to me and together, we entered the tavern.

The crowded pub was noisy with a raw, bawdy clientele. I was certainly not used to such a motley crew of people. One man had a peg leg. I noticed the profile of a very beautiful young woman, only to discover the right side of her face had been severely burned. Another man had no suspenders attached to his trousers and they fell down every time he stood up, making me blush as he wore no drawers. Had I not been a married woman, being seen in such a place as this would have been inexcusable. Actually, it was probably a terrible idea to be here regardless of my marital state. I looked around cautiously and decided the chances of William finding out were slim; these were not the sorts he cavorted with at all and word of my 'adventure' was unlikely to grace his ears.

As my eyes searched the room, I noticed a very large, portly woman trying to wake her husband who was sleeping in his chair. She kept knocking her knuckles on his ear. Finally, in a fit of frustration, she poured her beer on his head, which sent him into a fit of sputtering. The man stood up, roared like a lion, and shook himself like a wet dog, sending beer spraying in every direction. A few of the pub's patrons laughed, but I have to admit, I became quite annoyed when some of the ale splashed on my sleeve and I began to question my sanity for following my father into such a den of depravity as this. Then, just as suddenly as he had woken, the husband with the beer-soaked head, plopped back into his chair and — much to the chagrin of his wife — fell back to sleep like a baby.

I took a cloth from the bar to soak up the beer from my garment, and when I looked up, I saw a toothless man grinning at me. I couldn't understand how or why this man would venture out into public with such an empty, gaping hole for a mouth. Then I realised that some people simply could not afford such luxuries like dentures. The grinning man also caught Father's attention, causing him to pull me near him.

'Keep close,' he said into my ear. I could feel his lips touching my earlobe as he spoke, and all worries about the pub's rough patrons faded from thought. For a brief moment, I imagined being a little girl and having Father read me a bedtime story, then kissing me goodnight on my forehead. Oh, the years we had lost!

Father then summoned the barman. 'Absinthe,' he said.

'One glass or two?' said the barman.

'The bottle,' growled Father as he laid some money on the bar. I felt an echo of Mother's disapproval cross my mind as I thought of his money woes, but quickly banished them. This was my father. Who was I to question how he spent his money? By then, father had picked up the emerald green bottle and was making his way to a table. The barman handed me a tray with two empty glasses, two slotted spoons and several lumps of sugar wrapped in newspaper, which I accepted as graciously as I could, though I didn't know what they were for. I then followed Father through the crowd to an empty table at the back of the tavern where he introduced me to the Flaming Green Fairy.

I was completely beside myself as Father instructed me on

how to prepare and drink this curious elixir. I loved fairies and was eager to taste the green liquid that supposedly allowed you to see a Green Fairy, though I was doubtful I would. Father poured about two-fingers worth into each glass. Over the glasses, he laid the wooden slotted spoons, upon which he placed a lump of sugar. The lumps had been soaked in alcohol and smelled like liquorice. Father picked up the small beeswax candle that sat at the middle of our table and, much to my surprise, lit the sugar lumps on fire! A flame shot up, scaring me – I nearly jumped out of my seat.

'What on earth?' I asked, startled.

'Follow me,' he said then proceeded to spit into his glass, putting out the flame. Quickly, he tossed back the hot liquid and let out an, 'Ahhhh!'

I had never expelled saliva in front of anyone before, let alone into a cup and drink it. Father looked at me, expectantly.

'Waiting for hell to freeze, girl?' he asked.

I looked at him, and then down at the cup. It took some mustering, but I used my hand to cover the cup so Father would not see as I pressed my lips together and managed a dainty spittle into the drink. After a moment, the flame was extinguished, but more from me covering the cup with my hand, depriving the fire of oxygen and less due to my saliva. I then stuck my pinky into the cup to see if it was too hot to put into my mouth – it was. I blew on the liquid a few times, as if it were a hot soup.

'For the love of dogs and onions, take—'

I lifted my cup and swallowed the drink whole. It was hot. It was strong. It tasted like liquorice-flavoured vinegar, tart and minty as I had imagined. I tried not to think about the fact that I was swallowing my own regurgitated saliva. I felt a fierce burn as the liquid slid down my esophagus and hit my belly like a bolt of lightening. I gasped for air.

'That's my girl,' he said with a laugh and poured two more cups. I'm certain a look of panic crossed my face. 'Don't worry,' he grinned, 'only the first drink is set ablaze.' I sighed in relief.

With some urging, I managed to take a few tiny sips of the liquid but couldn't again take down the whole cup at once. Father drank three or four within the same hour it took me to finish my second. By then, however, my body was beginning to feel the Green Fairy's intoxicating effects. I noticed a strange sensation — I felt light-headed and experienced a floating feeling, as if my head were being lifted up by a string. The concertina music sounded better now and I became oblivious to the raw, gritty people who surrounded me. My focus was solely on Father, who was just a wee bit blurry, but in a way that pleased me.

'I fear I may be getting drunk,' I said.

'Think of it as a lucid intermission,' he said.

I began to rub my beer-soaked sleeve, and had to remind myself why it was wet. Ah, yes! The wife poured it on her sleeping husband and he shook it off like a mutt. I laughed. That's when Father stood up, took off his fancy ruffled jacket and wrapped it around my shoulders. I smiled. I enjoyed it when he fussed over me.

'You are a gentleman, despite what Mother says.'

'I've been accused of many things, but never that.'

I thought about Father's reputation as a dandy and a libertine. I wondered if it was really just an act to create a persona more intriguing to the public – to make his poetry seem that much more exciting. Surely, no man is entirely wicked. He did like to live life on the edge, however, and I knew Mother certainly didn't approve of his risk-taking behaviour. But he married her, so he must have loved her a little bit... and she, him, for that matter.

As Father took another sip of the emerald green absinthe, I asked, 'Did you ever love my mother?'

The question ruffled him so much, he accidentally spit the alcohol out of his mouth. Some of it got on my face.

'I loved her as much as I love passing a kidney stone.'

'Why do you hate her so?'

His spine stiffened. 'Did she not tell you about the divorce? That's curious, she told all of England,' he said in a pointed tone.

'I heard a bit of it,' I said, wincing.

'She wanted to yoke me like a damn ox. A Byron will not be bridled,' he said pounding his fist on the table.

'I share your experience,' I said.

'Only I sit penniless, forbidden to claim any of my wealth. Unable to show my true self to anyone. It is a life undesired and without hope,' he said.

Before I could respond, the prostitute from earlier pushed her way through the crowd. Her eyes narrowed on Father and she managed to plop herself onto his lap. She was now very drunk.

'Kind sssir, could you ssspare a glasss of the frog's ssspit?' she slurred and reached for the bottle of absinthe.

Just then the Chaplain came out of nowhere and grabbed hold of the prostitute's arm. He yanked her out of Father's lap and threw her onto her rear. She screamed as she hit the floor. As Father stood up to go to the woman, the Chaplain put his hand on his shoulder.

'Leave her be, plume-plucker,' snarled the Chaplain, swinging his fist. He missed Father, allowing Father to punch the man between the eyes. The blow sent him flying backwards onto the rotund woman, who was also quite drunk. She stood up, pushing the Chaplain off of her.

'Rowdydow!' she trumpeted then threw her beer glass across the room. It smashed on the wall not far from my head. I screamed.

Other bar patrons took up their fists and began brawling with each other. The Chaplain and the prostitute were caught in the middle of the scuffling.

Father took my hand and led me out the back door to escape the drunken pandemonium. My heart pounded as father laughed against the wind like a man gone mad.

Outside, in the crisp night air, we ran from the building. After about a quarter mile, we stopped on a footbridge that sat above a small creek to catch our breath.

'That was a narrow escape!' I said between breaths.

'Indeed,' said Father, 'But you must admit, brawling is much more fun than your peevish parallelograms.'

'But I beg to differ! Think about the profundity of two perfectly straight lines, never to connect in all infinity. Like two tragic lovers, never to cross paths,' I said as I tripped on a loose board. Walking had never been quite so difficult for me. Luckily, Father caught me in his arms.

'My enchantress of numbers. What a gift you are,' he said.

I smiled, soaking in Father's love. 'I want to show you something, something magical,' I said before I hiccupped. We both laughed as I took his hand and dragged him off to find my carriage.

It was after midnight when we returned to Ashley Combe.

The night sky was clear, boasting a full silver moon. I thought that if we were very quiet, we could enter the house through the front door instead of climbing through my bedroom window. I was still quite tipsy and prayed my bout of hiccups would not return.

We entered the house and it was dark. Puff meowed. I knelt down to give him a little pet then led Father up the staircase. At the end of the hall was Mother's room. I motioned for Father to be quiet as I walked down the hall and leaned up against Mother's door. Luckily, I could hear Mother snoring. I sighed with relief and led Father down to the other end of the hall to my bedchamber.

Once inside my room, I closed the door and locked it. I then opened the French doors and went onto the balcony, motioning for Father to follow me.

'This is what I wanted to show you,' I said, pointing to the Leyden jar. Only, I had attached a coiled metal rod to the top of it.

'What is it?' Father asked.

'Lightening in a bottle. Now watch,' I said as I began to turn the hand crank on the electrostatic generator. It took several minutes, but soon the coil began producing sparks. The sparks were small at first, but the more I cranked, the larger the sparks became. Each burst of static electricity illuminated our faces and made a sharp, crackling sound.

'Lightening from a machine. I don't know how it works, but it is damned remarkable,' said Father.

'I told you machines weren't all bad,' I said.

Father reached his hand out to touch the electricity.

'No! You mustn't touch it,' I said.

'I must know how it feels,' he said.

'You'll get hurt, perhaps burned, even,' I warned.

'All the more. I'm not afraid of a little burn,' he said as he thrust his hand into the electrical current. 'Ah!' he said as he gasped from the pain of the current that pulsed through his flesh. He immediately pulled his hand back.

'Are you alright?' I asked as I stopped cranking and knelt down next to him.

'Radiant,' he said.

I inspected his hand. I shook my head and snuggled up to him. He wrapped his arms around me.

'It's far too dangerous to keep fire in a bottle,' I said.

'Or in your heart,' he said as he stroked my hair. I delighted in this fuzzy, perfect moment next to the man I longed for my entire life.

'Ada, I love you,' he said as he kissed my forehead. I closed my eyes and smiled, squeezing him tighter. He then kissed my cheek. I could feel his rough, unshaven skin against my skin, his breath was warm on my face.

Then, came another kiss.

This one was on my mouth. And it lingered uncomfortably. Then, instead of pulling his lips away from mine, he pressed them more firmly against my mouth. His mouth opened slightly and the kiss suddenly changed from a doting peck to wet and ripe debauchery – it felt similar to the way William kissed me on our wedding night. Alarmed, I opened my eyes and withdrew from him. Did he really just kiss me the way I thought he did?

I looked into Father's hazel eyes for confirmation that the kiss was a mistake. But instead of apologizing, he leaned in for another kiss. I immediately pulled away.

'What are you doing? This is wrong, we…we share the same blood!' I said in a panic.

'And pain,' he replied as he reached for my hand which I quickly pulled away.

I struggled to understand his intentions, but as he leaned in for another kiss on the lips, his intentions seemed frighteningly clear: he was trying to seduce me.

'Soul meets soul on lovers lips,' he said.

'No, no, no. This can't be. It is strange. Unholy. You're my father,' I said.

He looked at me seriously for a moment. Vulnerability flashed in his eyes.

'What if I were just a man. Just a man who loved you?' he said.

I shook my head, 'No, you cannot be just a man to me.'

'Use your imagination,' he said as he ran his fingers over my scalp, pulling the combs out of my braids.

I thought to myself that it must be the absinthe causing him to behave so horribly. Surely he couldn't really want what he was asking?

'You're so beautiful, you walk in beauty like the night,' he whispered.

'No, no, no,' I said again, and began to crawl away from him.

'We belong together,' he said.

'Not like this,' I said and stood up. 'You must leave.'

'But, I —'

'Go now, please. You're drunk. I'm less drunk. Go, now!'

Sombrely, without saying a word, Father stood up and brushed off his pants. I honestly had no idea what he was thinking. He looked disappointed, angry even. He cracked his jaw, turned and walked to the edge of the balcony. He then climbed down a lattice that led to the ground. I watched as he disappeared into the tunnels in the moonlight.

My head was spinning. I didn't know what to think. I had read once that absinthe can have hallucinogenic properties. Perhaps I hallucinated the kiss? Perhaps he was hallucinating I was a former lover of his? Or my mother? I didn't know. All I could do was fall onto my bed, crawl under the covers and sleep.

The next morning, I awoke to a blue jay singing on my windowsill. Suddenly, my eyes popped open. I jolted straight up as the faint memory of last night began to hit me. I moved too quickly, now my head was pounding. I certainly spent too much time with the Green Fairy who now seemed more like a green devil. My eyes had trouble focusing. What exactly happened last night? I tried to piece the events together. There was the crude tavern. Then the fight. Then the ride back home where I showed Father the Leyden jar. It was then I remembered the kiss. Holding my breath, I looked at the other side of the bed: it was empty, thank goodness. I then heard someone clear their throat. I looked over to the chaise lounge to find Mother.

I rubbed my own forehead, 'Mother, I didn't hear you knock. I thought I locked that door,' I said with a raspy voice.

'I have a key to all the doors. We need to discuss a matter.'

'I need my tea first.'

'I know who you brought to your bedchamber last night.'

I bit into my tongue. Did Mother really know or was she just fishing for information? Then Mother held up a ruffled man's jacket, the one Father was wearing before he lent it to me. I felt my stomach churn. I did everything I could to keep from vomiting.

'I knew Babbage didn't desire you for your brain,' said Mother and she walked out of my room.

Breathe, I told myself, breathe. I was finally able to inhale. At least Mother didn't know about Father, but thinking I'd been inappropriate with Babbage was equally as terrible. This could jeopardize everything. What to do, what to do? I panicked.

24

With Mother downstairs thinking I'd committed an infidelity, I decided to take a very long bath to try and cure my spinning head and intense nausea – after a glance in the mirror I realised I was more green than the Green Fairy herself. At one point, I even knelt over my chamber pot, trying to force myself to vomit, but it was no use. I simply felt like I was in hell. Once I had dressed, it was lunchtime. I carefully made my way down the staircase, gripping the wooden railing the entire time, then marched into the dining room. It was Sunday and William would be returning Monday morning.

Mother ate her savoury fish stew while I just stared at my bowl.

'At least eat some bread.'

'It's not what you think, Mother. Babbage is like a father to me,' I said.

'It's not your fault. You've been preyed upon. The same way Lord Byron preyed upon me. It is this very thing from which I've been trying to protect you your entire life,' said Mother matter-of-factly.

I thought about Father. A sadness washed over me, worse than the nausea.

'What was it about Father that you loved, if ever so briefly?' I asked.

Mother looked at me, rubbed the crook of her arm. She

closed her eyes.

'In him, I saw an opportunity,' said Mother.

'For freedom?' I asked.

She opened her eyes, 'For redemption,' she said, 'I was going to rescue him from his depravity. Such a fool I was. At least I was able to save you.'

Tears began to well in my eyes. Could it be possible Mother was right all these years? That Lord Byron was in fact a poison and a debauched person? He was called, 'mad, bad and dangerous to know' after all. Oh God, I thought, could I have really been this blind? I was desperate to know my father, so desperate perhaps that I failed to see any of his shortcomings despite having been warned my entire life. But I still wanted to believe Lord Byron's intentions with me were pure. I am his *daughter*.

'Come,' said Mother, 'I want to show you something. It's time.'

I followed her up to the attic. I had not been in this part of the house before. It was much bigger than I anticipated. Mother wasn't sure where anything was, she simply knew this was where my less important belongings were stored. Amongst the items was a trunk full of my childhood toys, a small green trunk and an unopened wooden crate that was labeled 'Export of Greece'.

'Ah, here it is,' said Mother as she dusted off the small green trunk and opened it. I watched mystified as Mother pulled out a scrapbook. 'It's time for you to know your dark and dreadful history.'

She opened the book that was filled with newspaper clippings all related to her divorce. Some read, *Lady Byron Seeks to Divorce Beloved Poet, Lord Byron Denies Rumours of Divorce,* and *What will Happen to Poet's Babe Ada?*

I was stunned, 'There was a headline about me?'

'Several,' said Mother.

I turned the pages of the scrapbook to read more headlines like, *Ada: The Girl Caught in the Middle,* and *Wee Ada Says 'Fare Thee Well' to Poet Father.*

'I had no idea,' I said, flabbergasted.

Mother gave me a stern look and said, 'It gets worse. Lest I forget the rumours of sodomy. But his appetite for Greek love didn't make the papers,' she said.

Father committed sexual congress with another man? But he spoke to me of fancying women. I was terribly perplexed.

I swallowed hard as Mother turned the page to reveal a scandalous headline that read, 'Lord Byron fathers child with mistress!'

'My father had, a…a bastard?' I asked, barely able to get the words out of my mouth.

'A girl born shortly after you,' she said. For the first time, I could feel the pain in Mother's eyes. It was hard to take.

Then came the most shocking headline of all. Nothing could have prepared me for what I was about to read next.

Mother turned another page. The headline read, *'Is "She Who Walks in Beauty" Byron's Own Sister?'* And another, *'Byron Accused of Fathering a Girl with his Sister!'* Below the headline was the same portrait of my aunt Augusta Leigh from Lord Byron's locket. Had Father committed incest with my aunt and created a baby? My body convulsed, as if I might vomit. I tried to take it all in, but it was too dense, too dark. Too frightening. 'Surely, this last one is a lie,' I said.

'Not only is it true, it is the reason why I retained custody of you.'

All the pieces of the puzzle were coming together now.

'Don't you see?' said Mother, 'Lord Byron was a monster, twisting all natural behaviour into vice. He preyed on the weak. His own sister suffered the consequences of his vile depravity,' she said. 'Perhaps now you understand why I couldn't let him near you,' said Mother, as she rested her hand on my shoulder.

My breath quickened. I understood far too well.

That night, I laid in bed, unable to sleep. My breathing was fast and shallow. I sat up then donned my wool robe and slippers.

I went to my study, where I tried to work. I reviewed some of Babbage's illustrations. It was still unclear whether or not Mother was going to tell William what she thought she knew. A man's jacket doesn't confirm an affair and it would be counterintuitive for Mother to stir up unconfirmed problems in her own daughter's marriage. But Mother often acted out of her need to be correct in all matters to prove she was smarter than me. I really hoped Mother would let this matter go and let me off with a warning.

As these thoughts ran through my mind, I found myself clutching the doll Father gave me. When I had picked it up, or how I came to be holding it so tightly, I didn't know. But as soon as I noticed the raggedy thing in my hand that once seemed so precious to me, I threw it at the wall. It hit with a tiny thud then slid to the ground, like a dead bird that flew headfirst into a window – never seeing its own death coming right before its tiny eyes.

I turned my attention to some papers titled 'Menabrea's Notes on the Analytical Engine.' Babbage had asked me to translate them from French into English, so more people would be able to read them. But I didn't want to just convert them from one language to another; I wanted to really impress upon the scientific community how important, how revolutionary this thinking machine would be. For all that was good and holy, I wanted the Analytical Engine to be constructed.

How was I going to accomplish this? I only knew of one way to find an answer. I had to imagine it. I rested my head onto my desk and closed my eyes, drifting into the realm of sensations that cannot be experienced through sight, hearing or other senses.

Here, inside my own, personal domain, my mind filled with colourful images of flying machines. Some were wild and bat-like; others were streamlined, like a long narrow boat with wings studded with brass bolts. Some didn't have wings at all, instead they were circular and could hover above the Earth, propelled by a powerful wind. My day-dreaming mind dipped and twirled with each imagined flying machine, soaring on wings of imagination ever deeper into that curious place where my mind was free to explore the deepest of mysteries.

The flying machines gave way to images of steam trains, big and hulky, churning out clouds of sinewy steam as I rode my mental currents ever deeper. The engine's steam stretched out, uncoiling like a snake or a never-ending ribbon, and I was reminded of Monsieur Jacquard's weaving loom and the large spools of silk thread that it turned into beautiful patterns like pastoral scenes or family crests. I could see all of these things and more, as my consciousness placed one foot into a dream-state while the other was firmly planted in my study, straddling the place between alertness and sleep. In this space where the impossible can be realised, I saw myself walk over to the imagined loom that was weaving a brocade of deep blues. A crimson spool of thread also fed into the pattern on the fabric. It appeared to be creating numbers and letters that were all jumbled up. A number two, then a number five, then an 'S'. Something was wrong. A few more letters came out, was it trying to spell a word? Yes, a word was emerging. I stepped closer to the fabric, fearful but not knowing why, and reached out to touch the letters with my fingertips: 'I-N-C.' Then out came 'E-S-T.' I put the letters together, my stomach filled with ice. The word was very clear, now: *Incest.* The fabric then burst into yellow flames that licked the word, scorching the 'C' and turning it black. Soon the loom itself was on fire. I could feel the heat from the flames. I had to escape before it consumed me! I awoke from my dream-state, startled.

I whispered the word 'incest' aloud then covered my mouth with my hands. I had been trying to answer a scientific question, but my mind was consumed with Father and that terrible, filthy word. I thought of the line Father had written in Childe Harold, 'And spoil'd her goodly lands to gild his waste.' Did he spoil his own sister's 'goodly lands' to 'gild his waste'? Could he really have made a baby with my aunt Augusta? Is this why I was named Augusta Ada after her? Chills ran down my spine. Technically, Augusta was a 'half' sister to Lord Byron, since they had different mothers. But still, the blood! They shared the same blood! I wondered if Augusta and Lord Byron's baby girl had any deformities like his clubfoot. Then, a thought slowly crept into my brain the way in which a venomous spider creeps toward a butterfly caught in its web: did Lord Byron want to make a baby with ME?

These thoughts were too intense to control, too heavy to hold. I was so thoroughly disgusted, I felt as if I were suffocating.

I sincerely thought I might go mad. Before I knew what was happening, I had jumped up from my desk, ran through the kitchen, and exited the house out the back door.

The cold night air brought a welcome slap to my flushed cheeks. I looked up at the sky, it was a moonless night, but the stars were bright above. I wondered if the stars knew what was in our hearts. If they were looking down on me in my agonized state with pity or contempt. Then I shook myself – the stars were just gassy giant balls of light. They didn't know anything.

The cold night air stung my nose and ears, but I needed it to breathe. I sucked the frigid, damp oxygen into my lungs before releasing it back out through my nostrils. I fell to my knees and began to hit the dirt with my hands. I hit it harder and harder until my hands ached. Finally, I just crouched over onto my forearms and into a puddle of tears. The tears burned my frosty face. I felt fire and ice at the same time. It was such a strange sensation, it took me out of my misery for just a brief moment. I tasted the saltiness of my tears on my lips and remembered I was alive – like fire.

A thought flashed in my mind. I could survive this betrayal. Yes, Father had a monster in his soul, but I didn't need to be destroyed by it. I could release the beast from my 'goodly' land and he would be forced to 'gild his waste' elsewhere. Yes, that is what I would do – release him from my life. But could I release him from my soul?

25

The next day, William returned from his trip. I was never so delighted to see him.

'I'm so very happy to see you, my love,' I said as I embraced him and kissed his cheek and lips. William seemed surprised by my display of affection.

'Perhaps I should go away more often,' he said.

'Please, don't leave me, ever again,' I said as I squeezed him tightly. In his arms, I felt safe.

Mother caught my eye mid-hug and gave me a nearly imperceptible nod as if to say, 'All is good, I won't tell.' But of course Mother could turn on a two-pence, and I knew I'd best not give her any reason to betray me.

'Well, I do come with news,' said William.

'Something exciting?' I asked.

'Yes, in fact. Very exciting. How would you like to be a countess?' he asked.

I could not believe my ears. A title?

Mother grinned. There's no way she would tell William about finding Father's jacket in my bedroom now.

William pulled a rolled-up letter on parchment paper with an official-looking wax seal from his jacket.

'Go ahead, open it,' he said.

I took the parchment from him and cracked open the wax. Carefully, I unrolled the letter to discover William and I were to be the proclaimed Earl and Countess of Lovelace.

'Lovelace,' I said out loud, 'I shall be Ada, Countess of Lovelace?'

'Indeed,' said William.

'Isn't the Earldom of Lovelace an extinct title?' asked Mother.

'Not anymore.' he said.

The idea of a new identity fascinated me, especially in light of all I learned about Father recently. This would be a new beginning, a reason to put my dark past behind me. At least, I hoped I could.

That night, dinner was a joy, and William doted on me as he always had. I made special efforts to listen to all that he had to say, and I didn't once mention the Analytical Engine. I vowed to be a better wife to him, and I knew in my heart that I had to say goodbye to Father forever.

Before bed, I brushed out my long, brown curls with a silver hairbrush. I needed to see Father one last time so that I could explain why I had to end our relationship. After William fell asleep, I wrote a letter to Father, requesting he meet me after I returned from attending to my husband's business in London. The business had to do with the paperwork regarding the change in our new titles, but I didn't feel it necessary to inform Lord Byron of this, nor did I mention the purpose of our meeting. I also enclosed ten pounds, considering he was my father, after all, and I didn't want him starving to death. Though I felt a tinge of sadness, I also felt relief. I knew ending our relationship in person would be the honourable thing to do. Oh, how I hated knowing Mother was right.

A week later, William, Mother and I left for London. After we tended to the business of adding our titles, the Darwins were to throw a party in honour of the Earl and Countess of Lovelace (my heart still lept every time I remembered that was us). I, however, wasn't looking forward to the party. My impending discussion with Father weighed heavily on me and I was beginning to second-guess my judgement. Also disturbing was the new nightmare I had the night before we left.

In my tormented dream, Father and I were on a train. It was night, and we were eating cakes. I noticed the train was speeding across the countryside at an unusually fast pace. At first, I did not feel alarmed, but then the train seemed to become unstable on its tracks and the ride became particularly bumpy. With each curve in the tracks, the train leaned impossibly close to the ground, so close in fact, I noticed that if I were to stick my arm out the window, I would be able to touch the ground.

While none of the other first class passengers seemed to be disturbed by the train's strange ride, I told Father I thought it best to check with the engineer, just to make sure the train was working properly. When Father and I reached the head of the train, I was horrified to find there was no engineer. The train was driving by itself and clearly out of control.

Immediately, I tried to slow the train, but I had no understanding of its braking instruments or how they worked. Soon, I could see a great granite mountain up ahead. Panic set in, for I knew if I couldn't stop the train before reaching the mountain, the train would crash and all aboard would face a grisly death.

When I begged Father to help me stop the train, he looked at me with a gentle pity and said, 'The flower in ripened bloom unmatched, must all the earliest prey; though by no hand untimely snatched, the leaves must drop away.'

With that, he reached into his jacket pocket, withdrew his pearl-handled pistol and put the barrel into his mouth. That's when I awoke, startled, sweaty and fearful.

Not only was he poisoning my life, he was now haunting my dreams. I knew I had no one to blame but myself. This made me feel twisted up inside, for I did love him, perhaps too much for my own good. I also knew I needed to protect my marriage and, well, Lord Byron was a man who couldn't be trusted. Any scandal he caused would surely ruin any chance the Analytical Engine had of getting funded or built. I didn't understand this before, only now was I realizing the devastating effect that Lord Byron could have on my life. When I was a girl, there was no Earl whose reputation I needed to protect, and there was no wild inventor with an idea for a machine to change the world. Now, as a young wife and business partner, things had become much more complicated.

At other times, I felt incredibly guilty about my decision to cut ties with Lord Byron. He was my father and I did feel a duty to him. He had no other family or financial resources from which to draw. I was all he had in the world and I was about to reject him entirely, just as my own mother did twenty years prior. I felt as if I had become just like Mother and it was killing my spirit.

Lost in these ominous thoughts, I dressed for the party at the Darwin home.

26

On a very chilly night, the Darwins greeted us warmly. Both Mother and I wore gowns made of a hunter-green velvet, trimmed with ermine, nearly making us twins. Mother had both dresses made; mine was a more youthful cut, with a medium neckline and three-quarter length sleeves, while Mother's dress encompassed her usual severe neckline and full-length sleeves. It never occurred to me that Mother would wear her green dress to the same event where I would wear mine, so I was much surprised when I noticed Mother wearing it as she stepped into the carriage that would take us to the party. It was like looking into a mirror, only the reflection was twenty-five years into the future.

To me, it felt like some odd manipulation or way for her to steal attention and, once again, I felt the need to distance myself from her.

The Darwins lived in a London flat they called Macaw Cottage due to its brightly coloured wallpaper and furniture. It had tangerine walls and chase lounges the colour of limes – it was like living inside a fruit bowl. Even the pianoforte had been painted pink as a cherry blossom.

In addition to the tropical themed décor, the Darwins added a few touches of their own. Emma Darwin was the granddaughter of Josiah Wedgwood, a progressive-thinking man who made his fortune in pottery. I eyed a lovely cornflower-blue

Jasperware urn, made in the Greek style that was adorned with a sculpture of Pegasus. The beautiful horse, with its powerful wings spread wide, looked as if it were about to jump off the urn and fly to some far-off world. The urn sat on the tangerine-coloured mantle over the fireplace.

Of course, Charles' taste in knickknacks was slightly more exotic, given that he was a naturalist and had spent four years sailing around the world on the H.M.S. Beagle. He collected many unusual specimens, including strange, horned beetles (most of which were dead and displayed in glass jars), fossilized sloth teeth, a taxidermied capybara and a very well-preserved white-winged vampire bat. Needless to say, Macaw Cottage was a very unique place.

My inability to physically get away from Mother may have played a role in my decision to drink more champagne than usual that evening. Typically, when at a social event, I might have a glass of wine with dinner and a digestif after, usually a cognac. This was always plenty for me, as I'd then be exhausted and ready to retire to bed. But tonight, I started the party with a festive glass of bubbly champagne. The carbon dioxide bubbles danced on my tongue, exploding as they sailed down my throat. The champagne gave me a warm feeling in my stomach. I quickly moved on to a second glass.

My head felt light, almost like a balloon that was floating on a small gust of wind. I drifted over to the fireplace to get a closer look at the Wedgwood urn on the mantle. I ran my finger across Pegasus' wings. In that moment, I wished wings would sprout from my own shoulders and fly me away from my family troubles.

Mary Somerville had arrived to the party early. She spent

some time chatting with Charles and Emma before finding me alone in the parlor.

'Ada, why are you in here all alone?' she said, 'It's supposed to be your party.'

'Attempting to hide from Medusa. I fear she'll turn me to stone any moment,' I said.

'You must mean your mother,' said Mary, 'I bet she's incredibly proud of you. I know I am.'

Mary was so sweet and supportive. I cherished her.

Then William and Mother entered the parlor. 'Our guests are beginning to arrive,' said William. I nodded and went to him.

As William and I greeted our guests, Mother stood right by my side, commenting on the ladies' hairstyles and satchels.

'Such exquisite beading on your handbag, Lady Thomas,' and, 'What a lovely feathered hat, Madame Dubois,' chirped Mother, before she admonished me under her breath, 'Would it kill you to smile? And stand up straight, you look like you've been stricken with Ricketts.'

I wasn't in a smiling mood, however, and moved to stand on the other side of William. Mother moved with me, however – I wanted to scream. I felt cramped and stifled.

An elderly man who walked with the assistance of an ivory cane, Mr. Felbucket, eyed Mother and I, then exclaimed, 'What lovely dresses! I had no idea the Countess had a sister.'

Mother's face lit up. She knew it was flattery, of course, but I knew it was the kind of attention she had been secretly hoping for.

'Mr. Felbucket, I fear it may be time to acquire some specs, for I'm not the Countess' sister. I am her mother,' she said.

'Let met assure you, Lady Byron, no spectacles could improve my view tonight. From where I stand, you both look simply lovely,' he said and kissed her hand. I tried to smile and be polite, but somehow, William could read the annoyance on my face.

'Everything alright, Birdie?' he asked.

I nodded with a weak smile.

The party had a guest list of forty-four people, about thirty or so had arrived in the first half hour. Of course, the plucky Charles Dickens was there, along with several other people I had met at Babbage's soirees.

Emma Darwin approached me. She had a single dimple on her left cheek that appeared when she smiled. There was an earthiness to Emma, and a warmth, too. I got the feeling that Emma would prefer to be barefoot in a garden outdoors, rather than be all gussied up. But if Emma was anything, it was flexible and seemed able to mould herself to whatever the circumstances.

'It's nearly half past the hour. Why don't you and William go into the parlor and mingle with your guests. I'll greet the latecomers,' said Emma.

I looked to William. He nodded and took my arm. Mother responded by quickly taking William's free arm. He walked both of us into the parlor.

It was difficult not to notice the Darwins' many scientific treasures, as they were displayed in every nook and cranny of the parlor. Mother's eye quickly focused on a jar of leeches that rested on a tangerine-coloured shelf.

Charles Dickens was, per usual, the life of the party. He had discovered a live rhinoceros beetle in a glass box that Darwin had been using in his studies. The shiny black creature was the size of Dickens' palm and had what appeared to be large pincers coming out of its head. Every time the scarab crawled to one side, Dickens would rotate the box, again causing the beetle to continue to crawl across the glass wall.

I empathized with the ugly bug. I, too, felt stuck in a box, doomed to crawl in an endless loop, scrutinized by those around me.

Dickens then cleared his throat and announced to the room, 'They say that after time, owners and their pets begin to look alike.' He held up the beetle next to Darwin's face and continued, 'Here is proof!'

Darwin scoffed at his friend, used to being the butt of Dickens' jokes by now. But the guests had a hearty laugh. William turned to share his laugh with me, but I wasn't laughing.

'Ada,' said William, 'Did you hear the joke?'

'Yes, clever,' I said flatly.

'You could try it have fun,' he said. Then his voice lowered. 'You're in quite a mood. Is it your monthly?' he asked.

I grew offended and whispered, 'Do not speak to me in public about such things.'

'What things?' Mother asked, desperately wanting to be part of the conversation. Instead of answering, I went to get another glass of champagne. Everyone telling me how to behave, how to stand, how to feel was too much.

William went to speak with Charles Dickens, who was now the center of attention.

That's when Babbage entered the party with a woman I didn't recognise. The woman had very dark brown hair that had been done up in braids that were pinned underneath a black hat with a short, black, bobbinet-tulle veil that covered her eyes. Her dress was black silk, with tight sleeves that had black ruffles at the wrists. She was perhaps thirty-two or thirty-three. Her cocoa-coloured eyes were large and owl-like, dwarfing her tiny nose.

I was surprised that Babb had brought a lady since I had never heard him speak of courting anyone. He was a widower who missed his wife dearly, and I assumed he would stay that way.

I returned to Mother once I saw Mary speaking with her, the situation seemed safe enough. As Mother complimented Mary's dress, I felt a tap on my shoulder.

'There you are, my dear Countess. Have you met Miss Poe?' said Babb.

I nodded politely to the woman who was dressed all in black, wondering if she was in mourning.

Miss Poe eagerly clasped her gloved hands around my right hand, saying, 'How do you do?' with an American accent.

'Miss Poe's father is a poet in America,' Babb added, 'I bet you two have much in common.'

'I'm certain of it,' said Miss Poe. 'I only want to know, was your father as much of a lunatic as mine?' Miss Poe asked with a grin.

By lunatic I believe she meant mad. Unfortunately, my father's madness wasn't something I could easily discuss with a stranger, or anyone really. I wondered if all Americans were this forward. I stood silent, trying to figure out what to say to her as my emotions got the best of me.

Most embarrassingly, tears welled in my eyes. I knew Miss Poe meant nothing by her question, as impolite as it was, she was merely looking for a way to start a conversation, but the champagne had brought my hurt and sadness to the surface. Not sure how to handle myself, I excused myself and walked away.

'Forgive the Countess, she's not feeling well. I'll see to her,' said Mary.

'I'll go,' said Mother.

Babbage interrupted, saying, 'Please, let me,' and he followed me down the hallway.

As I wiped tears from my eyes, Babb did his best to comfort me.

'Whatever is the matter, my dear?'

'Forgive me, I'm not myself tonight. Miss Poe seems lovely. I just need a moment alone.'

He put his hand on my shoulder. That's when I looked up to see Mother speaking to a concerned William, who began to head toward us. He did not look happy as he approached us.

'May I have a word in private with my wife?'

Babb nodded and went back to Miss Poe.

'Your mother told me you saw Babb enter the party with that woman and you burst into tears. What am I to make of that?' said William in a sharp tone.

'It's nothing, really. I'm just feeling emotional tonight. I apologise.'

'Are you jealous he's with that woman?'

'Absolutely not, William. My tears had nothing to do with either of them.'

'Then what has you so upset?'

'May we please have this conversation another--'

That's when Emma Darwin announced dinner was to be served.

'Very well,' said William, and we went to the dining room.

Once all the guests were seated, the first course of julienne vegetable soup was ladled into Wedgwood bowls and served. The second course was red mullet. The entrée was a choice of mutton cutlets or whitebait fritters. The third course would consist of mayonnaise of chicken, green peas and strawberries. Madeira Wine was also served.

The joviality of most of the guests subdued a bit as they dined, each was hungry and eager to eat. As usual, Mother sat next to me on my left. Every time her fork and knife clanked on her plate, I cringed. William sat across from me and Babbage and Miss Poe sat to my right.

Just as I finished my glass of champagne, a servant poured me another. Mother took the glass from my place setting and set it just out of my reach. I moved it back and defiantly took another sip.

Having seen the interaction, Mary tried to fill the awkward moment.

'How is the Analytical Engine developing?'

'Ada and I are making quite a bit of progress. But we have yet to find a patron,' said Babbage as he looked sullenly to Miss Poe. She patted his hand to comfort him.

'Seems like a great many people would be interested in a machine that can think,' said Miss Poe.

'That's precisely the problem. They say is it un-Christian,' I said.

Miss Poe removed her hand from Babbage's. 'Is it?' she asked.

'Of course not,' said Babbage.

Mother could no longer hold her tongue. 'A machine cannot think any more than an animal,' she said.

'Surprisingly,' said Charles Darwin, 'there is much debate as of late on the mental abilities of some animals. Chimpanzees, for example, seem to exhibit some emotions similar to humans.' Mother shot him a sharp look.

'We are made in His holy image and you men of science seem eager to mock that image,' said Mother.

I knew I should let the whole business go, but I was angry

over the ridiculous matching dresses and her controlling behaviour.

'What I mock is the notion that God would give us a great intellect and not intend for us to make full use of it,' I said.

Before Mother could reply, Mary spoke.

'I must agree,' said Mary, 'The almighty Lord gave us powers of perception and the ability to process complicated thoughts. It is our duty to explore the universe he created for us.' Her tone was gentle and optimistic. But Mother wasn't having it. If there was one thing she loved above all else, it was being right.

'Well, I believe there is a line in which God has never intended man to cross. It seems this machine crosses that line.'

Suddenly, everyone spoke at once. Each guest had a differing opinion and soon it was clear no consensus could be reached. I closed my eyes as my head swam, the cacophony overwhelming my senses. I simply knew tonight's controversy would not bode well for me.

Fortunately, it was soon time for the entertainment. A servant rang a bell and requested the guests exit the dining room and stroll into the parlor. A very special performance was about to begin.

A tribesman from the Amazonian tribe called the Zo'e began to beat a drum. His lip had been cut to accommodate a long, narrow disk made from the bone of a spider monkey, giving his lower lip the illusion that it was quite large. His head was decorated with a crown of vulture feathers and his skin had been rubbed with a red paste. He wore nothing else but a pair of britches.

As the tribesman drummed, Emma sat at her pianoforte and played music to compliment the drumming.

Two Zo'e tribeswomen, dressed in simple shifts that barely covered their private parts, danced to the music. They did rhythmic gyrations that involved shaking their shoulders and hips in unison, and I found myself leaning forward in my seat, mesmerized by the dance. To the average person, this exhibit of physical expression could seem incredibly shocking. Offensive, even. In fact, a few women in the audience excused themselves out of propriety. Mother did not seem to enjoy the performance, but she at least endured it. On the other hand, because many of the guests were members of the scientific community, most of the audience watched in fascination. The rituals of the Zo'e tribe had been seen only by a handful of Europeans and I was terribly excited to be one of them.

I imagined watching these tribesmen dance to be the closest thing to travelling back in time because this ritual could have been created centuries ago. My heart began to lift as thoughts of Father melted away, chased out by the spectacle before me. And the champagne.

Then the two Zo'e female dancers began doing a hop-step, hopping on one leg three times before switching to the other. The coordination required to accomplish such a feat was impressive. Then, they looked at the audience and stretched out their arms. The women motioned for the audience to join them, and I so longed to kick free of my corset and follow their lead. Of course no one, not even the daughter of Lord Byron, dared accept their offer.

Just then, however, I saw Dickens lean over to Charles Darwin and say, 'I should like to accompany you on your next expedition to South America.'

Much to my surprise, William weighed in, 'You've collected

some very fine specimens, indeed.' He was clearly referring to the nearly naked women.

The men laughed. I took offence to their comments, finding them disrespectful to women. I turned to Mary for her reaction.

She just shook her head and whispered, 'Now you know the real reason women are kept out of the sciences.'

'Not to worry,' I replied, 'I'll make my way in.'

I then stood up and, shedding all good sense, headed toward the performance area to answer the Zo'e tribeswomen's call to join in the ritualistic dance. Mother's eyes filled with horror when she saw me. She scuttled her way over to William.

I watched as she pleaded with him, but there was little he could do.

The tribal women welcomed me, rubbing some of their red pigment on my face and neck. It felt warm and earthy on my skin. They tried to show me how to do the moves, which were a lot different than the dance steps Frau Schmidt taught me years ago. My corset constricted a lot of my movement, but the fact that I was trying to hop and shake my hips garnered applause from the guests. I could feel my heart beating faster and faster as my breath quickened.

Excited by the crowd, the drummer sped up his beat, Emma played the pianoforte faster and the dancers, myself included, began hopping and dancing in a frenzy.

Just then, Mary stood up in defiance and headed to the performance area. The crowd cheered when she joined me and the Zo'e women. Though Mary was a bit stiffer than me in her movements, she seemed to be enjoying herself. We exchanged a wicked glance, as if we were both misbehaved children. She laughed as did I. I was finally having a sensation, the thing

Father always talked about.

Then Charles Dickens joined us in the dance, eliciting all sorts of hoots and cheers from the audience, and it wasn't long before Babbage and Miss Poe were on their feet as well. The two did their best with the exotic movements, but looked so silly that they couldn't help but laugh. After a minute, some of the women took off their uncomfortable, toe-pinching pointy shoes and hopped and shimmied in their stockinged-feet. I was thrilled to see the ten or so other party-guests join us in dance.

William watched silently as I participated in this terribly bohemian and wild act of revelry. Many of the people dancing were perspiring! I was having fun, but from the look on my husband's face, he clearly was not. I knew that sour expression of his. I then watched him exit out of the party. Worried I had gone too far, I stopped dancing and ran after him. Mary called after me, 'Ada?' but I ignored her.

I made my way outside of Macaw Cottage, the cold air stinging my hot face. I saw William heading to the carriage and ran up to him.

'Where are you going?' I asked, though I knew he was looking for his own escape.

'I refuse to let you continue to openly disrespect me,' he said angrily.

'I was having a sensation, you should try it some time,' I retorted.

'And you should try showing me some respect. That was no way for a Countess to behave,' he said as he climbed into the carriage, stomping on the steps.

'William!' I called out to him, 'We must at least say goodbye to the Darwins.'

Then Mother stepped up behind me and said, 'I thanked our hosts and told them William had a fever coming on. Now, get in the carriage before all of bloody London thinks you're mad.'

I reluctantly climbed into the carriage, in my now sweat-soaked green dress that had a layer of red dust over it from the body paint. The other green dress followed right behind me. The ride home was long and silent. Little did I know, the worst part of the night was yet to come.

27

We returned to Ashley Combe that night, bringing a rainstorm with us. Tears flooded out of my eyes, some for William's harsh words, some for Mother's harsh words, and some for just not understanding how to make my way in the world. No matter how hard I searched for it, the path to pleasing others while also pleasing myself didn't seem to exist. I prayed it were a road yet to be constructed. In the meantime, I felt as if I were stranded in a ditch.

Once inside the house, I was desperate to take refuge in the solace of my study, but before I could turn down the hallway, William took my arm.

'Go to bed. I don't want you in there,' he said.

'What are you afraid I'm going to do? Start dancing?' I shouted with irreverence.

'That room and everything in it feeds your disobedience. You sit in there and pay no mind to the world around you.'

'I am to obey you now, like a dog?'

'You are my wife. You must learn your place.'

'Is that a place where I exist only as a prop to bolster your image? To drip off your arm – smiling every moment – and be paraded around for other men to covet?'

'Don't be a child. I've never treated you that way and you know it. I've given you everything you've asked for and you've taken me for granted. It's time for you to be restrained.'

'But, William,' I said as he walked to the pantry. There, he found where the servants kept a few tools. He picked up a hammer and nails then dumped some vegetables out of a wooden crate. He stomped the crate to break it apart and gathered the wooden slats. I continued to argue with him.

'I saw you looking at those tribal women, jesting with the men about going on Darwin's next expedition to collect specimens.'

'They were jokes, Ada. That is the way all men speak to each other.'

'Yes, and it is hurtful. Disrespectful.'

'So that's your excuse for making a damned fool out of me tonight? You had to get drunk like a commoner then jump up and behave like some savage because I made a joke?'

'What I did had nothing to do with you.'

'Everything you do, speak or think involves me, whether you like it or not.'

William walked toward my study with the hammer and boards.

'What are you doing?' I asked in a panic.

William didn't answer me, he instead took the boards and began nailing them over the door of the study.

'You can't!'

'Watch me.'

Tears began to flow again, soaking my face.

'Please, William. Please don't take away the one thing that is keeping me alive.'

'The one thing. Do I matter so little to you?' Before I could explain myself, he said, 'Don't answer.'

He continued to board up the study.

I ran past him, then past Mother, who had been watching the

entire argument, and ran up the stairs to my room. I slammed the door for extra effect.

Once inside my room, I heard a voice say, 'You'll wake the dead.'

It was Lord Byron.

My heart stopped. I turned to see Father sitting in a chair with his feet up on the ottoman. Not the person I wanted to see.

'How dare he board up your study. You need your work like you need air.'

'Father, you can't be here. I'm in so much trouble as it is. If he discovers you—'

There was a knock at my bedroom door.

'I have some warm milk for you,' called Mother.

On edge, I yelled toward the door, 'Go away!'

'You are behaving most impetuously. I want a doctor to bleed you.'

I motioned to Father to hide as I yelled to Mother, 'Leave me alone.'

Mother began to open the door, but I threw myself at it, shutting it. I locked the lock then remembered she had a key. I pushed an oak chest in front to the door.

'I will pray for your soul,' said Mother and walked off.

Still a bit lightheaded from the champagne, I turned my attentions back to Father. I spoke in a low, pointed whisper.

'You must leave at once.'

'You said you wanted to speak with me.'

'My night has been a disaster.'

'Let me comfort you, Pippin.'

He stood, attempting to embrace me, but I resisted.

'What is it, dear girl? Are you afraid of a father's hug?'

I felt my heart leap into my throat. This was the moment

I was going to have to tell him what I discovered about the divorce. I was terrified to disappoint him, but knew I mustn't wait another second, or I'd I lose my courage.

'Mother has told me the details of your divorce. She has told me about my half-sister. That you and your own sister…' I couldn't speak the final words, they were too gruesome. I wondered for a moment how I became part of this strange and dark tale. The pain of it was too intense; merely breathing hurt.

A rage began to race through Lord Byron's body. His green and brown eyes got big and red. A vein on his forehead began to pulsate. I had never seen this side of him before. It frightened me. He spoke slowly, with great intensity.

'Your mother created that entire scandal.'

'For what ungodly purpose?'

'Don't be obtuse. She wanted to ruin my reputation and gain sole custody of you. She painted me as a monster in every newspaper. She enjoyed it like a sport. Has she told you about how she employed Catherine Lamb in her scheme?'

I shook my head, no.

'Catherine's an obsessive woman who enjoyed my bedchamber behind her husband's back and couldn't understand why I didn't want to spend every waking moment playing her fool. Your mother recruited Catherine to create falsehoods and scandal, to ensure the court would have her sympathy.'

So many emotions swirled through my mind, I was beginning to feel seasick.

'I don't know what to believe. Regardless, what happened between us the other night, the way you kissed me, it was wrong.'

Father's demeanour softened. Whatever kind of twisted love he felt for me, he seemed to feel it quite strongly.

'Wrong in the mind, but right in my heart.'

'It cannot happen again,' I implored.

'You are the keeper of my soul. I will obey your rules,' he said as he took my hand. I quickly pulled it away.

'I have but one request, child. One simple thing I need from my daughter.'

I was terrified to hear what he wanted. Then he spoke.

'Help return my property to me. Provide me the deed to Newstead Abbey.'

I squirmed inside my own body. In the back of my mind, I had thought of selling the property in hopes of funding the Analytical Engine if no other funding source materialized. Father's request changed everything. Of course he wanted it. This must why he contacted me in the first place. I felt like a fool for not seeing this coming.

'We could live there together,' he said as a softness returned to his eyes, 'You could do as you pleased. Numbers, machines, horses. You could live the life you've dreamed of. With me.'

'You know I cannot.'

'You can, it's your mother and husband who have led you to believe you must serve them. A Byron serves herself first.'

'Even if I wanted to return the property to you, I don't see how.'

'You will sort it out.'

'There isn't any—'

'You will sort it out or I will expose you,' he said as he held my chin in his hand, 'Don't forget, I own your dark secret.'

Lord Byron stuck out his tongue and licked the side of my face, from my chin to my forehead. It sent shivers up my spine.

'Good night, daughter,' and he leaned in for a kiss, but I

recoiled as if a viper was trying to attack. He laughed then walked out onto the veranda, climbed down the trellis and escaped into the tunnels.

I dropped onto my bed, grabbed a pillow and began to beat it fiercely with my fists. He had me right where he wanted me.

28

The sun finally rose to peek through the last of the rain clouds that had nearly drowned half of England, and yet it was still quite dark and stormy inside Ashley Combe.

I refused to come out of my bedchamber for a fortnight. William, who was obviously still quite angry with me, didn't attempt to coax me out of my self-imposed exile. I was furious with him for boarding up my study, but the fact that he hadn't tried to get me to come out of my bedchamber worried me as well. What on earth had he and Mother been up to this past week that no one had seen fit to try and make amends with me?

The following Monday, William would get up at dawn to take a carriage three towns over where he would survey some properties for his oldest architectural client. He would be away for four days. I waited for Monday, convinced William would at least try and reconcile with me before he left, but instead of a tearful reunion before his departure, I heard only the clatter of horses as his carriage took him away.

With him out of the house, I finally managed to leave my room and go about my day, but I was struggling to hold onto a sense of myself. A darkness had begun to creep into my heart — my life's purpose was fading away. Father had betrayed me with his depravity. My husband had boarded-up my study. And Babb and I struggled to find support for our machine. My life suddenly seemed in shambles at the hand of all these men, and it felt like an elephant was sitting on my chest. I could barely breathe at the injustice of it all. I decided to take a walk outside to get some fresh air.

Yes, the breeze on my face helped. A brisk walk on the grounds and through the trees after taking in the view of the Bristol Channel led me to discover a striped caterpillar on the shrubbery. I gently picked up the creature and carried it back into the house and upstairs to my room. I placed it into a jar I had on my dresser and put a stick and some leaves inside.

Caterpillars are capable of great transformation and highly inspirational to scientists and poets alike. Perhaps, I thought, if such a simple creature could completely redesign its own biology and purpose in life, shouldn't I be able to do the same? I knew I had the power inside me. What I needed was the time and space to transform. Could I simply will it to happen? Or were there greater forces at work? My body and life had changed before when I became a woman, certainly it could change again.

I began to obsess on this change. It was like a fever inhabiting my head, controlling my thoughts and actions. I closed my eyes and engaged my imagination. I saw numbers, like fairies, flitting about, often singing but sometimes screaming. The numbers seemed to represent all the ideas and feelings inside me, trying to form into some type of elegant equation – to make sense, but sadly, they did not. At least not yet.

Mathematics, I thought, was the study of the unseen relationships between all that existed, like a secret language of the universe. But to be fluent in that language, I must be able to feel, to seize even, the mystery of all that existed in my unconscious mind. On the gossamer wings of my imagination, I hoped to soar into my new self. Like Pandora's box, I decided I would unleash my creative angels – and demons – and let them carry me into metamorphoses. For I knew if I did not change, I would die.

I would use my study as my cocoon. Instantly, I knew I must rip down the boards William put up and nestle inside where I would wait for the transformation to take place.

Once Mother and the servants went to bed, I found the hammer William used to put up the boards. I went to my study and began to rip the boards off the walls, one by one, using the claw-side of the hammer. The sound of the nails and wood being torn out of the wall sounded like bone and cartilage breaking.

Finally, I made my way into the study. I was alone at last.

I did not sleep that night. By morning, my stringy hair was wrapped into a loose bun that was tied around a pencil. Red pimples were forming on my forehead, but I didn't care. I was determined to write a piece of work that explained in detail how the Analytical Engine worked and why the world needed this machine. Why the future of the world depended on this machine. Why the only hope for our future was this machine.

I looked at the piece of paper labeled 'Monsieur Menabrea's Notes on the Analytical Engine.' I then refocused my eyes on another, larger stack of papers that was titled, 'Notes from the translator, Augusta Ada Lovelace.' It was on this stack I continued to write.

Here is a portion of what I wrote:

Those who view mathematical science not merely as a vast body of abstract and immutable truths, whose intrinsic beauty, symmetry and logical completeness, entitle them to a prominent place in the interest of all profound and logical minds, but as possessing a yet deeper interest for the human race, when it is remembered that this science constitutes the language through which alone we can adequately express the great facts of the natural world.

The distinctive characteristic of the Analytical Engine, and that which has rendered it possible to endow mechanism with such extensive faculties as bid fair to make this engine the executive right-hand of abstract algebra, is the introduction of the principle which Jacquard devised for regulating, by means of punched cards, the most complicated patterns in the fabrication of brocaded stuffs.

The bounds of arithmetic were however out-stepped the moment the idea of applying the cards had occurred; and the Analytical Engine does not occupy common ground with mere 'calculating machines.' It holds a position wholly its own; and the considerations it suggests are most interesting in their nature. In enabling mechanism to combine together general symbols, in successions of unlimited variety and extent, a uniting link is established between the operations of matter and the abstract mental processes of the most abstract branch of mathematical science.

We may say most aptly, that the Analytical Engine weaves algebraical patterns just as the Jacquard-loom weaves flowers and leaves. Those who think mathematical truth is the key to understanding the Creator's works, will regard this machine as the translation of His principles into explicit, practical forms.

In this machine, a new, vast, and powerful language is developed for the future use of analysis. A language to wield its truths for the purposes of exposing mankind to a new and wondrous future.

For the honour of our country's reputation in the future pages of history, we hope these causes will not lead to the completion of a computing machine by some other nation or government. This could only be a matter of great regret.

And from there I continued to write in a fervor. I reached a new state of mind in which I was entirely focused on the words I was writing. I was amazed to see that I was able to completely block the outside world: Father, the fight with William – it all vanished. The only thing in the world was the Analytical Engine. It was as if the machine itself possessed my mind. It was speaking through me. Would it be powerful enough to transform me?

I wrote and wrote and wrote, smearing ink on the paper and my hand.

It was Mother who first discovered my infraction. She nearly choked at the sight of the boards as they lay on the floor with their sharp, pointed nails still sticking out of them like claws. Mother was utterly shocked. To her, it was as if I tore Jesus off the cross with my bare hands and he was sitting there with me.

'Dear God, what have you done?'

I regarded her in a cool manner. 'There is an awful lot of power in this little body of mine,' I said.

Mother just stared at me, not comprehending my words. 'It's my duty to report this to William.'

I said nothing and continued to write.

'It must be a fever,' said Mother as she reached to feel my forehead, but I swatted her hand away.

'Surely there's a devil in this machine for it has bewitched you. Forget the doctor, I'm sending for a priest.'

'God himself cannot exorcise this machine from my soul. I live only because of it.'

Mother stared at me with a truly frightened expression. This was an extreme she had never seen in me before, but I couldn't take time to explain myself.

'I believe you've gone mad. What are on these vile pages?' said Mother as she grabbed a stack of my writings and tried to read them.

'Give those back!' I raged. We struggled over the notes, some pages ripped. My hair tumbled down onto my shoulders.

Many more pages would have been shredded if Kate had not entered the room just then and interrupted us.

'Countess, forgive me, but you have a visitor,' said Kate, not sure what to make of the scene.

Distracted, Mother's grip on the pages loosened and I was able to take them back. I gathered up all the pages and trotted into the parlor where I found Charles Babbage waiting for me.

Mother followed me and was none too pleased to see Babbage.

'Good afternoon, Mr. Babbage. Please forgive us but Ada is not feeling well,' said Mother.

'On the contrary, I've never felt better,' I said.

'How was Menabrea's paper on the Analytical Engine?' he asked, a little unsure of what was going on between Mother and me. The tension was thick.

'I found it was quite limited in scope,' I said.

Disappointment washed over Babbage's face, I know he so hoped this analysis would be the answer to his prayers. That's when I handed him the ten-page long translation labeled Menabrea's Notes.

'However, I have written some additional instructions on the usage of the machine, as well as many of the possible implications for future uses.'

I handed him a large stack of pages labeled *Notes from the Translator, Augusta Ada Lovelace.*

'I don't understand,' said Babbage, 'If they were so limited, what are these?'

'Where Menabrea lacked in explanation, I simply filled in the gaps,' I said.

He counted the pages, ten, twenty, thirty. He couldn't believe his eyes.

'This is your analysis?' he asked.

'Yes. It includes the suggestion for a new language. One both people and machines may speak.'

Mother nearly fainted.

Babbage flipped through the many pages I wrote. I created numerous equations and diagrams, all to help the reader understand the machine.

'It's so very detailed. Tell me, why didn't you just write an original piece from the start?' he asked.

I considered the question, then confessed, 'I didn't imagine I could.'

'This is very good news my dear, very good news!' he said, 'I'll read them over and take them straight to the publisher. Good work, my girl,' he said as he exited the house.

Without saying two words to Mother, I stood up and returned to my study to finish my transformation.

William returned home the next night. I overheard Mother alerting him immediately to Babbage's visit and the fact that I was again in my study, against his wishes.

William marched into my study, not bothering to knock.

'I need to speak with you.'

'Then speak.'

I looked at him defiantly. I was ready for battle.

'I know about you and Babbage. I've been a damned fool.'

'There is nothing between us, other than this machine.'

'Not according to Kate.'

I looked at him, stunned. What ever could he mean? That's when he held up my gold and ivory bracelet.

'She says you've been bribing her while you stay out late with him. Sometimes all night. He sends you letters written in some diabolical code.'

He threw the bracelet at the wall. The delicate gold clasp broke. That's when I realised Kate had confused Lord Byron with Babbage. I knew I needed to tread very, very carefully.

'It's not true,' I said.

'I confronted Annabella and she confirmed it.'

'Mother has always tried to stir up problems between us, you know that.'

The pain on his face was so great, the burden so heavy on his shoulders, I knew I had to confess my relationship with Father. I could not let him think I had broken my marriage vows.

'I do have a confession to make.' I had to be very careful, a lot was at risk, but I could lie no more. 'I have been meeting a man. But the man I've been meeting in secret isn't Babbage,' I said, harboring a great deal of shame.

His wounded, slate-blue eyes looked up at me.

'Annabella told me he was just here yesterday,' he said.

'Yes, Babbage was. But the man I've seen at night, for which I gave Kate the bracelet to keep quiet, is actually my father. I have been meeting Lord Byron in secret,' I said.

William just looked at me in disgust and shook his head.

'Lord Byron is dead!' he shouted, appalled at what he thought was a ridiculous lie. I had to convince him of the truth – my marriage depended on it.

'It's what he wants the world to think, you see he faked his own death because—' but William wasn't having any of it. I was finally telling him the truth but he didn't believe me. I panicked, having no idea how to fix this.

My husband looked like he was some kind of injured animal. His voice got very soft and shaky.

'What does he give you that I…that I don't? A bloody machine?'

'You must believe me, I don't love Babbage.'

'Of course not. You only love yourself.'

That's when I ripped an illustration of the Analytical Engine off the wall and put it before his face.

'What I love is the future. I dream it, feel it on my flesh, taste it in my mouth. Scratch me…' I dug my nails into my own forearm and drew blood. 'I bleed the future out of my veins.'

'You think you know the future?' His hurt spiraled into a fit of rage. William ripped all my illustrations off the walls and screamed, 'You are nothing but a spoiled brat!'

Just then, he swiped all my notes and books off my desk, and, with his boot, kicked the desk over onto its side. But he didn't stop there. He took the fairy painting off of the wall and busted it over his knee.

'The half-mad daughter of a depraved lunatic,' William shouted, 'My family all said "Don't marry the Byron girl." Hell, your own mother tried to warn me. She would have tried harder if she hadn't been so desperate to get rid of you.'

I slapped his face. William raised his hand to slap me back, but stopped himself. I had never seen William so out of control.

'You bring out the worst in me,' he said.

William steadied himself, then gave me an ultimatum.

'Choose, Ada. Babbage and his damned machines… or me. This marriage doesn't have room for both.'

With that, he thundered out. I looked sorrowfully at the drawing of the Analytical Engine lying on the floor. How could I possibly give up my dream?

29

Two long weeks passed without William and I speaking to each other. I skipped breakfast and William took his lunch in the parlor. Mother barely came out of her room. My study remained in a disheveled state. I dared not enter it.

I felt so isolated, like I didn't have a friend in the world except for my cat. Luckily, Puff still appreciated my soft touch and chin scratches. Of course William didn't believe that I was meeting Father. No one in their right mind would think Lord Byron was clever enough to pull off such a feat. It only made me look more desperate. Perhaps I had gone too far with my secret meetings with him and now my relationship with Babbage would need to terminate if I wanted to please William. The tears came in the morning and at night. What was left for me now without the Analytical Engine? I knew I was expected to have children, which I very much wanted, but I also wanted to study and write and see the best of science put to use.

At the heart of all this was my depraved father. He was the reason I was in so much distress. I knew I had to see him one last time, to settle the business with Newstead Abbey. On a Wednesday, while William was again seeing to some business affairs out of town, I rode my horse, Sylph, to the tavern where he said he resided.

The Sea Witch Tavern was a small and run down place where mostly sailors stayed in between voyages. The rooms and ale were cheap and this was certainly was no place for a Countess to dwell. But I had to say goodbye and make my peace with Father.

An elderly man who appeared to be a Spanish Moor was working in the lobby. He gave me a strange look as I entered. It was almost as if he'd never seen a young lady in the inn before. Father was using the name Harold Childe as his cover. When I said the name, the Moor pointed down toward the south end of the structure, 'Room eleven, at the end.'

When I got to the room, I knocked on the door, hoping he would be in. He did not know that I was coming.

That's when a woman with curly dark hair in her fifties answered the door, opening it just a crack. She brushed a rogue wisp of hair behind her ear and said, 'May I help you, Miss?'

I was startled to find a stranger in room eleven. Was Father no longer staying at the same tavern?

'I'm sorry. I was looking for my father.'

Then I heard Father's voice say, 'Wait. Come in.'

The door opened and I entered the small room with one bed. In father's hand was a pistol with pearl handles, which he placed into his jacket pocket. Why did he have a gun and who was this women? I was terribly confused.

'Who is she?' I asked.

'She is my seamstress. Teresa, please leave us a moment?'

Teresa reluctantly exited the room. I could barely speak. I had made up my mind about how to resolve our relationship, but still it was difficult to get the words out. That's when I saw what must have been Teresa's sewing table. On it, was a basket of dolls that looked nearly identical to the one Father gave me.

My heart sank. That doll was no precious artifact he had kept from years ago. The doll was just one of many and lacked any significance. He had lied to me.

'What is the matter, dear girl? What brings you here?' he said.

'I...I no longer have use for the property at Newstead. I am returning it to you,' I said with a sadness in my voice.

Father smiled and looked relieved, 'This is wonderful news.'

He went to hug me, but I backed away from him.

I gathered my courage to speak the rest of my thoughts.

'The morning of my twenty-eighth birthday, I'll meet you at the north side of the fens behind my home to sign over the deed to the property. But on one condition,' I said with a warning.

'What?' he asked.

I paused. The sad, fatherless little girl inside my soul was kicking and screaming, begging me not to say it.

'It will be our last meeting,' I said with tears in my eyes.

'My angel, no,' he said.

'It must be this way,' I said and ran out of the room.

I returned to Ashley Combe with a heavy heart but with some relief that this affair would be over in a couple weeks. Mother had been right; Lord Byron was as dangerous as a venomous snake.

Months passed and my birthday was quickly approaching. It was currently December 1st and in exactly nine days, I would be twenty-eight and receive my inheritance. William had continued his cool treatment, but one night, I crawled into his bed.

I said nothing as I pulled off my nightgown in the moonlight that streamed in through the window. He also said nothing, but did not stop me. I kissed him, gently at first. He resisted a bit, but I began to stroke his chest. After a moment, William found peace in my arms and embraced me with all the passion he could muster. I realised in this moment, that sometimes words are not enough to express romantic love. I was learning to connect with my husband through my body, realizing how much I enjoy the closeness that coupling brought us. I think it also reminded both of us how much we really did love and care for each other, despite all the arguments and secrets. I now understood how important intimacy was in a marriage as a way to move through all the clutter and disappointments in a relationship. We would get past our hurt and anger because we loved each other.

As the days crawled on, William began to soften, but I continued to avoid my study, wanting to let the wound heal. Three days before my birthday, Babbage arrived at Ashley Combe as William and I were eating bowls of oxtail stew with dumplings for lunch. Mother was out, receiving one of her water cures.

Babbage knocked frantically on the front door. Our new servant Colleen, Kate's replacement, went to answer it, but William stopped her. Instead, he went to the door himself.

Through the window, he could see it was Babbage. He opened the door.

'Mr. Babbage, we are not receiving visitors today. If you have something to say to my wife, put a letter in the post addressed to me,' said William as he tried to shut the door. But Babbage put his foot in the door, so it couldn't close.

'It's terribly important I speak to her today,' shouted Babbage, hoping I was there and would hear him.

'I don't want you in my house. Now, go,' said William, firmly.

But Babbage did not give up. He moved along the side of the house to the window. He pounded on the glass, shouting, 'Please!'

I went to the window and opened it.

'He's right Charles, you must go,' I said sadly.

William looked at me, surprised. It was my intention for my actions and demeanour to prove to William that I had chosen him over the machine. This seemed to please William.

I closed the window and turned to head up the stairs.

Babbage continued to bang on the window.

'But Blackwell the publisher has contacted me. He's interested in printing your notes on the Analytical Engine next month,' he said excitedly.

I stopped in my tracks, my heart began to race. I looked to William, eyes pleading. But after a moment, my eyes surrendered to his. It took every ounce of strength in me to walk away from Babbage. I continued up the stairs.

Then, William, either taking pity on me or actually curious himself, said, 'Ada, wait.'

My heart lifted and I ran back down the stairs.

William opened the front door and Babbage rushed in.

'You will be brief,' said William.

In the parlor, William sat between Babbage and me.

'Having my notes published is wonderful news! Let me be so bold as to suggest sending a copy to every science institution on the continent and in America.'

'Patience,' said Babbage, 'It seems the publisher requires one revision.'

Babb then hesitated.

'Well, what is it?'

Babbage let out a heavy sigh. 'He refuses to print a scientific work that bears a...' he was having trouble getting the words out of his mouth. 'That bears a woman's name,' he finally said.

My heart sank. Surprisingly, William looked devastated as well.

'But why?' William asked, 'If it's good enough to be published why does the authorship matter?'

'Blackwell feels it may compromise the perceived validity of the piece, thereby rendering it unsalable,' said Babbage.

This was awful news.

'It pains me greatly to tell you this. But I beg you to put your own interests aside and act in the best interest of the machine,' Babb pleaded.

I weighed his words, then made a decision.

'No,' I said. 'Either my name is attached, or I won't allow the printing.'

'Ada please. Be reasonable,' urged Babb.

'You want me to just stand by while you take credit for my labours? I won't have it. All these years, I've been looking for a way into the sciences. This is it,' I said sternly, thinking about all the women who'd been denied because of their biology. All the women who were kept out of the sciences, out of university, out of intellectual endeavours of all kind. I knew I had to be strong, to be an example of a woman who refused to accept the status quo.

A pained look then crossed Babbage's face. He could not look me in the eyes.

'Please, please, forgive me when I tell you this. But I have already made it so. It will be printed without your name,' he said.

In that moment, with those three sentences, the sky crashed down on me. It felt as though the stars themselves were pummeling my skull from above, driving me deeper and deeper into the earth where I felt I would be stuck forever. How could Babbage have done something so unforgivable behind my back? As the second stretched into millennia, I thought of all I had done to help this man and felt my sadness turn to rage, which I unleashed on Babbage with rancour.

'How could you! I trusted you! You gave me your word,' I yelled.

Babbage only sputtered, red-faced and stunned.

William stood up, disgusted, 'Leave at once or I shan't be responsible for what I do,' he said.

'In time, she'll understand I had no choice,' said Babbage.

'Get out!' shouted William as he shuffled Babb out the door.

That night, on the eve of my birthday, I cried alone in my bed. I could hear William and Mother speaking heatedly down the hall. I got up and opened the door to hear them better curious about what they were discussing.

'I will take legal recourse against Mr. Babbage. How dare he take advantage of her by stealing her hard work and claiming it as his own. If he could have written the notes himself, he would have,' said William to Mother.

Mother shook her head, 'It's deplorable, I agree, but a high-profile lawsuit like this will most certainly be dragged through all the papers and turn into a public spectacle.'

'All the better to expose him as the scoundrel he really is,' he said.

'I beg you to consider her health. A public trial could be the very ruin of her,' she said.

'Ada will want to claim her work as her own,' he said.

'But what if he retaliates by attacking her virtue? Lest we forget she's a Byron and that name sells papers,' she said.

I had heard enough. I closed the door to my room and thought carefully. I knew where Mother kept the deed to Newstead Abbey; I saw her put it into a drawer in the library after we returned from Mr. Lushington's office. While Mother was trying to convince William not to pursue a lawsuit against Babbage, I snuck downstairs to retrieve the deed.

In the library, I quietly opened the wooden drawer and carefully rolled up the deed before tying it with a piece of string. I slid the deed up my sleeve and made my way back to my room.

I pulled out a small trunk from under my bed. I began to fill it with clothing, some money and finally, the deed. I pushed the trunk back under my bed and crawled back in between the covers.

Later that evening, after the sun sank from the sky and the moon forgot to rise, Mother brought some Devonshire crab soup to my room. She sat next to me on the bed, laid a cloth over my lap, then attempted to spoon-feed me. I refused each spoonful.

'Too hot? I'll blow on it,' Mother said and brought the spoon to her own puckered lips.

'Mother, I don't want it.'

'You must eat. Come now, just a couple of spoonfuls.'

But my stomach was in knots. First, Father's betrayal now Babbage's. Neither turned out be the men I thought they were. Or hoped they were, anyhow. Was William the only man in my life who could be trusted? Or would he eventually betray me as well? I wanted nothing more than to disappear. Just run away and never come back. So much for my grand metamorphosis,

I thought. Tears filled my eyes again. I tried to hide them from Mother, but it was no use.

'It tortures me to see you like this,' said Mother.

I rolled over onto my side, facing the wall.

'If you eat some soup, just a little bit, I will give you a most exciting birthday surprise,' she said.

I hated being treated like a child.

'A surprise? I've had enough of those lately,' I said.

'I mean a gift,' she said.

'New crochet needles, perhaps? Bring them quickly so I can stab one into my eye,' I said.

'No. It's regarding your father.'

I rolled over, to look at her. Had Mother discovered he was still alive? Was she going to tell me this news? Had Father contacted her? Or had she read that someone had spotted him? Or worse? My mind was suddenly filled with dozens of dreadful scenarios.

Mother must have noticed the worried look on my face.

'Don't worry. It has nothing to do with the terrible things we discussed before. This will be something you might appreciate, in time.'

I wasn't convinced.

Mother finally left me alone and, after a few moments, I managed to slurp down a few gulps of soup that tasted better than I had anticipated. The savoury liquid on my tongue triggered my appetite and I relished the little bits of crab. I ended up finishing the entire bowl.

A bit curious and a bit fearful as to what kind of 'gift' Mother had for me, I made my way downstairs with the empty bowl on the tray.

'I ate it all, thank you,' I said. That's when I noticed something was hanging on the wall in the parlor. It appeared to be a painting with a cloth covering it.

'Is that my gift? A painting?' I asked, curiously, wondering why it was covered up.

'Today, you inherit the last remnants of a madman,' said Mother.

'It belonged to my father?' I asked, not sure if I wanted to imagine the strange artwork my father would have collected.

'It is your father's portrait. And your mother says it is an exquisite likeness,' said William.

I was relieved the gift was as harmless as a portrait. I wondered if I should act surprised when I saw Father's face or just give no reaction at all. I decided no reaction was best.

'Are you ready?' Mother asked.

'Indeed,' I said, feeling a little guilty for pretending not to know the landscape of Lord Byron's face, feigning to be unfamiliar with the way the green and brown of his eyes danced, depending on the colour of jacket he was wearing. I thought it cruelly ironic that I would be given Lord Byron's portrait on the eve of the end of our secret relationship. Perhaps it was a sign from the heavens that though I won't continue to see him in the flesh, I can still glance into his wide-set, hazel eyes simply by looking at the wall. From there, he cannot harm me.

William pulled the sheet off the portrait, revealing his face. I looked at the portrait but something was wrong. I tilted my head, squinted, blinking to refocus my eyes.

Yes, there must be some mistake.

The image was of a man so striking in appearance, so damned handsome, he was nearly pretty. Dressed in a scarlet-red and gold uniform of Albanian styling, the man's head was wrapped in a silk scarf that was patterned with reds and turquoises. The tail of the scarf hung down on his left shoulder. A single, brown wisp of a curl peeked out from underneath the scarf, resting on his high forehead. His nose was strong and straight and hung over a thin, dark moustache and cleft chin. His wine-coloured lips were so full and lush, they seemed to recently have been stung by a bee. A silvery-steel ceremonial sword rested in his pale hands and he appeared to be standing in front of some ancient Greek ruins beneath a turbulent sky that most likely meant to reflect his own stormy temperament.

As my eyes drank in the image on the canvas, there was something about his eyes that struck me – something wasn't right about them. I looked to her mother for confirmation.

'Well? What do you think of England's greatest poet? You have his eyes, you know. Blue as the Mediterranean Sea,' said Mother.

That's when the hair stood up on the back of my neck. Chills poked my spine like a thousand sharp needles. The tray I was holding suddenly slipped from my fingers. It fell to the floor causing the bowl to bounce and shatter into a hundred pieces. The sound of the porcelain fracturing against the wooden floor pierced my ears; it was like someone had pounded on numerous black keys on the far right side of our pianoforte. The sound was the last thing I remembered before I regurgitated my Devonshire crab soup and fainted to the floor.

30

When I woke up, I was in my bed. I struggled to remember the night before. Ah, yes, the portrait. My father's portrait.

The sun was just starting to rise. The white and grey sky stretched downward, like an angry old face. Black rain clouds loomed nearby.

The chrysalis in the jar next to my bed had begun to break apart. The damp, sticky creature made its daring escape from the case that held the mystery of its transformation. With slow, determined movements, the insect began unfolding its new, wet wings. Green, blue and black gossamer began to expand inside the jar. It flapped its wings to dry them before it attempted to take flight. After several minutes, up flew the butterfly, but the jar's lid kept it from escaping. It tried again and again. Apparently, the sound of the metamorphosed insect thrusting its body against the top of the jar was loud enough to wake me.

I rolled over to investigate the butterfly. Something about the little thing's determination lifted my heart just the slightest bit.

'Today you begin your new life,' I whispered as I took the jar over to the window, 'And I will begin mine.' I opened the window then unscrewed the lid and watched the butterfly flee from the jar and soar out the window. Transformation was literally in the air.

I dressed and put on my heaviest coat before retrieving my

small trunk from under the bed. I opened it and took out the deed to Newstead Abbey, clutching it firmly. Like the butterfly, I also escaped out my window with the trunk and deed, in search of a new life on my twenty-eighth birthday.

I walked through the gardens, then through the tunnels. My boots kicked mud and rocks out of my path. The small trunk made a trail in the earth as I dragged it behind me.

Frogs were sounding-off in the fens; the insects buzzed about.

The plan was for me to meet Father at the north end of the fen. My heart was pounding. Just like the butterfly though, I was determined. I had one thought on my mind and one thought only: Lord Byron's clubfoot.

I could hear the sound of pounding horse hooves up ahead, followed by a whinny. I looked up to see the man I had come to know as my father, high on horseback.

'Pippin! I was afraid you wouldn't come. You look beautiful this morning. Happy birthday, my dear.'

I just stared at him and said nothing.

'Do you have the deed to Newstead Abbey?' he asked.

I lifted the rolled-up deed for him to see.

'Very good, hand it over,' he said as he reached out his hand. I stopped in my tracks.

'First, take off your boots,' I said evenly, as if my heart wasn't pounding against my ribcage.

He looked alarmed.

'Don't be silly. I must away before it's too late,' he said sternly.

'Take them off!' I hissed.

His jade and pine-coloured eyes darted back and forth as he continued to argue for hurrying off.

'Come, there is no time! What if we get caught?' he said.

I then threw down the deed and grabbed at his right leg. I yanked his boot with all my might. He clung to the horse, trying his best to shake me off of him. But I wasn't going to let go. As I pulled on his boot, the horse was led round and round in a circle.

'Let go! You don't know what you're doing,' he said.

This was the moment I let it all out. The pain. The rage. A deep, unwavering voice came out of my gut for the first time. I was finally certain.

'I saw my father's portrait. You are an imposter!' My words were like a whip, slashing his ears.

I gave another firm yank as the horse stumbled on the uneven marsh. After a fierce struggle, I managed to pull him off his horse. He landed on the ground.

He grabbed me by the shoulders and shook me, saying, 'I am your father!'

I pushed him down and crawled on top of his legs. I then untied his right boot. He managed to use his body to buck me off of him. I rolled into the mud but came right back at him. This time, he was able to pin me down on my back. My only recourse was to reach inside his coat pocket where I knew he kept is pearl-handled pistol. I had it in my right hand as I rolled out from under him.

I jumped up and, though my hands were shaking, I pointed the gun's barrel directly at him.

'Take off your boots,' I demanded.

'You don't know how to fire a gun. You're more likely to shoot yourself than me, put it down!' He said.

He was right, but I had seen others use rifles when hunting. I knew at least how to cock it, which I did. It made a definitive click.

He looked me in the eyes, apparently underestimating me, because he slowly began to stand and walk towards me. That's when I pointed the gun at the ground near him and fired. The sound and kickback of the gun made me jump. He jumped back in terror as his horse ran off. That's right – I was a *true* Byron and capable of anything, I thought. He sat back down.

'Take off your boots,' I said.

After a long, silent moment, he reluctantly pulled off both boots, then the stockings. His feet were perfectly normal.

Defeat filled the mystery man's face.

'Who are you?' I said, still pointing the gun at him.

'A man who loves you,' he said.

'Tell me your name!' The words exploded out of my mouth.

A vulnerable look flashed on the man's face.

'I... I am Scrope Davies,' he said as if they were the saddest words in the world. His hazel eyes winced.

I then tossed the pistol aside and began beating him with my fists.

'My father's eyes are blue, you bastard! Blue like the English sky after rain, blue like a Royal sapphire in the Queen's crown and true-blue like my own eyes. I should have known, I should have known you weren't really him,' I said, before descending into tears. I dropped my head, wiped the tears from my cheeks, then looked back at him.

'How could you deceive me like this? How could you give a girl her father, then take him away?' I asked.

Scrope tried to speak softly, to not further instigate my anger.

'I knew your father,' he said, hoping that would please me. It didn't and I kicked him with all my might.

'Not good enough!' I spat, then tried to collect myself. 'That night we first met – what would you have done if I insisted you remove the entire stocking from your foot?'

He let out a breath. 'I was fairly certain that feigning pain would make you reconsider. It was a gamble that paid off.'

'How could I have been so stupid?' I said, more to myself than him.

'Listen to me. Your father loved you and wanted desperately to know you,' he said, trying to sound reasonable.

'You're lying. You're just another swindler. While the others wanted my money, you took my soul,' I said.

He pulled the locket with the two portraits from his jacket: one portrait was of me as a baby and the other was of my Aunt Augusta.

'If I didn't know your father, how would I have this?'

I snatched the locket from his hand.

'I admit I came here with less than virtuous intensions. But your father left me with a great debt. He burned through my assets and destroyed my property, leaving me penniless. He ruined my life. I thought this would be money easily obtained.'

'By preying on his pitiful little girl?'

'Yes, it sounds terrible, I know. But a pitiful little girl isn't who I found here. You are grace. You are intellect. You walk in beauty, like the night of cloudless climbs and starry skies.'

His sad attempt to quote from Byron's poem failed to impress me.

'Spare my ears. You do not know the guilt, the shame I have felt these last few months. It has nearly killed me.'

'I never, never thought for one moment I would fall in love with you. But that's what happened. I think about you from the moment I wake up to the moment I fall asleep. All those times I told you how beautiful you looked, I meant every word. Pretending to be your father has felt like a prison to me. So many times, I almost confessed my true identity in case there was any chance you could love me like a woman and not a daughter. The hugs, the kisses, the smiles you gave to me became a kind of torture. That night I kissed you… I had to. But now, don't you see? We are free.'

I hushed and grew quite serious. I needed a moment to process it all.

Finally, I looked up at Scrope. There was only one thing I needed confirmed.

'My father's really dead, then?' I knew the answer, but needed to hear it from him.

He nodded, yes, 'I'm sorry. So very sorry.'

Then I wept for my father. I was like a sad little girl, longing for the solace of a father she never knew. Scrope tried to comfort me, but I pushed him away.

'Ada, it's not too late for us. We can leave together, right now. I know you're not happy here. I don't care about money, I just want to love you. To spend my life with you.'

Off in the distance, we could hear a voice. It was William calling my name.

Scrope swallowed hard, his pulse quickening, nervous what William would do if he discovered him.

'Come, run away with me. Live the life you were meant to live!'

I shook my head, 'No, no, no. I do not wish to cling to a phantom any longer.'

William called again, his voice getting louder, 'Ada!'

Scrope knew he had just a few seconds to escape. He bent down to pick up his pistol, and spotted the deed to Newstead

Abbey lying on the ground. I saw him eye it and shot him a challenging look.

'Could you truly be so vile?' I asked.

Scrope cracked his jaw and left the deed lying on the ground before running off to find his horse.

Stunned for a moment, I picked up the deed and stuffed it into my trunk. I then began to walk. Not towards William. Not towards Scrope. But in my own direction.

As I walked, rain began to fall. It did not occur to me to stop or return home. I just kept marching on, like a soldier fighting for my soul.

After an hour, the sky opened up and began to pour. Streaks of white-hot lightning flashed above me as I walked, it was as if a war was taking place in the sky. I marveled at the electricity that was shooting out from the heavens, as if it were an omen that mirrored my own inner fire. As if each deafening clap of thunder were Thor, the Norse god of thunder, taunting me.

I was headed to Blackwell the publisher. I was going to confront him, make him know that I wanted my name published on my notes. I wouldn't take no for an answer. I was going to make it clear that I was a woman, no, a human, to be reckoned with. A veritable force of nature. Let it rain! I thought as I imagined myself to be the actual storm: blustery, electric and powerful. Once this image came to my mind, the drops of rain no longer stung my flesh. Instead, I felt like I was riding a rain cloud like a horse, able to shoot bolts of electricity out of my fingertips at will. No one could say no to a woman who shoots lightning from her hands. The image pleased me. Despite being soaking wet with a drenched wool coat, I felt more powerful than I ever had in my entire life.

I walked for over four hours, which was how long it took to get to the center of town. Each time the wind whipped in my face, I twirled in delight. Each element of nature added to my own storm-like force.

Finally, I made it to Ironmonger Lane, where I knew Blackwell had his printing shop. I looked at the numbers on the doors. Twenty-one, twenty-two. I still had a short ways to go; I was looking for the number forty-nine, the square of seven and the fourth squared prime number. Individually, the numbers four and nine were also squares in their own right. I felt my mind alive with the mathematic perfection of it all.

As I read the shops' awnings, I stumbled, accidentally bumping into a stranger, pushing him into a puddle. The old man grumbled at me, 'Mind your step. Can't you see there's a storm?' I turned to the man and said, 'I am the storm,' and I proceeded down Ironmonger Lane, occasionally leaning on the storefront windows to help steady me.

Finally, I found number forty-nine. I wiped the rain out of my eyes to ensure the blurry numbers before me were in fact those I had been searching for. The sign above read Blackwell's, so I knew I was in the right place.

As I tried to push the door open, I suddenly grew dizzy. It was the same feeling I had after viewing the portrait. Instead of vomiting however, I collapsed in the doorway. Blackwell, a man in his sixties with white hair and beard, was standing inside with his apprentice, a teenage boy with shiny brown eyes, when he noticed me through the window.

'Who's there?' said Blackwell as he motioned for his apprentice to investigate.

The apprentice opened the door and pulled me, soaked and shivering, inside.

'I swear on the Virgin, I don't know her,' said the apprentice.

I reached out and clenched Blackwell's apron with my hands and said, 'I am the storm.'

'What is she saying?' asked the apprentice.

I repeated myself, 'I am the storm, I am the storm.'

Blackwell just shook his head. I continued.

'She walks in power like the storm with windy tresses and lightening eyes. And all that's best of mechanical forms her mind distils to scrutinize. About the Analytical Engine she writes, while the man Blackwell denies,' I recited with a rhythmic pulse that petered out at the end of the last line. I was quite delirious.

'My name, the notes on the Analytical Engine must bear my name!' That's when Blackwell realised who I was.

'I know who she is. She's the girl who writes with Babbage. Fetch her husband, the Earl of Lovelace,' said Blackwell to his apprentice, who donned his coat and hat before running out into the storm.

'My name... Augusta Ada Lovelace is my name,' and that's the last thing I remembered saying before I passed out.

31

I regained consciousness before I had the strength to open my eyes, allowing me the odd sensation of knowing I was in bed, though I wasn't sure just how I got there. The first thing I noticed, besides the soft cushion beneath me, was the sound of Mother's voice. She sounded so worried, so sad, that I wished to pat her hand… to tell her it would all be alright, but my body revolted at the mere thought of lifting my head. After a few minutes, I could finally make out her words.

'I shouldn't have waited so long to show her the portrait. Seeing it now, in her condition, was too much of a shock,' she said.

'You've protected her as best you could,' said a man. William? No, it was Dr. Poole. That's when I knew something must be very wrong. I hoped I wasn't dead. I tried to move, but was too weak.

'No, I've only protected myself. I forced her to bear my hurt and shame because I was too weak to do it. If her child doesn't live, I have no one to blame but myself,' she said.

I was very confused about whom they were speaking. Who did she protect? Who had a child? Before I could figure out the answers, I drifted back to sleep.

Some time later, I heard another voice. This one was William's. 'Just hold on, Birdie, just hold on. Please,' he said. I could feel his hand on my forehead. Then stroking my hair. It was the sweetest touch I had ever felt.

After dozing some more, I heard William's sweet voice again.

'How is she?' William asked.

'Her fever broke,' said Mother.

'I think both are going to live,' said Dr. Poole.

William shrieked with glee. Finally, I had the strength to open my eyes. I tried to focus on William, but he was still a bit blurry. I attempted to speak, but my throat was too dry. I coughed instead.

'She's awake! Give her a sip of the claret,' said Dr. Poole.

One of them put the cup to my mouth. I sipped it, then said, 'Would someone bring me my chamber pot? I need to have a wee.'

Both William and Dr. Poole laughed. Mother did not.

I stayed in bed for a fortnight. On New Year's Day, 1843, it was William who told me the good news – that I was with child! I was quite surprised to hear it. I'd assumed I would have been able to tell such a thing. The idea that a baby was growing inside of me was the most profound and wild idea I'd ever held in my mind. I was surprised by how happy I was to be carrying William's child, proud even. William looked at me differently. There was a new sparkle in his eye. It bonded us, as if the baby were a joyous secret only the two of us shared.

As excited and nervous as I was to become a mother, I found being confined to my bed exasperating. My mind and imagination needed to be worked. Surprisingly, William never asked me why I walked for hours in the rain to Blackwell's print shop. He seemed to just be happy I was at home, safe with his child.

I could tell that William was being very careful not to arouse any strong emotions in me, due to my fragile health.

Dr. Poole remained at the house, giving me daily doses of laudanum and claret. These made my mind a bit fuzzy and usually put me to sleep. I was permitted to read books on calculus, but the medicine made the equations blurry.

One afternoon, as the sun hid behind clouds laden with water and I huddled under an extra wool blanket, William came upstairs with a blank book.

'For you to write in,' he said.

When I realised William was giving me permission to write again, to go back to my work investigating the future, I perked up. I was so excited that I declined that night's dose of laudanum and claret. That sent Dr. Poole and Mother into an uproar.

'The laudanum is essential to your recovery,' said Dr. Poole.

'So is my work,' I said.

Still on bed rest, all my calculus books were spread out around me. I relished consulting the books before writing furiously in my notebook.

'You must think of the baby now,' said Mother as Dr. Poole held the glass of rust coloured liquid in front of my face.

I looked to William, my eyes begging him not to make me take the wine laced with opium.

'Dr. Poole, I prefer to regard Ada's wishes concerning her treatment,' said William.

'It would be very unwise to go against my orders,' said Dr. Poole.

'We'll take the risk,' said William.

Dr. Poole nodded. William looked at me, unsure if he was making the correct choice. I gave him a tiny smile and nod that his decision pleased me greatly.

As the season turned warmer, I was allowed to take tea in

the garden. I was so happy to be outdoors, I was reluctant to return indoors, even after the sun had set. I preferred the fresh air and the time to write in my notebook.

After six more months, as my pregnancy neared its end and my belly became as big as a hot air balloon, I sat outside in the beloved garden, writing in my fourth blank book, occasionally looking up to see a butterfly flutter by.

This day was quite warm and the sun had a saffron colour to it. While Dr. Poole and William played a game of chess, Mother arranged some daffodils into a vase. She had begun to wear shorter sleeves, exposing a small bandage over the area of her arm where she used to let the leech suckle. With Dr. Poole's help, she hadn't used a leech to bleed herself in weeks. She miraculously seemed more lively, as she had a new well of energy from which to draw. To be honest, I think simply having Dr. Poole back in her life was the true reason.

William said, 'Check' to Dr. Poole as he studied the chessboard.

'Poppycock,' said Dr. Poole, not wanting to believe William was about to win the match. That's when Colleen scurried out of the house and onto the patio.

'Sorry to disturb you, but Mr. Babbage is calling. He wishes to see the Countess,' she said.

Without lifting his eyes from the chessboard, William said, 'Send him away.'

'I tried to Sir, but he refuses. He is like a dog after a fox,' she said.

Just then, we heard the rattle of a large hedge nearby. As we all turned to look, we were shocked to witness a pink-faced Charles Babbage summiting the hedge before falling over it, landing him near the patio area. He howled in pain, but I couldn't help but laugh.

'Sir! You are to leave at once,' admonished Colleen.

William and Dr. Poole walked towards Babbage.

'Haven't you done enough damage?' asked William, fiercely.

'This is for Ada. Show her, please,' said Babbage as he held up a pamphlet titled, 'Notes on the Analytical Engine.'

The pain of Babbage publishing my work under his name resurfaced. I wondered if Babbage was really here to twist the knife in my wound? William must have wondered the same thing.

'You ought to be ashamed of yourself, flaunting the work you exploited from my wife,' said William.

'There's been a…' but before Babbage could get the sentence out, William punched him in the face. Babbage fell to the ground, again shrieking in pain.

Colleen was unaccustomed to violence and screamed before running back into the house.

Babbage held his jaw and said, 'The pamphlet, Ada! Look at it! Blackwell agreed to compromise.'

'Get out,' called William.

'Read the cover!' said Babb.

Mother picked up the pamphlet and flipped through the pages.

'Wait,' she said.

Dr. Poole helped Babbage up by the collar and held him.

Mother examined the pamphlet sceptically while I curiously looked on, wondering what had Babb so excited.

William cocked his fist, ready to punch Babbage again. Babbage covered his face with his arms.

Mother then cracked a rare smile and said, 'My daughter is a published scientist. Now, that's something to be very proud of!'

She gave me the pamphlet. I eagerly looked first at the title and then at the line beneath the title. They read, 'Notes on the Analytical Engine, by A. A. L.'

'A. A. L. Those are my initials. Mine!'

Babbage peeked at me through his arms that were protecting his face.

'Yes, yours. Augusta Ada Lovelace!' called Babbage.

William lowered his fist.

'It was the best Blackwell would agree to,' said Babbage.

'A. A. L.' I repeated and said, 'Finally, I have a profession of my own.' I had never felt more triumphant in my entire life.

I smiled, then rubbed my large, pregnant belly. Babbage breathed a sigh of relief. William handed Babbage his handkerchief, but did not apologise.

'This calls for a celebration,' said Dr. Poole.

William softened and agreed, 'I'll have Colleen open a bottle of champagne.'

Though still on edge, Colleen brought out the finest champagne flutes she could find for the impromptu party. When she arrived with the bottle of bubbly wine, Babbage asked if he could do the honours. In a gesture of good will, William agreed and Colleen handed the bottle to Babb. Using a cloth, he gently eased the cork out of the bottle and when it suddenly 'popped', everyone cheered.

But before I could taste the bubbles on my tongue, I noticed a stream of water hitting the ground. The fluid was coming from deep inside my belly. My knees buckled a little. I steadied myself by leaning onto the champagne cart.

William noticed immediately, 'Ada?' he said, taking me by the arm.

I then felt a cramping in my stomach.

'I believe the celebration shall have to wait,' I said.

'Excuse us, Mr. Babbage. The baby seems eager to join the party,' said Mother.

'Indeed!' said Babbage before following Colleen to the front door.

Once upstairs, William stood in the hallway while Dr. Poole and Mother went to work to deliver my baby. Within four hours, my son arrived. He was a healthy baby with perfect fingers and toes. He even had thick brown fuzz on his pink head. Dr. Poole used a surgical knife to cut the umbilical cord, releasing the wee lad from my body. The babe roared loudly, using his lungs and vocal chords for the first time. He handed the boy to Mother, who received him in a soft, cotton blanket. She held him over a bowl of warm water and washed him clean. After drying him off, she handed him to me. His tiny hands, his little nose and eyelashes, his perfect mouth all seemed like the greatest miracle. I could hardly believe I was holding my son. In that moment, my soul was truly transformed. I was born anew.

William came to my bedside. He also marveled at the boy. There was something so primal yet beautiful in seeing our son for the first time.

It was then I realised we hadn't settled on a name for him.

'Well, what shall we call him?' I asked William.

'I couldn't choose,' he said.

'I have a suggestion,' said Mother, 'What about Byron? Byron King Lovelace?'

William seemed a bit apprehensive, given the fiasco he believed was caused by Lord Byron's portrait.

I thought about Mother's suggestion. At first, I worried it would be a curse of name. Given all that I went through, with wanting to know my father so desperately that I unknowingly allowed a con man to deceive me. Though I was betrayed by Scrope Davies, did it mean I should hold my father in contempt? Now that I knew for certain he was dead, Lord Byron couldn't hurt me.

'Perhaps, there is a tiny piece, a good piece of my father within my son that I will get to know and love. If it pleases William, I would like to call him Byron. While I never knew my father, I will love and adore this Byron,' I said, knowing for certain that this was the absolute right name for him. Scrope Davies' stole the name for his own profane use of it. Now, I was stealing it back!

32

The next three years passed by faster than a steam train. My boy Byron was a healthy and curious toddler that brought William and I much joy. I managed to settle into my life as mother and wife, though my itch to reach into the future still remained. If only there were more hours in the day!

The much-anticipated Great Exhibition at the Crystal Palace was finally open. On this sunny day, William, Byron, Mother, Dr. Poole and I went to pay a visit.

Walking the grounds before entering the glass palace was its own fabulous adventure. I was enamored by the glorious erupting fountains that boasted statues of mermaids and mermen. A sculpture of a lounging Iguanodon, a giant, ancient reptile, rested near the fountain. Its claws were massive and shown in such detail! It was truly a work of art.

Slowly, my family and I climbed the steps of the magnificent entrance to the palace. For just a few shillings, we entered the largest glass structure ever built. All the walls and ceilings were made from giant plates of crystal clear glass, allowing the halls to require no indoor-lighting. Designed by Sir Joseph Paxton, the building was 1,851 feet long with an interior height of 128 feet. Even on rainy days, the daylight was all that was needed to light the nearly 15,000 exhibitions that contained treasures from around the world. Together, the building and the exhibits pointed to an exciting future fused with intelligence, hope, creativity and technology.

The main purpose of the fair was to show the newest and greatest ideas, engines and machinery, in hopes of inspiring a better England and a safer, more peaceful world.

It was thrilling to be amongst such exciting inventions and newly discovered relics. I was most excited to see the reconstructed bones of giant, ancient creatures a scientist named Sir Richard Owen had assembled. He named this class of prehistoric reptiles 'dinosaurs,' a word that meant 'terrible lizard' in Greek. William enjoyed examining the glass architecture of the palace itself, as well as investigating the brand new flush toilets their inventor, George Jennings, called 'Monkey Closets.'

Young Byron was now three-years-old and fast as a racehorse. William and I often joked how the tot with pecan-coloured hair and thick, brown eyelashes, never learned to walk; he simply went from crawling to running and there was nothing in between. Like me, he was terribly curious and never allowed anyone to do anything for him. Even if it meant spending two hours dressing himself or taking an entire day to build a castle out of pinecones and stones, Byron was fiercely independent. A trait William said came from his mother.

William and I knew we needed to keep a close eye on our son at the exhibition so he wouldn't become lost in the crowd of visitors.

Mother and Dr. Poole continued to spend time together and Mother never seemed happier.

As I marveled at the fruits of the Industrial Revolution, I came across a familiar invention.

'I see Monsieur Jacquard's weaving loom made it into

the Crystal Palace,' I said, hoping not to run into Monsieur Jacquard, himself.

'What about the Analytical Engine? Is it not here?' Asked Dr. Poole.

A man behind the loom answered the question, 'You won't find the Analytical Engine here,' he said before revealing his face. It was Babbage.

I smiled. William and Mother regarded him coolly.

'It's good to see you, old friend,' I said.

'Why shouldn't the Analytical Engine be included? At the very least, Ada's analysis should be on display,' said Mother. This was very high praise, coming from her.

Most regrettably, the Analytical Engine was not constructed in time for the exhibit because Babbage still didn't have funding. While many notable scientists did read my publication, there seemed to be a general inability for most people to grasp the meaning and purpose of the machine. It was as if Babbage and I managed to see into the future, while the others of our time lacked the same clairvoyance.

'It seems to be an invention ahead of its time,' I said.

'Not at all,' said Babbage, 'Some Americans have expressed their interest. I sail to New York at the end of the month.'

'That's great news,' I said.

There was an awkward moment between William and Babbage. Then, William relaxed. 'I wish you the best of luck,' he said.

William extended his hand to Babbage like an olive branch. They shook hands like gentlemen.

I suddenly realised Byron wasn't in my field of vision.

'Byron?' I called.

'Here, Mama,' he answered, 'Come and look at this!'

I followed his voice to find my son admiring a model of a flying machine, created by a man called William Henson. William, Babbage and Dr. Poole all followed me.

'What is it?' Byron asked.

I read the display, 'It's called an Aerial Steam Transit Engine,' I said, admiring its intricate latticed wings and bird-like tail.

I crouched down to Byron's eye level and said, 'Someday, a flying machine like this one will take us all the way up to the moon.'

William laughed, wagging his finger at me, 'Don't fill the boy's mind with fantasies.'

'But it's true!' I said.

'Really, Mummy?' my blue-eyed boy asked sceptically.

'Yes. We just have to imagine it,' I said.

Little Byron stared at the machine for another moment, giggled, then ran off toward a dinosaur statue. William flashed me a smile before we both chased after our son through a hall that celebrated the future. Our wonderful future.

THE END

Afterword

Despite all of Ada and Babb's efforts, it is an unfortunate fact that Charles Babbage's Analytical Engine was never built in their lifetimes. The computer age would have to wait nearly one hundred years to get under way. Had this technology been adapted in the nineteenth century, the modern world would certainly look quite a lot different than it does today.

Some consider Ada to be the first computer programmer, however, that's not exactly accurate. She is remarkable because she was the first person to understand that machines could be applied in ways that were not limited to calculations. She also created the first published algorithm for a machine to carry out. She was also the only person of her time period to fully comprehend the machine's endless possibilities and to see how important the computer would become. Ada's detailed notes on the Analytical Engine remains her only published work, due to her untimely death at age thirty-six from cancer. At her own request, Ada was buried next to her father, Lord Byron, who also died at thirty-six. Lady Byron did not attend Ada's funeral.

On a personal note, I'm terrible at math. So terrible, that I was only able to pass high school geometry by writing a play about Pythagoras called *Heavenly Angle*. In light of this, it may seem odd that I chose to write my first novel about a mathematician, but I recognised early on in my research that Ada's story is so much more than equations and logarithms.

In film school at UCLA, I wrote a screenplay about Ada, later a teleplay; sadly, both remain unproduced. However, I know Ada would be able to relate to my situation considering Charles Babbage's Analytical Engine was never built in her lifetime. Also, like Ada, I was determined to see my project through one way or another, so I wrote this book as a way to tell her story from my perspective. Lord Byron was too delicious of a character not to include and any fatherless girl knows the torment of not having that paternal love and guidance. I've always had a difficult relationship with my own father, so perhaps it is at this axis where I feel connected to Ada the most. I hope that I have been able to breathe life into Ada in a way that sheds light on her humanity, her longing for her father's love and, of course, her genius.

In addition to writing about Ada, I also dress up as the Countess in Victorian garb and visit public schools in the Los Angeles area to teach kids about her life and work. The children are fascinated by her; when I tell them she was only allowed to study math and French, they all groan. One boy even shouted, 'That sucks!' to which everyone laughed. It's a great deal of fun.

Today, computers run every part of our lives and flying machines are planning to take us to Mars in a few short years. I often wonder if Ada were alive today, if she'd be some tech mogul in Silicon Valley or a European Space Agency astronaut, working on the mission to Mars. I also dream of travelling back in time to show her my iPhone just to watch her eyes light up when she discovered all the magical things it can do. But this is just a fantasy. The reality is that Ada was a woman ahead of her time.

Ada's story didn't end with her death. In 1980, Admiral Grace Hopper of the U.S. Department of Defense recognised Ada's ability to see into the future and named an early computer language 'Ada' in her honour.

In 1992, the Analytical Engine's predecessor, the Difference Engine, was constructed using only materials available in Ada's time, from Charles Babbage's plans financed by individuals in the technology industry. It works perfectly and is on view at the British Science Museum in London for all to see. I was able to marvel the elegant machine myself and hear the music of its spinning cranks, gears and number wheels. Also on display is most of Babbage's brain.

A second working model of the Difference Engine had been temporarily on view at the Computer History Museum in Mountain View, California, but it is now kept privately by Seattle's Nathan Myhrvold, the former Microsoft Chief Technology Officer, who funded its construction.

The Analytical Engine is now currently being constructed in England. Computer scientists, including Dr. Doron Swade and John Graham-Cumming, formed a non-profit organization called Plan 28 with the aim of finally bringing Babbage and Ada Lovelace's dream into reality.

Who knows how or if Ada's life and work will continue to inspire future generations? There's no way to be certain, but I can only imagine it will.

–SJE